# Don Pendleton's Mack
# Bolan®
## Treason Play

A GOLD EAGLE BOOK FROM
# WORLDWIDE®

TORONTO • NEW YORK • LONDON
AMSTERDAM • PARIS • SYDNEY • HAMBURG
STOCKHOLM • ATHENS • TOKYO • MILAN
MADRID • WARSAW • BUDAPEST • AUCKLAND

Recycling programs
for this product may
not exist in your area.

First edition October 2011

ISBN-13: 978-0-373-61548-3

Special thanks and acknowledgment to
Tim Tresslar for his contribution to this work.

TREASON PLAY

**Printed in U.S.A.**

# Bolan yanked Khan from the car.

Once he had dragged the man a safe distance from the vehicle, he stretched him along the ground. The soldier pulled a small flashlight from a pocket, clicked it on and ran it over Khan's blood-soaked form. Three bullet holes had pierced the man's chest.

Khan's eyes fluttered open. Bolan noticed that the former ISI agent's gaze looked unfocused. His breath came in shallow puffs. After a second, Bolan's presence registered with him, and he turned his head slightly to look at the big American.

"Cooper," Khan told him. "It's not over."

"It is for you," Bolan growled.

"Not for you. Not even close."

A shudder passed through Khan, and he was gone.

*Other titles available in
this series:*

I know that there are angry spirits
And turbulent mutterers of stifled treason,
Who lurk in narrow places, and walk out
Muffled to whisper curses to the night;
Disbanded soldiers, discontented ruffians…
—Lord Byron,
1788–1824

Conspirators lurk in the shadows, biding their time, hiding their faces. I'll drag the criminals into the light of day and unmask them for all to see.
—Mack Bolan

# *PROLOGUE*

*Dubai, United Arab Emirates*

Terry Lang pretended not to notice the man following him.

In fact, it was the third man he'd pretended not to see in the past couple of hours. Whoever had taken it upon themselves to track his every move at least had shown enough sense to switch out the agents following him, a small attempt to hide that they were tailing him. But their skill had ended there. The first and the third had fallen all over themselves to not make eye contact with Lang, averting their gazes as if burned whenever he looked directly at them.

Lang stopped and bought a bottle of root beer from a street vendor. Unscrewing the cap, he brought the glass bottle to his lips, drained some of it and resumed walking. After two more blocks he spotted what he'd been looking for, an alley. Slipping inside, he advanced several yards. Along the way, he tipped the root beer bottle and drained its contents onto the cracked asphalt. It made a fizzing noise and welled up in a whitish foam. The odor of garbage cooking under Dubai's midday heat registered with him and his nostrils wrinkled reflexively at the stench.

He found a recessed doorway and pressed himself inside its shade.

He switched the empty bottle to his other hand, his ears strained as he waited. Surely his tail hadn't fallen back? He doubted it. They hadn't followed him halfway across the city just to fall back when he disappeared into an alley. They didn't strike him as particularly skilled, but they seemed committed.

Sweat beaded underneath his hairline, then rolled down his temples, cheeks and jawline. His pulse quickened. Moments later he heard the soft shuffling of shoe soles brushing against the pavement. The muscles of his legs, arms and torso bunched up as he prepared to pounce. A dark shadow stretched along the ground past his hiding place.

The sound of movement halted.

A small grunt telegraphed the guy's next movement. By the time his pursuer rounded the doorway, a small, black automatic pistol clutched in his hand, Lang was prepared. He brought the bottle down in a wide arc. The fat end of the bottle exploded into a constellation of glass shards that glinted in the sunlight. Lang's downward swing continued, the edges of the broken bottle raking flesh, opening crimson ravines in his face.

The man yelped in pain and surprise. He whipped his head away and covered the wound with his hand. Blood immediately seeped between his fingers. In the same instant he started to raise his shooting hand so he could get a bead on his mark.

Lang's hand snaked out and he caught the guy's wrist in his grip, squeezing hard. His other hand, the one clutching the neck of the bottle, came around in a horizontal arc. Lang buried the jagged end into his attacker's eye socket.

The man screamed and wheeled away. His grip on his pistol loosened and the weapon fell to the ground. Lang gave the injured man a hard shove in the chest that sent him reeling.

Grinning, Lang tossed aside the remnants of the bottle. He scooped up the man's discarded pistol and grabbed a handful of the man's blood-soaked shirt and yanked him to his feet.

Shoving the guy into a wall, he pressed the gun's muzzle into the man's throat.

"Who sent you?" Lang asked, his voice barely a whisper.

The man, his face and neck streaked with blood, spit in Lang's face. With the back of his fist, Lang wiped the glob of blood and saliva from his forehead.

"You stupid son of a bitch," he said. "Who sent you? What do you want with me?"

The man's lips curved outward as though he was ready to spit again. This time Lang drove a knee into the guy's groin, eliciting a sharp draw of air, followed by a gut-churning moan.

"I can do this all day," Lang said.

And to prove his point, he kneed the guy a second time. Groaning again, the man sagged and Lang let him crumple to the ground.

The squeal of tires on asphalt caused Lang to spin. A big midnight-blue sedan jerked to a stop at the mouth of the alley. Front and back doors snapped open and four men spilled from the vehicle's interior, guns drawn, sites trained on him.

"Drop it!" someone yelled in English.

He guessed he could take out one, maybe two, before they killed him. More likely one. And then he'd end up on a slab. He still had no idea what this was all about and it was possible that, since he hadn't killed anyone, he could talk his way out of this. He knelt and set the pistol on the asphalt. Raising his hands, he came back up to his full height.

A rail-thin man in navy-blue slacks and a white dress shirt broke from the group of shooters and approached Lang. Keeping his gun trained on the American, the small man scooped up the fallen pistol and shoved it into the waistband of his pants. He barked in Arabic—a language in which Lang was fluent—for someone to call an ambulance.

The guy gave Lang a murderous look. In return, he flipped the guy the middle finger.

"No ambulance," a voice called in Arabic. "This one's not worth the trouble."

Lang turned and looked at the new speaker. A flash of recognition immediately morphed into dread.

A Caucasian man with sandy-brown hair, a wide face and flushed cheeks rounded the front of the sedan blocking the alley. He wore a blue polo shirt, tan slacks and brown loafers. If he carried a weapon, it wasn't visible.

"Hello, Terry," Daniel Masters said, his British accent obvious.

Lang nodded, but said nothing.

"You've caused us some problems," Masters said.

"Sorry, Daniel," Lang said. "I didn't know you were in Dubai. Perhaps we can talk about this."

If the Englishman was surprised Lang knew his name, he showed no outward signs. Instead, Masters nodded at the man on the ground. By now, the man was tucked into a fetal position, groaning, one hand clasped over his injured eye.

"Think I'll pass," Masters said. "I see how you talk."

Lang shrugged. "Sorry about your man. I didn't want to do it, but he pulled a gun on me."

Masters made a dismissive gesture. "To hell with this idiot. You could kill fifty like him for all I care. Maim them, whatever. Best man won, as far as I can tell."

"Very understanding."

"You're tough. For a reporter."

"Special Forces. Army. Long time ago, but I still have a few tricks I can use. You probably already knew that, though."

"I did. But I think it goes deeper than that."

"I'm sure I don't know what you mean."

"I think you do."

Lang knew where the conversation was going and he

didn't like it. Fear fluttered in his stomach and sweat slicked his palms. His hands closed into fists. Masters was close, but not close enough to take a swing at without taking a couple of steps forward, telegraphing the attack. Because it didn't fit his cover, Lang didn't carry a gun, though he thought longingly of the one hidden back in his apartment.

One of the men was moving in a wide circle around Lang, moving behind him. A third had broken away and was approaching from the side. All kept their distance, forcing him to lunge in any one direction if he wanted to strike first. That gave them ample time to put a bullet in his head before he could complete any attack.

Masters apparently sensed the calculations racing through Lang's head.

"You can't make it," he said. "Even if you took one of us, the others would put you down in a heartbeat."

Lang flashed what he hoped was his best disarming grin. He spread his hands wide. No threat here, his body language said.

"Hey, if this is about something I did, something I wrote, we can talk about it."

A humorless laugh escaped Masters's lips. "What you write in your shitty little newspaper isn't the issue. It's what you're reporting elsewhere that's giving us heartburn."

"I don't—"

"Khan tried to shut you down, tried to stop your snooping. It didn't work. He tried to do it the easy way. Evidently, you're too damn thick to get the message. So here we are."

Lang put some steel in his voice. "Khan doesn't tell me where to go, who to talk to. If he doesn't like it, he can go to hell."

"And aren't you the crusader?" Masters said. "Playing the part to the very end. There's a good lad."

He nodded and the men who'd surrounded Lang closed in. Lang figured the charade was over. Lang hoped that because Masters had spent so much time jawboning and getting his men into position, that Masters wanted him alive. If that and Lang's lack of a discernible weapon caused the men to hesitate even slightly, he'd exploit it as best he could.

If not, well, he probably wasn't going to come out of this alive anyway. Given the choice of dying now or dying in captivity, he'd just as soon get it over with. The end result was the same.

The gunman closest to him brought his shooting hand up to shoulder level and locked his pistol on Lang. The CIA agent stepped sideways and brought the gleaming blade down in an arc, burying it in the soft tissue of the man's neck. Yanking the blade, he brought it forward until steel burst through flesh in a spray of crimson. The man's gun thundered, discharging a round within inches of Lang's face. The close-range blast caused his ears to ring and disoriented him.

At the same instant something blunt, hard, punched the back of his skull. The impact caused a flash of white light to explode from behind his eyes. His legs turned rubbery and he crashed first to his knees, then to all fours.

Gasping, vision blurred, he only was vaguely aware of a shape that loomed overhead. When the second blow to the head was struck, his limbs went loose and he crashed to the ground. A black veil of unconsciousness settled over him.

# CHAPTER ONE

Mack Bolan, aka the Executioner, was the last to arrive at the War Room. When he entered, he found Hal Brognola, his sleeves rolled up to the middle of his forearms, a tattered cigar clenched between his teeth, already seated at the table. Barbara Price, Stony Man Farm's honey-blonde mission controller, was also seated at the table. She was setting a coffee carafe on the table, and judging from the steam wafting from her mug had just filled it with coffee. Her full lips turned up in a warm smile, which Bolan returned.

Brognola, who'd been staring into the contents of his coffee mug, his brow furrowed, looked up at Bolan and gave him a tight smile. Aaron "the Bear" Kurtzman, head of Stony Man Farm's cyberteam, shot the big Fed a look. When he spoke, he laced his voice with mock indignation.

"What the hell, Hal?" he said. "You're looking at the coffee like you expect the Loch Ness monster to pop out of there."

"I don't think Nessie could survive in this swill," Brognola retorted.

"Where is the love?" Kurtzman replied.

Bolan found his seat and, against his better judgment, poured himself of a cup of Kurtzman's coffee. Once the soldier got settled in, Brognola turned to him, his face grim.

"We've got a lot to discuss, Striker," the big Fed said.

"I expected as much." Bolan leaned forward and rested his forearms on the table. His old friend slid a folder across the tabletop and it came to rest inches away from Bolan. The soldier opened the folder and leafed through the contents, which included several top-secret intelligence reports, several printouts of news stories from newspaper websites and half a dozen or so pictures. Bolan picked up the pictures and scanned through them one at a time. The image of a Caucasian man with ruddy cheeks, blond hair and pale blue eyes stared back at him.

"His name's Terry Lang," Brognola said.

"The journalist?"

"Among other things. There's more to this guy than meets the eye. Lots more."

"Meaning?"

Brognola turned his gaze in Price's direction. "You want to field this one?"

Price set down her coffee mug. She tucked a lock of hair behind her ear and scanned several papers arrayed in front of her before looking up and meeting Bolan's gaze. "What Hal means is that Mr. Lang has one hell of a freelance gig going on the side."

Bolan scowled. "You two aren't making a lot of sense."

"You're right," Price said. "We really aren't. Sorry."

"I know Lang is a reporter for the *London Messenger*. He writes mostly about energy and foreign policy. Occasionally he writes about nukes and nonproliferation issues, too. Works out of the Middle East a lot, I guess because of the energy coverage."

Price seemed impressed. "When do you have time to read anything other than top-secret dossiers?"

"His articles have been in more than one of my mission packets," Bolan said. "Occasionally he publishes a clunker or two. But most of his stuff seems to track with what I've seen. I always guessed he either had impeccable sources or he was a spook."

"Give the man a cigar," Brognola said.

"So he really is a spook?"

Price nodded.

"He works for the Central Intelligence Agency. He operates in a nonofficial cover capacity, and he tracks nuclear proliferation and smuggling for them. Or he did."

"Did?" Bolan said. "I don't like where this is going."

"It gets even worse," Brognola interjected. "Lang relocated to Dubai several months ago. It gave him a better perch to watch for any illicit shipping of nuclear technology or radioactive materials. Despite all the glitz, the country has become a hotbed for arms and drug smugglers and their fellow travelers. That's included nuclear smuggling, too."

Bolan nodded.

"Lang has lots of sources," Brognola continued. "Some damn fine ones. White hats and black hats. And he could consort with them easily because of his cover. With all that information coming in, he had a lot of irons in the fire, a lot of cases working. The guy dug up loads of good information."

Bolan arched an eyebrow. "And the problem is?"

"He went missing about forty-eight hours ago," Brognola said. "Bam, just disappeared. That's not necessarily a big deal, considering the nature of his cover. But he was supposed to check in with his handlers in Langley and never did. According to the CIA, Lang never, and I mean ever, misses a check-in call. He always made his contacts, except this time."

"And now everyone's worried."

"Yes."

"He clean?"

Brognola nodded. "Best we can tell. The counterintelligence people are poring over their files. They want to make sure they haven't missed anything. According to what the President has told me, though, the Agency has yet to come up with anything bad on the guy."

Bolan considered what he was being told. "You need what from me?"

"Go to Dubai," Brognola said. "Find out whatever you can. Frankly, there doesn't look to be any good outcomes here. If the guy has disappeared of his own accord, it's probably because he's gone rogue. If he's vanished because he's been kidnapped, that could be even worse. Regardless, we need to know what happened to him. You game?"

"How soon can Jack fire up a plane and fly me to Dubai?"

# CHAPTER TWO

*Dubai, United Arab Emirates*

The C-37 jet airplane stood on the tarmac at Dubai International Airport, parked near a hangar that housed government-owned planes. Heat rose from its engines and caused the air above them to shimmer. The craft's side door popped open and a small stairwell dropped from the plane.

A tall figure, his eyes obscured behind aviator-style sunglasses, a large duffel bag slung over one shoulder, disembarked from the craft's air-conditioned interior. He scowled involuntarily as he collided with a wall of scorching heat. A sheen of perspiration formed on his forehead almost immediately. *Dry heat, my ass,* he thought.

The Executioner descended the steps, walked onto the tarmac and swept his gaze over his surroundings. The soldier spotted a black sedan parked perhaps a dozen yards away. A short slender man, with hair trimmed down to stubble, stood next to the vehicle, his arms crossed over his chest. Light gleamed off the lenses of his mirrored sunglasses.

When Bolan reached the car, the man bent his head a bit and peered over the rims of his glasses at Bolan.

"You Cooper?" he asked Bolan, referring to the soldier's Matt Cooper alias. Bolan nodded.

"You Carl Potts?"

"None other," Potts said. He produced a black wallet, unfolded it and showed Bolan his FBI credentials.

"Special agent in charge," Potts said. "That means I work ninety hours a week instead of seventy like the rest of my people do."

"You probably have two alimony payments to prove it."

"Three," Potts said, holding up as many fingers. "Fortunately, I think this job will kill me before I get a fourth."

"We all need a bright spot."

Potts nodded over Bolan's shoulder at the plane. "You got more gear?"

"The pilot can take care of it," Bolan said. "You guys get us a rental?"

"Better," Potts replied. He nodded toward a gleaming black Mercedes parked next to a terminal building. "Just remember to fill the tank and wash the windows before you bring it back."

"Nice," Bolan said.

"Just don't say Carl Potts doesn't take care of his friends. Or friends of friends. How's Mr. Brognola doing these days?"

"Works like a dog."

Potts shook his head. "Some things never change." He tossed the soldier the keys for the car. Bolan caught them with his free hand.

"We appropriated it," Potts said. He made air quotes with his fingers when he said *appropriated*. "Got it from some Russian gunrunner. He forfeited it."

"I don't have the greatest track record with cars," Bolan said.

Potts scowled and shook his head. "Washington always sends me the prizes."

THE FBI's DUBAI OFFICE was located on the top floor of the U.S. Embassy. Bolan was in Potts's office, seated across the desk from him. The Executioner studied the various certificates and awards on the office wall. He noted that Potts had a bachelor's degree in international studies from Princeton University and a law degree from Harvard University.

"You didn't strike me as an Ivy Leaguer," Bolan said.

"You can see how far it's gotten me," Potts replied. "The second wife tried to take the law degree and divorce. She offered me a dog in return. Hell of a deal in retrospect. You want some coffee?"

Bolan nodded. Potts picked up a mug that stood next to the coffeemaker, peered inside it, wrinkled his nose as though he had seen something disgusting. Shrugging, he filled it with coffee and handed it to Bolan. The soldier waited while the federal agent rounded his desk and fell into his chair. Leaning forward, Potts reached into a side drawer, grabbed a folder and set it on his desk. He opened it and picked through the contents, his brows furrowed in concentration. From his vantage point, Bolan could see several pictures mixed in with the paperwork.

Finally, Potts stopped rooting through the dossier. He removed a picture and tossed it across the desk at Bolan, who studied it.

The picture depicted three men. The man closest to the lens, his head topped by a thick, gray mane, was scowling. Bolan pegged him in mid-fifties. The other two men looked younger, with full heads of hair, sunglasses covering their eyes. Bolan guessed they were the muscle even before Potts told him as much.

"The silver-haired devil's the guy you want. That's Khan. Just how you get to the guy, I can't say. He moves around a lot both in this city and throughout the Middle East. There's rumors that he has body doubles, but I have no idea whether that's true. A lot of these gunrunners have massive egos. They like to lie to one an other, build legends about themselves. Seems pretty damn silly."

"So what's the best path to finding Khan?"

"Funny you should ask, my friend," Potts said. Shuffling through the folder, he found another photo. This one contained three men. With what appeared to be a black permanent marker, someone had circled the face of a thickset bald man. The guy was cradling an FNC assault rifle and grinning from ear to ear.

"It's a surveillance shot," Potts said. "The moron in his natural habitat, I call it. Guy's name is Adnan Shahi. He's one of Khan's lieutenants. If Khan passes gas, this guy probably can tell you what the old man's been eating."

Potts paused, sipping some coffee while Bolan studied the photo, memorizing the guy's face.

"He doesn't look like much," Potts said. "That's because he's not. But he tends to travel very heavily guarded. He knows everything Khan does. If Khan took Lang, Shahi will know about it. He'll know which doors to kick in."

"You have a location for him?"

Potts nodded. "We've had him under surveillance for the past several hours, ever since I first got the call from Washington. Like I said, though, if the heat's on, he's not going to be calling his BFFs and talking about it. He's going to stay quiet. He's a bad human being, but he's not a moron. Once I heard about Lang's disappearance, and that Khan might be involved, I wanted to go in and shake down Shahi. Hal asked me to stay cool. Goes against my grain, but I did it anyway. He thought it best that you make the first contact."

"That bothers you."

Potts smirked. "Past tense, brother. Now that you're here, I can see why Hal wanted me to wait."

"Because?"

"Because you're a spooky bastard. I can lean on them, but you're going to break them. Every last one of them. And hopefully find Lang in the process."

"Hopefully," Bolan replied.

"You can do this for me, can't you?" Ahmed Haqqani asked.

"I'll do it," Nawaz Khan replied. He stood at one of his windows, his hands behind his back, the fingers of his left hand wrapped around his right wrist, and stared at the sky-scrapers that surrounded the building.

He heard Haqqani take a step, saw the man's reflection close in on his own.

"If you can't do it, I need to know," Haqqani stated.

Khan spun and faced the other man. "I said I will do it."

Haqqani nodded. "I just know how hard it will be to get this. Some say it doesn't even exist."

"It exists. Trust me. I know for a fact it does."

Haqqani shot Khan a curious look.

"When I was with the ISI, we had very good information that it existed. I never saw it personally, of course. But the intelligence was solid."

"How solid?"

Khan ignored the question. "Just make sure you have the money. Leave the rest to me."

"How soon can you have it?"

"Soon," Khan replied.

"How soon?"

"You ask too many questions, Ahmed. That makes me nervous."

"I meant no offense."

"I'm not offended, just suspicious."

The other man apologized again, but Khan dismissed him with a wave. "Never mind. I know this is important to you. You want to do this for your father."

"Yes," Haqqani said.

"Leave it to me."

# CHAPTER THREE

Sometimes Adnan Shahi wondered whether it was worth all the bullshit.

He stood on the balcony of his penthouse and stared at Dubai's skyline. At that elevation, the sound emanating from the traffic below was muted, broken only by the occasional honking of horns. He barely heard it. Instead, all he heard was the constant chatter of his thoughts as they relentlessly raced through his head. As Nawaz Khan's second in command, he had plenty of worries and they never seemed to stop battering him, like waves hitting rocks, one after another.

Just running Khan's business, what essentially was a massive logistics operation, and endless march of trucks and airplanes and ships, was a big enough task. Add to that the fact that every flight contained illegal contraband and the whole thing suddenly exploded into a mammoth pain in the ass. Just thinking about it caused the acid in his stomach to bubble and churn, like a witch's brew in a cauldron, hot enough that he expected steam to shoot out from between his clenched teeth.

Then Khan decided to kidnap an American. And not just any American, but a damn CIA agent. Suddenly, Shahi found himself waking up in hell on a daily basis. Unconsciously his open hand drifted to his stomach and he patted it. He shook his head in disgust. An American spy. They'd snatched the damn guy off the street and Shahi knew that'd be the end of it. Where they were taking the American, he was as good as dead.

Shahi slid a hand into the right hip pocket of his pants and pulled from it a pack of cigarettes and a lighter. Sliding a cigarette between his lips, he torched the end of it, took a long drag and blew tendrils of smoke through his nostrils. He returned the cigarettes and the lighter back into his pocket and turned his attention back to the traffic below.

There was just nothing good that could come of this, he thought. Normally he trusted Khan, in part because experience told him he could and in part because the guy called the shots. But this time Shahi couldn't help but wonder whether Khan had miscalculated, whether he was going to walk them off a cliff. Khan's decision to cozy up to the Russians made Shahi especially nervous.

But surely Khan had thought all this through? Sure, he could be ill-tempered and stubborn, but the man wasn't a fool. He hadn't become a major player in the ISI without being able to think strategically.

"He's no fool," Shahi muttered, as though saying it out loud would make it a fact.

The crash of glass shattering reached out from inside the apartment and yanked Shahi from his thoughts. That noise was followed by a man's scream.

What was that? he wondered.

He stepped to the double doors that led from the balcony into the penthouse. He pulled open the door in time to see one of his gunmen stagger toward him. The guy had a hand clutched over his chest. Rivulets of blood seeped through his fingers and rolled down his forearms. He dropped to the ground and released a final death rattle before his body went limp.

A thrill of fear raced down Shahi's spine. He dropped to one knee next to the fallen man, one of his guards, and rum-

maged beneath the man's bloodied coat, looking for his gun.
It was gone, as was his mobile phone.

Shahi didn't want to go inside. But, if he was under attack, he also knew he couldn't continue to hide on the balcony. If his attackers found him out there, he'd have no place
to run. Swallowing hard, he slipped through the door and
into his home. Another of his guards was curled up on the
floor, his body still, blood pooling around him. Another was
draped over the back of the couch, the shirt on his back
soaked in blood, the top of his head pressing into a seat
cushion.

He saw something else and froze.

A man dressed in black stood several yards away. A pistol was clutched in his hand and aimed directly at Shahi's
head. The Pakistani's eyes darted to a pistol that lay several
yards away on the floor, discarded. The man in black apparently read his intentions and shook his head.

"Don't," he said.

Shahi swallowed hard, his mind racing through the numbers one final time as he brought up his hands in surrender.
The math didn't make sense. This son of a bitch had just
knocked out three of his guards—and those were the ones
he'd seen—and looked none the worse for it. No obvious injuries. No hesitation in his graveyard voice or his eyes.

Instinctively, Shahi knew he couldn't bridge the distance
between himself and the discarded pistol before the other
man shot him. The only thing he'd get from that was the satisfaction of knowing he'd gone down fighting. He was too
much of a pragmatist to consider that a fair trade for his life.
He had to think of another way out.

BOLAN SIGHTED DOWN THE barrel at Shahi, the pistol's snout
locked dead center on the guy's face.

As grim as hell, the soldier marched toward the Pakistani. Along the way, he bent and picked up the pistol that Shahi was eyeing, shoving it into his belt.

"Who the hell are you?" Shahi sputtered.

"Where's Lang?"

Fear flickered in the guy's eyes. He licked his lips.

"That's what this is about? You're looking for the reporter? You shoot my place up just to ask me about that?"

Bolan looked left, then right, surveying the carnage. "It appears so."

"You can't come in here and shoot my place up. Do you know who I am? I own the fucking police around here. They'll string you up by your balls."

"You talk too much, Shahi," Bolan said, "about all the wrong things. Tell me something interesting."

"What if I don't know anything?"

"You do."

Shahi's eyes seemed to search Bolan's face for several strained seconds. Bolan guessed the guy was running a cost-benefit analysis of turning on his boss versus taking a few extra breaths.

The change in Shahi's expression was almost imperceptible. His eyes drifted from Bolan and looked over the American's shoulder. Was it a trick?

Spurred by instinct, the soldier spun, the Beretta's snout looking to acquire a target. He caught sight of a man in a navy-blue business suit, a small submachine gun clutched in both hands. The guy was trying to draw a bead on the Executioner.

Bolan triggered the Beretta and the pistol coughed a trio of 9 mm rounds, two of which drilled into the man's chest. His legs suddenly went rubbery and he collapsed to the floor in a boneless heap, his hands clutching at the torn flesh of his torso. The SMG skittered across the floor.

A grunt of exertion spurred Bolan to whip back around. In the same motion he fisted the Desert Eagle and cocked back the hammer. By the time he'd come around, he found Shahi had sprung to his feet. The Desert Eagle's muzzle hovered only inches from the guy's nose. Shahi's eyes bulged and he raised his hands in surrender.

"Can you tell how pissed I am?" Bolan asked.

The other man nodded.

"Good. Now, where's Lang?"

Shahi opened his mouth as if to answer, but checked himself. He shook his head. "Forget it."

"Loyal to the end, huh?"

"Not even close," Shahi said. "I just know it's not worth it. Not worth it for you to know."

The guy paused. Bolan stayed quiet and stared, letting the uncomfortable silence expand.

"Wherever he is, he's dead," Shahi said. "Understand?"

"Where'd they take him?"

Shahi shook his head vigorously. "Forget it. Where he was going, he's already dead or he will be by the time you get there. Quit wasting your time. Quit killing people for no reason. If you ever find him, he'll be nothing but a sack of flesh and bones. And I'm not going to tell you anything. Take me to jail and Khan will have me out in twenty-four hours."

"You have a good line of bullshit," the soldier said. "But here's some straight talk. Tell me where I can find Lang or I will fire this thing point-blank at your head. In case you haven't realized it, I didn't put handcuffs on any of your guys and they're not going to jail. "

"You'll kill me anyway."

"Not if you answer my questions."

Shahi heaved a sigh and his shoulders sagged. He muttered the address, which Bolan memorized.

"Why did Khan go after Lang?" Bolan asked.

"I don't know. Lang had been looking into us, but that's all I know."

Bolan nodded. His finger tightened on the Desert Eagle's trigger and a peal of thunder swelled in the room, then died out. A foot-long tongue of flame lashed from the hand cannon's barrel. The slug drilled into a wall. Shahi screamed and crossed his forearms over his face protectively. Dropping to his knees, he cupped his hands over his eyes and sobbed.

"Apparently you take me for a saint or an idiot. Either way, you're wrong. I'm not going to listen to your endless stream of bullshit."

By now, the soldier was unsure whether the other man could even hear or understand him, having been exposed to the handgun's roar at such close range. Bolan was used to the weapon, but even his ears rang. For someone exposed to a shot up close and personal, the noise could be disorienting.

"Tell your friend Khan I'm coming for him," Bolan said. "I'll dismantle his organization piece by piece and put him in the ground."

Shahi nodded without looking at Bolan.

The soldier backed a few steps away from Shahi and holstered the Israeli-made handgun. He walked out past the indoor pool, through a massive sitting room filled with brightly colored rugs, a plasma-screen television and leather-upholstered furniture. When he reached the front door, he pushed it open and exited the apartment.

Message delivered.

HIS HANDS SHAKING, SHAHI picked himself up from the floor. His cheeks burned hot with shame and anger churned in his gut. The American had gotten the best of him. He became aware of a warm sensation in his crotch. Looking down, he saw that the fabric of the front of his pants was dark where he'd involuntarily urinated, guessed it had happened when the bastard had fired the gun at his head.

The carnage around him was stunning. Dead bodies were

sprawled at different points on the floor. Shards of glass littered the floor. Through one of the doors, he saw a corpse bobbing facedown in the pool, blood clouding the water around the body.

His breath came fast as adrenaline raced through him, causing his hands to shake and his heart to pound in his chest until he swore it would explode.

He stumbled to one of the fallen guards, knelt next to him and reached beneath the guy's sport coat. Shahi found a mobile phone on the guy's belt, stored in a black leather clip-on case. Picking it up, Shahi pounded in a number. With each ring the anxiety and impatience grew in him.

Finally, on the fourth ring, someone answered the phone.

"Yes?" Khan asked.

"We have trouble," Shahi replied.

# CHAPTER FOUR

Bolan crept up the stairs of the three-story apartment building, screams still echoing in his ears.

He fisted the Beretta 93-R, raised it in front of him, let it lead the way. As he neared the top of the stairs, another scream—this one more frantic and agonized—stabbed into his ears, lingering.

The solider muttered a curse. He already was losing time and likely was at risk of blowing the mission. From the third-floor landing, he heard the rumble of a throat clearing. Hugging the wall, he crept about halfway up the final flight of stairs, stopped and listened for a couple of heartbeats. A throat cleared again and the sole of a shoe scraped against the floorboards.

Bolan surged up the final steps. As he crested the stairs, he spotted a beefy man, his hair slicked straight back, coughing into a clenched fist. The guy apparently sensed the motion and wheeled in Bolan's direction. His hand grabbed for a pistol holstered on his hip.

The Beretta sighed and a trio of subsonic 9 mm rounds lanced from its barrel. The swarm of slugs stabbed into the man's mouth and cheek and exploded from the back of his skull in a spray of crimson. The guard's legs suddenly turned rubbery and his body collapsed to the floor in a boneless heap. A Glock slipped from the man's lifeless fingers and thudded to the floor.

The soldier cursed under his breath, but continued to march toward the source of the agonized screams.

In a perfect world, he would have preferred to have caught the guard unaware and put him down soundlessly with a knife to the throat.

In a perfect world, yeah. As if the soldier had ever seen such a thing.

Here in the real world, there was every possibility that the noised had alerted the band of killers hiding out in the apartment, every possibility he'd lost the element of surprise. So, okay, it was time to try the direct approach. Kneeling next to the corpse, he dug through the man's pockets until he found a wallet, which he pocketed, figuring he could comb through its contents for possible intel later, and a ring of keys. Stepping near the door, he pressed his ear against it and listened.

By now the screaming had stopped, but he heard murmurs of conversation. It was impossible to decipher the words or to discern the emotional state of the speaker. As best he could tell, Nawaz Khan or whoever had outfitted this slaughterhouse, had positioned a couple of security cameras on the building's exterior, but nothing inside, at least nothing he could see. It was possible the guys inside had no idea their comrade had just been gunned down.

His fingers curled softly around the knob and he tried to turn it, but found it locked. His mind flitted back to the ring of keys he'd found on the dead guard, but he dismissed the notion immediately. He had no time to test half a dozen keys in the hope that one of them might open the door. To hell with it, he decided. He needed to move now.

The Executioner tapped the Beretta and set loose a trio of slugs that chewed into the doorknob and lock. The tattered lock only held the door closed barely and Bolan hammered it with a kick of his booted foot.

The door flew inward. Bolan followed right behind it. Icy-blue eyes took in his surroundings and he saw he was in a room furnished with a card table, a trio of metal folding chairs and a big blue plastic cooler. Two gunners, one seated, one standing, were also in the room.

A slender man in blue jeans and a red T-shirt who'd had his back turned when Bolan stormed the place, whirled. His hand snaked out, something black gripped in it. The Executioner's Beretta coughed out a line of bullets that lanced into the thug's chest, causing him to fall in a boneless heap. The hardman who'd been sitting on a chair simultaneously dived sideways and squeezed off a couple of shots from his automatic pistol. The slugs whistled within inches of Bolan's skull. The soldier returned the favor with another triburst from the Beretta that pulverized the man's chest and caused him to slump to the floor in a heap.

As the man hit the floor, the Executioner was in motion. First, he checked a small adjoining room and made sure it was empty. Then, retracing his steps, he returned to the entryway before veering into another corridor that branched off from the open area. Bolan took a step forward and a foul but not unfamiliar smell registered with him, causing his nose to wrinkle.

A pair of doors lined the right side of the corridor and another door stood to the left. Light spilled into the dark hallway from beneath the two doors to Bolan's right. The soldier snapped a fresh clip into the Beretta and checked through the rooms, but found them unoccupied. He crossed the hallway and, with the Beretta leveled in front of him, and gave the third door a closer look. It had been pulled closed, but not latched.

Standing off to one side, Bolan nudged the door open with a toe. This time the smell smacked him like a sledgehammer. It was a mixture of excrement and charred flesh and God knew what else. The contents of Bolan's stomach began to push at the top of his throat. He swallowed hard and pushed his way into the room. With a sweeping gaze, Bolan took in the room's interior.

The plastic painting tarps that covered the floor crunched under the soles of his shoes. A hospital bed, side rails pulled up, stood in the middle of the room. Surgical instruments—scalpels, forceps, a small saw—stood on a wooden nightstand, the top covered with plastic sheeting. Next to the traditional surgical tools lay a soldering iron and a small torch.

Bolan fixed his gaze on the figure on the bed, felt his stomach clench as he took in the horrible sight. Death's rigor had caused the arms to curl up. Strips of skin, uniform in length and cut with precision, had been peeled from the chest, abdomen and forearms. The exposed tissue, still wet with blood, glistened beneath the big halogen lamps that burned overhead. Flesh seared by the soldering iron was black and puckered. Thick hair soaked with blood was matted against the skull. Blood had soaked the mattress beneath the man and pooled beneath the surgical bed.

The soldier marched around to the other side of the bed and studied the man's profile. The crazy butcher responsible for this savagery had left the one side of the man's face untouched. Bolan studied the man's features so he could confirm his identity.

The soldier set his jaw to hold back the rage that boiled inside him.

He keyed his throat mike. "Eagle One," he said.

"Eagle One," Jack Grimaldi replied. "Go, Striker."

"I found the package."

"And?"

"Expired," Bolan stated.

"Damn."

"I took out multiple targets up here," the soldier said. "We're missing at least one. As best I can tell, these guys all are muscle. Whoever did this—" he snapped a look at Terry Lang, then looked away "—isn't among them."

"You know this how?"

"The muscle's clothes weren't bloody," he replied. "I heard Lang's last death screams, so whoever did this likely had no time to wash off. Keep an eye out. The sadistic bastard who did this may still be in the building or will be exiting it soon."

Bolan found a discarded pile of clothes lying in one corner of the room. He guessed they were Lang's and searched the pockets, but found nothing inside them. Exiting the torture room, the soldier returned to the hallway. From outside the building, he could hear the murmur of car traffic and the hum of an air conditioner.

He took a couple more steps and suddenly his combat senses screamed for his attention, followed by the grunt of someone exerting himself. The soldier whirled and glimpsed a large shape hurtling toward him. Metal glinted, a knife blade poised to fall on the soldier. Bolan reacted, taking a step back. The blade whistled through the air just an inch or so from his face. The attacker pressed his advantage and stabbed at Bolan twice more, the frenzied action forcing the soldier to take a couple of steps back.

The guy slashed wildly at the Executioner and continued to press forward. Bolan sidestepped the attack and drove his fist into the guy's floating ribs. The man grunted and fell back, his eyes bulging with fear. His free hand flew up to cover his injured ribs. A scream of pain and fear exploded from his mouth as he renewed his attack. He lunged at Bolan, the tip of the knife hurtling at the Executioner's midsection. The soldier stepped aside and the gleaming blade whooshed past his torso, slicing open the nylon windbreaker he wore, but leaving his flesh intact. The soldier drove another fist into the guy's now-injured ribs and heard his opponent gasp with pain. The man dropped the knife and spun away.

Bolan drew the Beretta and leveled it at the man. The

knife fell to the floor with a clatter and the man brought his hands up.

"You and I," Bolan said, "are going to talk."

BOLAN WENT TO THE stainless-steel sink in the torture room. He filled a white foam cup with cold water from the tap and returned to the hallway where Ayub Sharif lay in the hallway.

By now, Grimaldi had arrived. He leaned one shoulder into the wall and crossed his arms over his chest. Bolan stood over Sharif and threw the contents of the water into the guy's face. Sharif's eyes popped open and his expression quickly flashed through shock, fear and finally rage as he took in his surroundings and assessed his situation. He looked at Bolan, then at Grimaldi and finally back at the Executioner.

"Hello, Ayub," Grimaldi said, his voice irritatingly bright. Sharif raised his forearm, dragged it across his face to wipe away the water that had been splashed on him.

"You know my name," he said. Though Bolan knew from his intel that the guy was a native of Pakistan, he spoke English with no trace of an accent. "How do you know my name?"

"Big fans," Grimaldi said.

"Your work speaks for itself," Bolan said. "Best cutter this side of Jack the Ripper. Besides, we have a file on you."

"Who are you?"

"Why don't you let me ask the questions?" Bolan said. "That's what I'd do if I were in your position."

"My position. And just what position might that be?" Sharif asked.

"Royally fucked."

"You don't scare me."

"Then you're an idiot," Bolan said. He jerked a thumb at the room where Lang had been tortured to death. "You killed Terrence Lang. Did it in cold blood. Kidnapped him. Tortured him. For God knows what reason. I could put a bullet in your head, dump your body in the river and celebrate with a steak dinner."

Sharif licked his lips. A sheen of perspiration had formed on his forehead and had beaded on his upper lip. "You can't prove I killed him."

Bolan knelt in front of Sharif. He rubbed his chin and studied the guy for several seconds. Finally he shook his head slowly, as though overwhelmed with disbelief.

"Sharif," he said, "I can't tell whether you're brave or stupid. Truth be told, I don't care which it is. You have blood under your fingernails. Your clothes and shoes are splattered with blood. Your file says that your best skills are torture and interrogation. So if you want to tell me you didn't kill Terry Lang, fine. I can live with that." Bolan slipped the Beretta from his shoulder holster. "I'm not here to put you on trial. The burden of proof I require before blowing your head off is light. I mean, life's too short for heavy burdens. Am I right?"

"What's in it for me?"

Bolan shook his head. "One breath, two breaths. Who knows?"

Grimaldi chimed in. "Best speak truth to power, Sharif."

Sharif scowled. Bolan watched as the cutter stared at his lap, thumbnail of one hand digging under the other while he considered his situation.

"Maybe I need to clarify," Bolan said. "I don't like you. You're a monster preying and profiting on the misery of others. You wore out my patience three minutes ago. If I had more time, or was a better interrogator, I'd establish a rapport with you, earn your trust, make you a lot of promises. I don't have that kind of time. So answer my questions. What's the game here?"

"He poked his nose into Khan's affairs."

"And?"

"Khan didn't like it."

"News flash."

"I mean, he betrayed Khan."

Bolan's brow furrowed. "Betrayed. You mean, they were working together?"

"That's what Khan thought. I mean, Lang was working through an intermediary, but Khan thought he had him, had leverage over him."

"What kind of leverage?" Grimaldi asked.

"When Lang first started poking around Khan's operations, Khan thought the guy was just another journalist sticking his nose where it didn't belong. We tried to throw him off the trail. We sent a couple of people his way, ones who gave him bad information, tried to send him in the wrong direction."

"And?" Bolan asked.

"And it didn't work. Not for long, anyway. Sure, he might follow the lead for a little while, but then he always came back around, asking the right people the right questions, going to the right places. It was uncanny."

"And Khan considered this a betrayal?"

Sharif shook his head. "No. After a while, Khan got tired of playing games with him and started having his people do their own digging, build their own case. Khan started to believe Lang was getting his information from an intelligence source or multiple sources."

"You thought he was a spy."

"Well, wasn't he? I mean, look at you two. You're not reporters, are you?"

Grimaldi looked at Bolan and grinned. "Pretty perceptive for a psychopath."

He turned to Sharif. "So Khan decides Lang's a spy and has him killed. And here we are. How's that a betrayal?"

"I don't know all the details."

"But you know some," the pilot replied.

"The way I understand it, Khan never knew for sure Lang was a spook or at least working with spooks. He made inquiries with his old ISI contacts, but they had nothing much on the guy. He'd been in Islamabad for a while, but their records had always pegged him as a journalist and nothing more. But Khan wasn't convinced, so he decided to try recruiting him."

"As a double agent," Grimaldi said.

Sharif nodded. "He wanted to see just how much Western intelligence really knew about him and he figured that, if Lang knew something, he'd share it, maybe even take bad information back to his handlers. If the right pressure was applied."

"Clever," Bolan said. "Risky, but clever."

"Too clever by half. Khan underestimated him. We thought we were turning him, but he was using us, penetrating the organization further all the time. He got what you Americans call the family jewels. Pieced together the organization's structure, found out who Khan did business with, what he sells and where. Surely some of this information you've seen."

Bolan gave a noncommittal shrug. "Khan knew all this stuff was going out the door?"

"Not at first, but he got the idea after a while. Hey, Khan had been an intelligence agent himself and had run operations against India while he was with the ISI. He knew the score. He's no fool."

"Not if he surrounds himself with top-shelf talent like you," Bolan said. "Didn't Khan think it was risky killing Lang? Who cares whether he was a reporter or a spy? Either way he's dead, and now you have me and a bunch of other folks breathing down your neck. Seems like a bad trade to me."

Sharif's lips parted as he prepared to reply to Bolan.

Before he could utter a sound, though, a small dark hole opened on his forehead, followed an instant later by the sound of glass breaking. Bolan whirled toward the sound and spotted the window behind him disintegrating in a waterfall of glass shards.

Grimaldi grabbed hold of Bolan's windbreaker and gave it a hard yank, causing him to reel backward. A bullet sizzled through the air and pierced the space where he'd been standing only a moment before.

Once the Executioner hit the ground, he rolled across the floor and got out of direct site of the now-shattered window.

Grimaldi simultaneously was on the move, his hand filled with a Browning Hi-Power as he sought cover. Bolan saw from the corner of his eye that his friend was safe, which freed him to deal with the shooter. Three more rifle slugs lanced through the window and drilled into the floor and walls. None of them came close to hitting the Stony Man warriors, though the shooter did succeed in keeping them out of sight of the window.

The shooting was over in a matter of seconds.

"You okay?" Bolan asked his old friend.

"Yeah. You?"

The Beretta leveled in front of him in a two-handed grip, Bolan was up on one knee, looking through the window and scanning the rooftops of nearby buildings. A trained sniper himself, his mind was running through a rough series of calculations, trying to determine the angle from which the shots had come so he could best identify the building from which the shooter had attacked. He saw no movement on any of the nearby rooftops, but within a couple of seconds thought he'd identified the sniper's perch.

He shot to his feet and moved toward the window. By the time he'd reached it, he heard tires squeal from the street below. He looked down in time to see a forest-green sedan rocket out of a nearby alley, cutting off an oncoming car before disappearing in traffic.

"There goes our shooter," Grimaldi said.

Bolan nodded. He stowed his weapon, ran outside and crossed the street to the alley from where the green sedan had shot into traffic. He searched the building's perimeter while Grimaldi continued to watch from above.

Minutes later Bolan keyed his throat mike. "I got nothing," he said. "But I do hear sirens. I guess it's time we made our exit."

# CHAPTER FIVE

"What about the other two men?" Nawaz Khan asked.

Daniel Masters shook his head. "Couldn't get them," he said. "Never got a clear shot."

Seated behind his wide mahogany desk, Khan leaned back in his chair and scowled. He pressed his fingertips together, his hands forming a steeple, and stared over them at Daniel Masters.

"This is not good," he said.

"Thanks for the bloody understatement," Masters snapped back. "These two men stormed the building, killed some of our best and brightest without breaking a sweat, and interrogated someone familiar with our plans. So, yeah, I'd say this is not good."

Khan fixed a hard stare on the Englishman as he pondered the words. If his glowering bothered Masters, he gave no outward sign of it. Instead the Englishman downed a Scotch whiskey on the rocks, wiped his mouth on his shirtsleeve and rose to make himself another.

"Who were they?" Khan asked.

Masters shrugged. "CIA. Delta Force. Who the hell can say? You were in intelligence before you went to the dark side. You know the players as well as I do. They could be private security contractors hired by the newspaper to rescue their guy. I mean, right? What we do know is that they are here, and they just tore a big damn hole in your operation."

"It can be dealt with."

"Can it? Look, first Lang infiltrates your organization. You kidnap him, hold him for a couple of days and kill him. Now you've probably brought the righteous wrath of the U.S. government down on our necks and you think it can be dealt with. You have the operational security of a toy store. My people are getting very nervous, Khan. They were before all this happened, which is why they sent me here in the first place."

An angry knot formed in Khan's gut as he listened to the Englishman vent. When he spoke, an edge had crept into his voice. "Your people need to leave this to me."

The corners of Masters's lips turned up in a mirthless grin. "Because leaving it to you has worked so well so far," Masters said.

"No. I have the contacts. I can make things happen. If you want to pull this off without me—" he made a sweeping gesture with his hand "—then be my guest. Otherwise, leave this in my hands."

"Which are so capable."

Khan leaned forward.

"I tolerate you because you can supply the things I need. Not because I think you bring anything else to this operation."

Undeterred, Masters leaned forward, too, rested his elbows on the top of Khan's desk and locked eyes with the guy. His face was perhaps a foot or so from Khan's, well within striking distance should he decide to take a swing at the arrogant prick's jaw, he thought.

"Tell you what, Nawaz. Tell me to pound sand, please. I'll catch a damn flight back to Moscow and tell Mr. Lebed that you've decided to cut short our little partnership, that you've decided you need your own space. My guess is he'll send five more guys back here within twenty-four hours that'll make our little American friends look like cream puffs. And they'll wipe out your whole gang. As for this arms sale of yours, we'd be happy to bow out, take the product back with us and be done with your silliness once and for all. Maybe you can hop on the internet and buy some radioactive material there. What do you say, lad? That sound like a fine plan to you?"

By now Khan had let his hand slip off the desk. He reached beneath the desktop and his fingers encircled the pistol grip on a 12-gauge sawed-off Ithaca shotgun that was suspended underneath the desk. Khan knew that one stroke of the trigger and the Ithaca would unleash a blast that would tear through the desk's modesty panel and spray this limey fuck's insides all over the walls of his office. He'd have the place scrubbed down, repainted and refurnished in twenty-four hours or less.

Just enough time for Lebed to realize he'd strayed off the reservation and for him to dispatch a hit team to Dubai, just like the Englishman had suggested. Maybe he and his people would be able to fend off the Russian's army of mercenaries and spies. Maybe.

He loosened his grip on the shotgun and forced himself to smile at Masters, who'd hardly stopped to take a damn breath since he'd first launched into his tirade. The former English spy uncoiled from his chair and walked to the bar to make another drink.

"You have the item then?"

Masters nodded without bothering to look at him. Instead he focused on his bartending pursuits. "It's nasty stuff, you know. It's not like highly enriched uranium or plutonium. Just a little bit of this stuff and—poof—you've got a mini Armageddon on your hands. And it's hard as hell to come by. Most people don't think it exists, but it does."

Khan considered pointing out that Masters talked too damn much for a spy, but thought better of it and instead absorbed what he was being told.

"I will get it, though?" he asked when Masters stopped to take a breath.

"You will."

"And I will make sure you get your money."

Masters raised his glass and toasted Khan. "Even better. In the meantime, you need to deal with our new friends. We need them gone as soon as possible."

"Don't worry," Khan replied. "I'm already working on that."

# CHAPTER SIX

"The Man isn't going to like this," Brognola said. "Hell, I don't like it."

"None of us do, Hal," Bolan said. "It is what it is."

"Hell of a time to get philosophical on me, Striker."

Bolan allowed himself a smile, his first since he and Grimaldi had returned to a safehouse owned and operated by the U.S. government inside a walled community located in suburban Dubai. The place was three stories high, stuffed with luxurious furniture, surrounded by iron gates and bristling with tall iron fences topped with concertina wire. It was surrounded by other, similarly luxurious homes, most occupied by foreign executives working inside Dubai who made tempting targets for Islamic terrorists.

"Where's Jack?" Brognola asked.

"In the shower," Bolan replied. "Or maybe one of the pools. I'm not sure."

Brognola laughed. "How is it to sit in the lap of luxury?"

"Not a bad place as far as safehouses go," Bolan said. "I've definitely slept in worse. Did you send a clean-up crew to the address I gave you? I'd like it if we could recover Lang's body and send it home."

"We're on it. We have guys from the local FBI office on detail there. The local police are none too happy with us, obviously. First, we pull a covert move in their town and then we lock them out of a crime scene. But they are cooperating, which is about the best we can hope for. You already met Potts?"

"I did."

"He's handling things on our end. He's really got the touch with the locals."

"What about Lang? At least in some circles, he was a high-profile figure. He can't just disappear."

"Right. Fortunately he was a private pilot. According to a press release that should be going out within the next few hours, he died in an accident. His plane crashed while he was flying from Dubai to Tel Aviv to conduct an interview."

"Sounds plausible."

"The family will issue a press release, too. Because he worked in a nonofficial cover capacity, his family has no idea that he was an espionage agent. They think he was just a reporter, which is just as well for all involved. I guess everyone is sitting on the story until the next of kin are notified. Once that happens, the story goes out, runs a couple of days and should disappear after the family has a funeral for him."

"And since the plane was lost at sea, there's no need for them to ever see his body so they'll never need to know that he was tortured to death."

"If everything goes to plan," the big Fed said.

"We've had such good luck so far."

"Cynic. Look, I'll stress to Potts that if he or any of his crew find anything, they should pass it along to you."

"Good," Bolan replied. "I may need him to dig up some other information, too."

Bolan paused and tried to gather his thoughts. "Let me ask you something, Hal. What else do we know about Lang? I mean, about the guy."

"What are you driving at? Do you think he's dirty?"

"Not necessarily. Frankly, I'm not sure what to think. But I do wonder how the guy got so over his head in this whole thing. And I have to wonder whether everyone's telling us everything we need to know, including our friends in Washington."

"Do they ever? Brognola replied.

"Think about it. You have an experienced agent who goes up against Nawaz Khan, a major weapons dealer. And he does it all by himself? No support? Nothing? I have an arms-length relationship with the government and can do that stuff. But I can't envision Lang doing the same thing. I'm sure he wasn't stupid. But was he enough of a cowboy to go out and get himself killed? And he took important information with him to the grave."

"I don't like where you're going with this," Brognola said. "But damn it, I also can't refute it. Let me rattle some cages here and see what else I can learn."

"Thanks." Bolan raised his mug to his lips and slurped some coffee.

"Look, Bear has been looking through Lang's phone records, trying to chart out who the guy was talking to and when. The rest of the cyberteam is working through the guy's bank records and whatever else they can get their hands on. Maybe we'll know more later."

"Keep me posted," Bolan said before terminating the call.

SEVERAL MINUTES LATER Bolan's cell phone rang again. He took the call.

"Go."

"Jesus, Cooper, that's how you answer the phone?" It was Potts.

"You get the building cleaned out?"

"About fifty percent. Not too bad, considering the mess you left behind. It was like the Valentine's Day massacre on steroids. The harder part was convincing the state security forces that they needed to let you go about your business and ignore the death of an American journalist and several

Pakistani nationals. But I think we're in the clear, at least for the moment."

"How'd you manage it?"

"Would you believe I'm a good diplomat?"

"No."

"Would you believe I dropped some names of people in Washington? The kind who approve arms sales to the United Arab Emirates?"

"That I believe. You have that kind of clout?"

"Nah, I just said I dropped names. I didn't say I knew them."

"Just the same, thanks for sticking your neck out."

"Don't mention it. Hey, the real reason I called was to let you know a couple of things. First, I got a phone call from a reporter, a lady named Tamara Gillen. She left me a message, said she'd heard through the rumor mill that Terry Lang may have been lost in an airplane crash. She said she might have some important information about that."

"I guess I don't need to tell you to ignore the call."

"Aren't you a genius? Thanks for the tip. Maybe if the bottom falls out of the paramilitary business, you can jump over to public relations."

Bolan grinned.

"Anyway," Potts continued, "she said she thought that the whole notion that Terry died in a plane wreck was bullshit."

"She say why?"

"Negative. Probably because she doesn't want to believe the guy's dead."

"That a theory?" Bolan asked.

"Call it an educated guess."

"Based on?"

"On the fact that Terry boned everything in a skirt in Dubai. You call five people who knew him, and they'd tell you the same thing. The bastard couldn't keep it in his pants to save his life. I barely knew him, but he was notorious among the reporters, politicians and government people for screwing everything he could get his hands on," Potts said.

"Good to know," Bolan said. "You know anything about this reporter?"

"She's little more than a name to me. I went back through my Rolodex and I had a card in there from her. She probably interviewed me at a press conference or some such. I try to avoid the press like the plague, but sometimes it just can't be helped."

"You think she knows anything about Lang?"

"She probably knows a lot about him. Whether any of it's useful is another matter."

"Maybe it's time I checked."

# CHAPTER SEVEN

I can't stay here! The thought boomed in Tamara Gillen's head and jolted her into action. She stepped away from her window and grabbed a handful of the curtain, ready to pull it closed. She stopped herself.

React and they'll know you're on to them, she thought. If they know that, they'll move and be on you in a heartbeat. Then what?

She glided away from the window, and made her way down the hall to her bedroom. Inhaling deeply, she held the breath for a couple of seconds, exhaled heavily, hoping it would calm her racing mind and equally rapid heartbeat. It did neither.

Concentrate on what you know, she told herself. When she'd arrived home earlier, she'd spotted two men positioned on the sidewalk across the street from her building. She'd recognized the bigger of the two immediately. She'd seen him skulking around Lang's building on at least one occasion. The man looked like he'd come straight from central casting for a thug—wide shoulders and chest, thick hair gleaming from hair gel, and a white scar that bisected his forehead.

"He shouldn't be here," Lang had told her at the time.

"Who is he?"

"Never mind," Lang had replied through clenched teeth. "Just take my word for it, he shouldn't be here."

But her instincts had told her to press him. "What do you mean, Terry? Who is he?"

"Just trust me and stop with the Q&A." His voice had sounded strange to Gillen, a quiet menace tinged with fear. Uncharacteristically, he'd avoided looking into her eyes. The memory caused a shiver to travel down her spine. She'd heard Lang angry before. In fact, he often seemed to swing between a boisterous charm that attracted people to him and a righteous anger that made him an unwavering opponent in an argument, even when he was dead wrong.

But the fear, that was seared into her memory. Lang never, ever, showed fear. Sure, a shrink may have argued that his in-your-face confidence masked a hurt, vulnerable little boy, provided a bandage for his wounded psyche. And Gillen would have told that shrink he was full of it, right up until she'd heard the fear and the distress in Lang's voice.

So, yeah, she'd dropped the discussion at the time. Now she regretted it.

Lang was long gone and this creep had found her. She had no idea who he was, what he was capable of or why he wanted anything to do with her.

"Thanks, Terry," she muttered.

Inside her bedroom, she made her way to the dresser, yanked open the top drawer and rummaged through bras, panties and socks stuffed inside. Where the hell was it? Finally her fingertips grazed smooth, cold steel. She hesitated for a moment, but then used her fingers to rake back the clothing until she could see the gray metal box at the bottom of the drawer. Taking the box from the drawer, she carried it over to her unmade bed, swept aside the wadded sheets to clear herself a spot and sat on the edge of the mattress. Perching the box on her knees, she used her thumb and index finger to work the dial on the combination lock until the final tumbler fell.

The lid came up and she studied the contents of the box. A small stack of bills—mostly U.S. dollars—secured with a rubber band lay at a forty-five-degree angle on top of her passport. She removed both items and set them next to her thigh on the mattress. A .25-caliber automatic pistol was the next item she took out, along with two clips for the weapon. She balanced the gun in her palm and scowled. It wasn't much, but it fit her hand well and was easily hidden. Finally she removed a silver key and slipped it into the hip pocket of her snug jeans. Sealing the box, she set it on the bed and stood.

The cash, gun and passport all were items she'd started keeping years ago, a ritual that began when she'd been a foreign correspondent in Sierra Leone and again while covering clashes between the Israelis and Hezbollah. When she'd been a green reporter, an editor had told her to carry enough cash to bribe public officials or to buy an airline ticket. And if that didn't work, well, that was why she'd carried the gun, though she'd never used it on anything except tin cans, paper targets and an occasional watermelon.

She scanned the room. Should she pack her clothes? No time. It was best for her to simply get the hell out of the apartment, get out into the open where people would see if something happened to her. She could take a cab to the *Messenger*'s office and surround herself with colleagues and friends. It may not make her safer, but it at least would make her feel safer, which was no small thing. And she might be able to dig up some more information. Maybe someone had heard from Terry or they might know something about the key.

Her cell phone beeped and the sudden, sharp noise in the midst of silence caused her heart to skip a beat. By the third ring, she'd regained her breath and shook her head disgustedly at her edginess.

"Tammy, it's Kellogg."

It was Mike Kellogg, the *Messenger*'s bureau chief. The sound of a familiar voice should have relaxed her. But she heard the tension in his voice and it only stoked more fear in her.

"Mike, what's going on?"

"Terry's gone."

She hesitated for a moment and said, "I know."

"You knew? What the hell. Why didn't you say anything?"

"What's the big deal? You know Terry. He's like a cat. He disappears, and you don't see him for a few days and then he resurfaces."

"This is different," Kellogg said.

"Different how?"

"Couple of guys came around looking for him. They asked a lot of questions."

"Questions? Like?"

"Like, had we heard from him? Did we know who he'd been talking to? Where had he gone? They took Bonham into his office for a while and grilled him. He came out of there red-faced and sweating, like he'd run a damn marathon with these bastards."

"They didn't identify themselves?"

"Not to me they didn't. I'm sure they told Bonham who they were, but he wasn't in the mood to talk after they left. He shut his door and turned on the Do Not Disturb light on his phone. But he looked pretty shook up when it was all said and done."

"Damn," she said.

"What?"

"I don't know," she replied. "Last I saw Terry, it was two days ago. He was acting nervous, almost scared."

"Terry? Bullshit. That guy always was on an even keel."

"Not this time. Seriously, he was worried. Scared. I never saw anything like it. And now these guys show up looking for him. That worries me."

"What had him so scared?" Kellogg asked.

"I don't know for sure."

"For sure?"

"I mean, I don't know," she lied.

"Maybe he just overreacted. The guy was working his ass off. Maybe he just got edgy, a little paranoid. Could happen to anyone."

"Sure," Gillen replied, not at all convinced.

"Look, you sound pretty shook up. You at the apartment? How about I come over? It's no trouble."

She thought about the two men waiting outside the building for her. On the one hand, it seemed an attractive proposition. Maybe if they saw her leave the building with someone instead of by herself, they'd keep their distance from her. Maybe. Or perhaps they'd just come after Kellogg, too. And that assumed that they'd be content to wait outside until Kellogg arrived, which wasn't a certainty in and of itself. No, she needed to take care of herself and do it right now.

"I'm fine."

"Really, it's no trouble," Kellogg stated.

"I'm fine," she repeated, this time in a no-nonsense tone.

"Hey, I can take a hint," Kellogg said. The good-natured tone of his voice sounded forced. Was he angry or just trying to cover for his wounded ego? At this point, she had no time to worry about such a thing. She needed to act.

"Look," she said, "I'll call later. Is that okay?"

"So you're staying put?"

The question struck her as odd. "Sure," she said.

They said their goodbyes and hung up.

BOLAN ROLLED UP THE SIDEWALK toward Gillen's apartment building, a glass-and-steel monstrosity that jutted toward Dubai's clear, blue skies. He'd been watching the place, getting a feel for the property and its surroundings for an hour. Almost from the moment he'd arrived, he'd been struck by the neighborhood's Western feel. Gleaming apartment and office buildings lined either side of the street. Restaurants and shops, many of them the same fast-food restaurants and department stores found in the United States, lined the streets. If it wasn't for traffic and other signs written in Arabic or an occasional group of women, their features obscured behind veils, Bolan could just have easily been in any major U.S. city.

Beneath his black nylon windbreaker, which he wore unzipped, as a small concession to the heat, the soldier carried the Beretta 93-R in a shoulder rig. The Desert Eagle rode on his hip, obscured by the tails of his windbreaker.

It was his second trip around the block now. The two men who'd initially caught his attention still stood in the recessed doorway of a nearby men's clothing store, both trying to look like they hadn't noticed Bolan. The bigger of the two men used a handkerchief to dab at the sweat beading on his forehead, then tugged at the collar of his shirt with his index finger to allow some heat to escape from inside his clothing. The man looked miserable.

Though Bolan couldn't say for sure whether he posed a danger, the man definitely seemed out of place. A second man stood on the corner decked out in blue jeans, a baseball cap and a Hawaiian-style shirt, having an animated conversation on his cell phone. He shot a glance in Bolan's direction, turned and stared into a glass window behind him, allowing him to monitor the soldier's approach without looking directly at him.

Two more men, both wearing tan coveralls, with heavy leather tool belts wrapped around their waists, stood next to a panel van parked on the street. A casual glance would peg them as telephone or cable television repairman. But Bolan's trained eye could see the telltale bulges of a handgun holstered in their armpits beneath their coveralls. One of the fake repairmen, a slender man with bushy muttonchop sideburns, carried an empty canvas satchel over one shoulder.

The soldier took a couple of steps and angled himself so he could get a better look at the van. Behind the wheel, he saw a silhouette with only a part profile visible from his vantage point. Bolan took out a pack of smokes, tapped one into his palm and pocketed the rest. With his other hand, he pulled out his lighter, clicked it open and torched the end of the cigarette. He didn't smoke much these days, but a cigarette was a convenient prop. Tucking the lighter away, he pulled his baseball cap farther over his eyes and started for Gillen's building.

One of the men looked up as Bolan approached. The soldier felt his muscles tense, but he didn't break stride. Instead he continued walking right toward them. The man carrying the satchel looked at his partner and nodded politely as the other man spoke at a rapid tempo, occasionally punctuating the phrase with excited gestures from his hands. Bolan took a drag from the cigarette as he passed. He caught Mr. Sideburns' eye, gave him a nod and kept moving until he reached the nearest intersection.

The Executioner turned right and rolled down the street, passing the panel van, which now stood to his left, ignoring the driver. Then he walked past the front of Gillen's apartment building and kept going until he reached a nearby intersection, turned right and headed along the side of the building.

The building had a two-level parking garage beneath it that was accessible from the street. Bolan slipped into the parking garage. As he approached a glass door that led from the ground level of the garage, a woman was exiting the building. Smiling, she held the door open for Bolan. He thanked her and passed through it, stepping into the building's air-conditioned interior.

He keyed the throat mike.

"Jack?"

"Go, Sarge."

"There was a phone company van parked outside when I entered the building. How about now?"

"Gone, baby, gone."

"You see it move?" Bolan asked.

"Yeah. It turned the corner a couple of minutes ago, just after the repair guys disappeared into the building."

Bolan scowled. "You got it in sight?"

"Affirmative. It's pulling into the parking garage."

The soldier stopped and drew the Beretta from beneath his jacket. "Okay, my guess is it's heading for the sixth floor to pick up the two guys and Gillen."

"I'll head that way," the Stony Man pilot stated.

"Don't engage unless you have to. They may already know they've been identified. Until then, let's play it cool."

"Clear. By the way—"

"What?" By now he was on the move again, hugging the walls in the hallway, pressing the Beretta against his thigh to keep it out of sight.

"Couple more guys came in after the chumps in the repair outfits. Maybe two minutes later. Both had been standing on the opposite side of the street, but they converged on the building in unison."

"Sloppy."

"Probably," Grimaldi said. "But they're probably headed your way."

Bolan reached the end of the corridor. It branched off in two opposing directions, like the top of a *T*. Flattening against the wall, he peered around the corner and saw the two repairmen exit the elevator and turn in the direction of Gillen's apartment. Bolan kept the Beretta low at his side and rounded the corner. He started for the men as they came to a stop in front of Gillen's apartment.

THE SHARP KNOCK ON THE door startled Tamara Gillen. Who the hell could that be? she wondered. Kellogg? No way. There hadn't been enough time for him to have traveled from the bureau to her apartment. Uncoiling from the chair, she moved to the door. The .22-caliber pistol was tucked into the waistband of her pants and covered by her shirttails.

"Who is it?" she called before reaching the door.

"Phone company," a male voice replied.

Reaching the door, she peered through the peephole and saw two men in telephone company uniforms standing outside her door.

"I didn't call you."

"Of course you didn't," the man said with a laugh, "the phones are down."

Gillen scowled and walked over to the cordless telephone that stood on a small table in her kitchen that doubled as a desk when she worked from home or paid bills. She returned the phone to its charging base and stared at it for a moment. Her pulse quickened. None of this made sense, she thought. If all the phones were down, why check each apartment? She reached underneath her shirt and drew the small pistol. She began backing away from the door, figuring she should find her bag and leave via the fire escape if these guys became too insistent.

"Hang on," she said. "I need to put on a robe."

Something thudded against the door, striking it just above the knob. She took in a sharp breath of air and backed away from the door, then brought the pistol up in a two-handed grip.

A second thud registered with her and the wood around the latch exploded into splinters before the door swung inward. One of the men surged into the apartment. In his hand, he gripped he a pistol and he was moving it around, looking for a target. The second man barreled through the door just a couple of steps behind the first.

So little space separated them that Gillen didn't bother to yell for the men to stop. Her pistol popped twice and one of the intruders grunted as bullets drilled into him. However, his body continued to hurtle forward, powered by sheer momentum. She sidestepped him as a matador might move from the path of an angry bull, and he stumbled past her.

A dark blur flashed into her vision and something hard struck her wrist. She yelped, and the gun slipped from her fingers and hit the floor. Her attacker moved in close, grabbing a fistful of the fabric of her shirt, then hitting her in the ribs, hard, to knock her off balance. She stumbled back toward the wall. Her attacker grinned and stepped forward.

Then his head exploded in a fine red mist. His suddenly decapitated body lurched forward one more step before collapsing.

A big man stood behind the dead man's former position, a pistol in his outstretched hand. Smoke curled up from the handgun's barrel. The weapon coughed once more, sending a bullet into the man she'd shot a moment ago.

She saw the newcomer's lips move, thought she heard noise, but the words didn't register with her.

"Ms. Gillen. Tamara, we need to go," he said.

The sound of her own name jarred her from the shock that had startled to settle over her. His words sank in as he pulled her to her feet. She jerked her arm from his grip. He didn't resist.

"Who are you?" she asked.

He shook his head. "No time."

She stayed rooted to the spot. "Who are you?" she repeated.

"I'm a U.S. federal agent. I'm here because of Terry Lang."

"Terry?"

He nodded. "Let's go."

When they stepped into the hallway, the man stopped.

She noticed that even while standing still, he radiated an energy as though he were coiled, ready to strike. He wheeled ninety degrees, his gun coming up at the same time. Gillen stared after him and saw the cause of his consternation. A man was stepping into view from an adjoining hallway, an assault rifle clutched in his arms, the barrel tracking in on her and her companion.

BOLAN SENSED THE FIRST attacker before he came into view. He wheeled around, the Beretta's snout zeroing in on his target, a man toting an AK-47. The Executioner squeezed the trigger and the Beretta spit a triburst of 9 mm manglers. The slugs hammered into the man's chest and caused him to freeze in midstride before he collapsed to the floor.

A second shooter moved in on Bolan and Gillen. The hardman's machine pistol spewed fire and lead. Bullets sliced through the air inches above the soldier's head. A double tap of the Beretta's trigger and the gun coughed out a flurry of six rounds that didn't strike flesh, but drilled into the wall just behind his attacker, forcing him to take cover.

Bolan whipped his head toward Gillen.

"Move," he shouted, gesturing at the mouth of a nearby hallway.

Nodding, she turned and sprinted for the corridor.

The Executioner squeezed off two more bursts from the Beretta. The cover fire put his enemies on the defensive. He ejected the handgun's magazine and slammed another into the weapon's grip. In the same instant, another gunner mistook the lull in firing as a chance to catch his opponent by surprise. He came around the corner. The move exposed the shooter's face and his gun hand. Bolan's Beretta chugged out a volley of 9 mm rounds. Simultaneously the other man's own weapon cracked, spitting jagged tongues of flame from its muzzle. A couple of bullets from the AK ripped through the fabric of Bolan's windbreaker while other rounds slammed into plasterboard or ripped through carpet and wood.

The 9 mm slugs from the Beretta drilled into the gunner's face. The impact spun him violently. Even as the guy slammed to the floor, Bolan heard metal clicking on metal behind him. He wheeled and saw that Gillen had disappeared from view. Moving through the mouth of the corridor into which she'd just disappeared, he spotted a metal door with an exit sign fixed above it at the end of the hallway. The soldier marched toward the door, hoping he could catch up with the woman before Nawaz Khan and his people found her.

# CHAPTER EIGHT

Aleksander Mazorov knew he needed to move fast.

The big Russian raced up the stairs with a stealth that belied his size. In his right hand, he clutched a Browning Hi-Power. He heard a door snap closed from a couple of flights of stairs above. A smile ghosted his lips. He guessed, hoped, that the woman was coming his way, perhaps with the bastard who'd shot his men right at her side. His grip on the Browning tightened, but he kept it flat against his thigh while he continued to climb the steps. He needed to grab the woman and get the hell out of the building as soon as possible, before the local police arrived and he either got scooped up by them or had to shoot his way out of the situation.

From above, he could see a shadow moving over the wall, could hear the slap of her feet against the stairs as she rushed down.

He raised the Browning. A heartbeat later he saw calves clad in dark slacks fall across his line of sight. When the woman came into view, her eyes seemed to look first at the gun barrel and widen with surprise and terror as she realized what she'd come up against. She froze. Mazorov guessed her mind was racing, ticking through her options, weighing whether to pivot and run or to perhaps rush him. Or she could just be frozen with terror, though he somehow doubted it. Considering that she'd met her initial attackers with a pistol, he guessed she wasn't the shrinking violet type.

Maybe, he decided, she just needed some prompting.

"Hands up," he said. "Or I'll kill you."

She brought her hands up slowly, elbows cocked at nearly ninety-degree angles. He stepped to one side and motioned for her to move down the stairs. She brushed past him and continued down the steps.

He allowed himself a tight smile. Mission accomplished.

GRIMALDI CROUCHED BETWEEN a pair of parked cars. Peering around the rear of one of the cars, a red BMW, he watched as the panel van's rear door fanned open and four shooters piled from the vehicle onto the concrete. He keyed his throat mike.

"Striker?"

"Go."

"The van has more hostiles unloading. I count four."

"They coming my way?"

"Not if I can help it," Grimaldi said.

"Clear. Thanks."

With the Colt Commando leading the way, the lanky Stony Man pilot came up in a crouch and closed the distance between himself and the group of shooters. As he neared them, he heard snatches of muttered conversation. He recognized a couple of words as Russian. What the hell was going on? he wondered. What did the Russians have to do with this? Where they Russian *mafiya?*

One of the gunners gestured at the door leading from the garage into the apartment building. The others stood by, listening to his orders. Grimaldi listened just long enough to realize he'd garner no good information from them as long as they continued to speak Russian. He came up from the shadows, raised the Commando to his shoulder, the retractable buttstock snug against his body.

One of the hardmen saw him. The Russian simultaneously opened his mouth to shout a warning and brought up his hand, which clutched a submachine gun. Grimaldi triggered the Commando and unleashed a swarm of 5.56 mm rippers from the weapon that drilled into the guy's chest. His target jerked in place for a moment under the onslaught of autofire. Grimaldi turned slightly and caught a second hardman under a withering hail of fiery death.

Simultaneously the man who'd been handing out orders moved into action. He spun in Grimaldi's direction, dropped into a crouch and loosed a burst of autofire from an Uzi. The rounds hammered into the concrete just in front of Grimaldi. While the guy tried to improve his aim, the Stony Man pilot returned the favor with another burst from the Commando. The bullets sliced the air just past the man's face. Though they missed flesh, the guy jerked back hard to get out of the line of fire, and the motion caused him to lose his balance and stumble back a couple of steps. In the same instant Grimaldi triggered his weapon again. The ensuing burst stitched across the guy's torso, causing a trail of crimson geysers to explode from his chest before he collapsed to the ground.

Tires squealed, and Grimaldi responded by wheeling around toward the noise. The van was hurtling toward him, quickly gaining speed. The pilot dived sideways, throwing his body between a pair of cars. He grunted when his body hit the concrete, and bolts of pain shot out from his shoulder where it collided with the ground. The van roared by, just missing him.

Pulling himself to his feet, Grimaldi caught sight of the van. Brake lights glowed red and rubber squealed against concrete as the vehicle slowed. He rested the Commando on the roof of the parked car in front of him and tapped the trigger. The 5.56 mm slugs hammered into the van, sparking off its steel skin.

The weapon ran dry, and Grimaldi let the weapon hang on its strap while he replaced it with the Beretta 92 that rode in a shoulder holster. He raised the weapon and tried to draw a bead on the van. Before he could line up a good shot, the vehicle had turned a corner and was rolling down a ramp to a lower floor.

The pilot sprinted forward, but by the time he reached the ramp, the van had disappeared. He heard tires squealing from the floor below him. Whoever was driving obviously wanted to get the hell out of the garage and put some distance between themselves and the firefight.

Grimaldi ran to the nearest stairwell and sprinted down to the ground floor. Hitting the release bar on the door, he burst through the doorway, into another level of parking. He arrived in time to see the van hurtling out of the garage.

BOLAN GLIDED DOWN THE steps, the Beretta in a two-handed grip. A voice rose up from the floors below and the soldier froze, straining to hear. The voice definitely sounded female, and he guessed it was Gillen.

He had to descend another flight of steps before the voices gained more clarity.

"I told you," he heard Gillen say, "I don't know where Lang is."

"And I told you, I don't care. You're coming with me."

"Damn it!"

A sharp slapping sound reached Bolan's ears. Gillen yelped in surprise and pain. Bolan felt his face and neck flush hot with anger and his jaw clenched tight. By now, he had moved about one floor above Gillen and her captor. He deliberately slowed his pace so he could monitor the situation without alarming the gunman and putting Gillen in greater danger. They were continuing to descend the stairwell.

The sound of someone pressing on a door's release bar reached Bolan. He walked around the landing, spotted the man pushing open the door with one hand and motioning Gillen to go through it with the hand holding a gun. The Executioner stood fast for a couple of seconds to give Gillen enough time to pass through the door.

In the meantime, the big American locked the Beretta's barrel on Gillen's captor. Bolan cleared his throat.

The man spun, his pistol hunting for a target. Bolan tapped the Beretta's trigger and a triburst lanced into the guy's ribs, breaking bone and drilling into his torso. The hardman staggered back a step, hitting the wall behind him, then raised his weapon and snapped off a wild shot that sounded like a thunderclap in the cramped confines of the stairwell.

The Beretta sighed again. This time, the slugs punched into the man's heart and killed him. His body slammed against the wall, leaving a crimson smear as it slid to the floor.

Bolan raced down the steps and was through the door in seconds. He found himself on the bottom floor of the garage. The sound of footfalls thudding against the concrete reached him. He looked forty-five degrees to the right and saw Gillen moving at a dead run to get away from him. Before he could call out to her, she stole a glance over her shoulder, saw him standing there and kicked the speed up another notch.

The soldier muttered a curse and raced after her. He couldn't blame her for running. Despite his assurances that he was there to help, he was a complete stranger and she'd watched several people die violently at his hands in a short span of time. She'd also almost gotten kidnapped while under his "protection."

So, no, he couldn't blame her for running away. But it made his job much harder. The soldier poured on the speed to try to bridge the distance between them. He also holstered the Beretta, guessing that the sight of a gun wasn't helping matters, either. He began to gain on her, the distance between them shrinking to about ten yards. He could hear her breathing, loud, but measured, as though she'd trained as a runner.

She turned right and ran for an exit. The turn cost her some speed and she took it wide, providing Bolan a chance to pivot and head after her diagonally. She stopped to pull open the door and he was able to close in on her, wrapping his arms around her upper body and pinning her arms against her.

"Let me go," she shouted as she struggled.

"Gillen," Bolan said, "I'm here to help."

She continued to struggle. Raising her foot, she stomped down hard on the ground, just missing Bolan's foot.

"Damn it. Stop!"

Sirens wailed in the distance. From his peripheral vision, Bolan saw someone approaching. He whipped his head around, anticipating trouble. He found Grimaldi walking toward them, the Colt Commando slung over his shoulder, a wide grin playing on his lips.

"Unhand her, knave," Grimaldi said.

Bolan figured the struggle wasn't helping and he let her go. She'd been straining to break his grip and her suddenly free body hurtled forward, causing her to stumble a couple of steps before she stopped.

She wheeled around, her cheeks and neck scarlet with exertion and anger. She took a step forward and raised an open hand to deliver a hard slap at Bolan. The soldier noticed her hand was shaking and he guessed it was because of the adrenaline coursing through her. She didn't take another step, but the anger and fear didn't drain from her face, either.

"What the hell is the matter with you? You come into my apartment, my home, and start shooting people? Manhandle me?"

Bolan held up his hands, palms forward, in a placating gesturing. The sound of the sirens continued to grow louder.

"We need to go," he said. "You're in danger."

"Yeah, from you! I'm not going anywhere until you tell me what's going on."

Bolan shook his head. "Not now. Not here. You need to trust me."

She threw up her hands in frustration. "I don't even know you."

"If we stay here, we'll get picked up by the police. If my friend and I end up in jail, we can't help you. We lose valuable time. And Terry Lang died for nothing."

She opened her mouth to reply, hesitated. Her mouth closed and she shook her head slowly.

"Fine, damn it. Let's go."

"You won't regret this," Bolan said.

"Too late."

BOLAN WAS PACING THE hallway in the safehouse, speaking to Potts by cell phone.

"You realize you're giving me an ulcer," Potts said.

"Sorry."

"Oh, problem solved then."

"Look," Bolan replied, "just smooth things over with the locals. The last thing I need is them breathing down my neck while I'm trying to work on this. Will you handle it?"

Potts paused a couple of seconds. "Okay."

"Thanks."

"You're going to give me a heart attack. You know that? A big fat, fucking coronary. Which one of my ex-wives sent you here, anyway?"

"I thought I was giving you an ulcer," Bolan said, ending the call and slipping the phone into his pocket.

He walked to the kitchen, where he found Grimaldi and Gillen seated at a table. She'd pulled her long hair back into a ponytail and secured it with a rubber band. Her face looked freshly scrubbed, and she wore a white T-shirt that was too big for her. Flecks of blood had spattered on her other clothes and her exposed arms during the altercation at her apartment building.

A cup of coffee sat on the table in front of her. She'd wrapped her fingers around it and was staring glumly into the cup. When Bolan entered the room, she peered up at him, her expression stony.

"I gave her one of your extra shirts," Grimaldi said. "And some coffee."

Bolan pulled one of the chairs out from the table, spun it and sat on it. He rested his forearms on the top of the chair's back and looked at Gillen.

"Say it," she said.

"What?"

"Whatever the hell you're thinking, just spit it out."

"How well did you know Terry Lang?"

She thought about it for a couple of seconds, then shrugged. "We knew each other two years, maybe three. Worked together off and on during that time."

"That's not what I asked."

Her eyes dipped toward her coffee cup again. "We spent a lot of time together," she said.

Bolan detected something in her voice, maybe sadness, though he couldn't be sure.

"Were you sleeping together?"

Anger flashed in her eyes. She opened her mouth to say something, but the soldier cut her off.

"You're hiding something," he said. "If your big secret is that you two were lovers, then please spare me the modesty. I'm not a priest."

She pressed her lips together, forming a bloodless line.

"I feel violated," she said.

"I don't care," Bolan said.

"You're a son of a bitch."

Bolan said nothing. Grimaldi kept his mouth shut, but

turned his gaze from one to the other, as though he was watching a tennis match.

Finally she heaved a sigh and her shoulders sagged.

"We were sleeping together."

"And?"

She looked up a him. "And what?"

"What else? I mean, that's the big confession? What else is going on?"

Her face flushed and she crossed her arms over her chest.

"Look, he was married. Sleeping with him isn't something I'm proud of. We worked together, collaborated on a few things. It just happened."

"Maybe you weren't looking for it," Bolan said. "But Terry apparently was looking for it all over. Now some people are trying to kill you. Maybe it was because he was your bunk mate. Maybe not. Regardless, Terry's dead and someone apparently wants to kill you, too."

"Or at least capture you," Grimaldi added. "That wouldn't be pleasant, either."

"Did he tell you anything?" Bolan asked. "Say he was worried for his life?"

She hesitated. "The man, the one you shot on the stairs. We saw him a couple of days ago at a hotel. It really bothered Terry, unnerved him like I'd never seen before."

"He say why?" Bolan asked.

She shook her head. "No. I just noticed the change in him once he saw the guy. He got nervous, edgy. In retrospect, I can see why. The guy back there was a killer. He would have killed me."

Bolan nodded his agreement.

She raised her coffee mug to her lips, took a deep swallow and returned it to the table. Bolan noticed a small shudder pass through her and she hugged herself again.

"That's not the first close call," she said. "I was in Iraq, working for the wire services. The unit I was embedded with got ambushed. The soldiers I was with were killed, shot by a sniper. I was pinned down and scared out of my mind. Fortunately, another unit rolled in at the last minute and killed the snipers. I almost died that day."

"You were fortunate," Bolan said.

Nodding, she reached into the pocket of her jeans, fished around a couple of seconds and pulled her hand back out. She set a silver key on the table.

"What's it for?" Grimaldi asked.

"Not sure," she said with a shrug. "After we saw the Russians back at the hotel, Terry gave it to me. He told me to hang on to it, but that was all he said. He could be like that."

"And you didn't press him?" Grimaldi asked.

"No. Terry and I have known each other for a while. When he wasn't going to explain something, he made it obvious. You didn't force him to talk about something until he was ready."

Bolan nodded his understanding, though his gut told him the woman was still holding something back. He decided to take another stab in the dark.

"What are you working on right now?"

"Excuse me?" Gillen said.

"Stories. What stories are you working on."

Her eyes narrowed. "None of your business."

"Right now, it is. Were you collaborating on anything with Lang?" Bolan pressed.

She shook her head no.

"Working on any crime stories?"

"Nothing out of the ordinary," she replied. "Since I'm in a bureau, it has to be a big deal for me to cover a crime. If some guy gets mad and kills his brother-in-law, readers in London or Washington, D.C., don't want to know about it. Occasionally, some money guy or someone with a charity may get busted for shipping money to al Qaeda. When that happens, my editors want it. Over here, though, most of what I write about is commercial real estate and growth. The financial stuff, that's what people in London and Washington want to know about."

"Sure. How about Terry? What was he working on?"

Again, she shook her head. "Not sure," she replied. "We never talked about work."

"Bullshit."

She blinked. "Excuse me?"

"You heard what I said. You can't tell me that you two never talked shop, ever. You can't put two reporters in a room together for thirty seconds without them talking about work."

She'd been hugging herself, fingers encircling biceps. Bolan noticed her hands tighten and she leaned farther back in her chair.

"We didn't do that."

The soldier exhaled loudly. With his forefinger and thumb, he pinched the bridge of his nose and squeezed his eyes shut. Pulling his hand away, he opened his eyes and looked at the reporter.

"You must think you're extremely clever or I'm extremely stupid," he said. "Whatever. Either way, you're lying to me."

She licked her lips and stared at Bolan, her eyes not bulging, but wide enough to tell Bolan something was wrong. "I'm telling the truth."

The soldier nodded. Standing, he walked over to the coffee machine and poured himself a cup of coffee. He brought the cup to his lips, blew on it and stared ahead, studying the swirls in the wood grain of the cabinet doors.

"They peeled his skin off," Bolan said.

"What?"

"The people who took Terry, they peeled his skin off, while he was alive. They stabbed him more times than I can count. Not fatal wounds, mind you. Just enough and in the right spots to put him through agony. I'd guess he was miserable his last hours on Earth."

She turned in her seat and gave Bolan a look of shock and horror. "Why are you telling me this? What's wrong with you?"

Bolan set the coffee on the counter and turned slowly to face the woman.

"I'm not sure what your game is," he said. "But I know you're not being straight with me. Why, is anybody's guess. You haven't told me anything useful. Apparently you don't care that Lang's dead. So I figured why not share a few more details? You don't give a shit anyway."

"You're a bastard!"

"Sure I am," the soldier said. "Here's the thing, though. I'm trying to figure out what happened to Terry, find out who killed him and why. It bothers me that he died the way he did. You, on the other hand, seem at peace with the whole thing. So I thought I'd unburden myself. It worked. I feel better already."

With his hands, Bolan pushed off the counter and started across the room.

"Wait!" she called after him. "You can't keep me here. Am I under arrest? If not, then you can't keep me here."

His hand on the doorknob, Bolan paused, then shrugged. "So leave."

He opened the door, stepped out into the hallway and kept on walking. Grimaldi followed behind him a couple of heartbeats later.

"Wow," the pilot said, "which nugget of information should we follow up on first?"

"I'd send her packing," Bolan said. "But I think that'd be like putting a bullet in her head. Whoever tried to find her earlier, is going to come for her again. I'm sure of it."

"So what next?"

"You stay here," Bolan said. He handed Grimaldi the key

that the woman reporter had provided him. "If you can get her to spill her guts, great. In the meantime, I need to keep looking for Khan."

# CHAPTER NINE

Yuri Sokolov sat in the cabin of his Gulfstream executive jet. He listened to the engine's whine as the craft cut through the air over Asia. Thoughts of what lay ahead rolled through his mind. It comforted him to think of such things, distracting him from the horrible thing sealed in a special smuggling compartment built into the aircraft, one normally reserved for weapons or drugs.

Absently he grabbed at the cloth napkin folded over his left thigh, dabbed imaginary beads of sweat from his upper lip and returned the napkin to his lap. He'd meet Haqqani in Karachi in a matter of hours, at the airport, where he could pass along the horrible substance the plane carried.

Then he'd get back on the plane and get his ass back out of Karachi. Fast.

He noticed his left foot tapping out a rapid-fire beat and willed himself to stop. What the hell is the matter with you? he wondered. Quit acting like a damn child and do this.

A tumbler of vodka was clutched in his right hand. Bringing it to his lips, he drained it, thankful he was alone. If the others—the ones who signed his paychecks—saw him acting this way, jumping at shadows that existed only in his mind, they'd kill him.

A rueful smile crossed his lips. Rising to his feet, he crossed the cabin to a wet bar and poured more vodka. After ten years with the KGB and then with the FSB, you'd think you'd be used to danger, he told himself. And used to bad bosses. He'd had more than his share of both through the years.

But these people, the ones with the Seven, were the worst. It'd all seemed so good up front. They'd showered him with money. And with women, lots and lots of women, he thought, allowing himself another smile. And it'd all seemed pretty easy. Carry a couple of suitcases filled with the money to Sunnis insurgents in Iraq. Ferry precision-machined centrifuge parts to Iran. He essentially was a well-paid delivery man. Very well paid.

But this…

This could start a war. Start many wars.

Enough, he told himself. His job was to deliver, not to worry about consequences. He was a foot soldier and foot soldiers, in his view, did what they were told. They let smarter people worry about the consequences.

He sank back into one of the jet's plush seats. Besides, they'd assured him all this was temporary, essentially a ruse. He'd pass along the materials. They'd take them back later—by force if necessary. Sokolov ran his fingers through his thinning, reddish-brown hair. He didn't trust Daniel Masters as far as he could throw the little British fuck. Didn't trust any Englishman, for that matter, especially not one willing to undercut his homeland. But even that oily bastard wouldn't lie about something so important.

No, he told himself, Masters wouldn't lie about this.

And, if he did, frankly, it wouldn't matter. Masters had the Council of Seven convinced he knew what he was talking about. Therefore, he held all the cards. In Sokolov's little world that meant shutting up and doing as he was told.

And he'd do that.

Even if it brought Armageddon down on the whole world.

Sokolov watched Nawaz Khan push his way through the door of the aircraft, followed by an entourage of maybe a half dozen men.

The Russian made no effort to hide his disgust at the

Pakistani. Sokolov's brother, a Spetsnaz soldier, had been killed in Afghanistan, the personnel carrier he was traveling in pulverized by a Stinger missile, one presumably supplied by the United States. In light of that, he had little use for the Pakistanis, or the United States, for that matter.

Nawaz Khan marched up to within a foot of the Russian and stood, his fists cocked on his hips, and stared at Sokolov.

"You have it?" Khan asked finally.

"Yes."

Khan nodded approvingly. "And you can show us how to use this material?"

"Of course," Sokolov replied.

"Good."

A phone trilled from somewhere in the knot of men positioned behind Khan. From the corner of his eye, Sokolov saw one of the men bring a phone to his ear and heard him utter what the Russian assumed was a greeting, though he didn't understand the language. The man paused and listened. When he spoke again, the volume of his voice rose. Though Sokolov couldn't understand what the man was saying, he easily recognized the distress in the man's voice. By now Khan had turned to look at his assistant. The arch of the Pakistani's eyebrows, the ripple of his cheek muscles as he clenched and unclenched his jaw betrayed his worry, Sokolov thought.

When the man hung up the phone, he looked at Khan.

Khan gestured at Sokolov with an open palm. "Excuse me," he said. He turned and walked with his assistant to another section of the cabin, out of earshot of Sokolov, at least at first. As the conversation progressed, Khan's voice rose to a point where Sokolov could hear the conversation even though he couldn't interpret the words spoken. Khan occasionally punctuated his statements by jabbing his index finger into the man's chest. When the conversation ended, the man turned and exited the airplane while Khan came back to Sokolov, a strained smile plastered across his lips.

The Russian flashed a smile of his own. "Trouble?"

Khan shook his head. "Nothing we can't handle. This business we're in, it occasionally yields some surprises, yes?"

"Expect the unexpected," Sokolov replied.

"Certainly."

Sokolov stepped forward, bent his head until his face hovered within inches of Khan's own. The former KGB agent's smile faded. "If you have trouble on your hands," he growled through clenched teeth, "you better damn well deal with it before it becomes our trouble, too. You understand me, yes?"

Khan swallowed hard and nodded. "Yes."

"Good, I feel better already," Sokolov said.

Khan nodded in the direction of his entourage. "You can supervise them as they unload the cargo? You know better than they do how to handle the material."

"Damn straight I do."

# CHAPTER TEN

Binoculars pressed to his eyes, Bolan studied the warehouse. He was on the roof of a neighboring building, crouched next to a large chiller unit, his body enveloped by shadows.

He'd been situated there for hours, studying the number of guards, their patterns of movement, their weaponry, making note of it all in his mind.

Thus far, he'd logged two trucks within the past hour rolling into the warehouse. Both were nondescript, large tractor-trailer rigs, engines growling, pipes belching smoke into the air. He'd been unable to get a good look at the drivers, though that mattered little to him, either.

He was more concerned with what lay inside the warehouse than anything else.

According to intelligence gathered by Stony Man Farm, Khan owned the warehouse through a web of shell companies, and it was believed to be a transit point for some of the weapons the Pakistani shipped to conflict zones worldwide.

Hitting the facility would accomplish two goals as far as Bolan was concerned. One, he could hobble Khan's weapons-smuggling ring and—at least temporarily—prevent deadly weapons from getting into the hands of killers. Second, since Khan had submerged out of sight, Bolan figured his best tack was to drop some depth charges and bring the guy back to the surface. Sort of like fishing with hand grenades.

But first he wanted to make sure he had the right spot.

The intel he had was good, but he wanted to make sure it was right. The only way to do that was to check out the place himself.

He had changed into his combat blacksuit and smeared black camo paint on his cheeks, nose and forehead. The sun had fallen hours ago, taking down the heat considerably, making the surveillance gig more tolerable.

Grabbing his gear, the soldier got to his feet. He carried with him the usual handguns and also had brought along a Heckler & Koch MP-5 K. He looped the SMG's strap over his head and right shoulder, then pulled on a lightweight black trench coat to hide his weapons and other gear.

Walking up to the edge of the roof, he set both palms on the ledge, swung first one leg, then the other over the side and lowered himself slowly until he hung from his fingertips. Releasing his grip, he dropped to the top landing of the fire escape below, folding into a crouch. He scrambled down the stairs until he reached the final landing and, releasing the ladder, dropped to the alley below. Light in the alley was limited. Bolan glided along the wall of the building he'd just left. He stopped at the corner, flattened his back against the wall and stole a glance around the edge and saw that the target warehouse remained busy. A tractor-trailer idled outside the building.

The soldier surged across the street to the outer perimeter of the warehouse, using the big truck for cover.

From his surveillance, he'd gathered that one or two guards patrolled the exterior at any given time. They didn't wear uniforms, but instead dressed in khakis and royal-blue polo shirts. They looked as much like insurance salesmen as anything else, except for the pistols clipped to their belts. They appeared to communicate via mobile telephone rather than with radios. Both guards had deep brown skin and jet-black hair, and Bolan guessed they were of south Asian extraction.

One of the men was tall, wide and thick, built like a weightlifter. He wore his hair cut close to the scalp and rested the palm of his right hand on the butt of his pistol. The second guard was big, too, but soft, dumpy. A lit cigarette dangled from his lower lip.

He'd ignited that smoke with his previous one. The man paced continuously, his gaze sweeping over the area. Bolan was unsure whether the guard was careful or nervous or both.

The weightlifter stood in the center of one of the bay doors and glowered at the idling truck in front of him, as though he held it back with the sheer force of his will.

Bolan loosened his trench coat. His hand dipped inside and he fisted the MP-5's pistol grip, but kept the weapon hidden beneath the folds of the coat. When he reached the warehouse, he crept alongside its exterior, making sure to keep his ears attuned for any signs of danger such as footsteps from ahead or behind. Other than the rumble of the truck engine and an occasional shouted command from one of the guards, Bolan heard little else.

Earlier in the day, Aaron Kurtzman had tracked down a set of architectural drawings of the warehouse, and Bolan had done his best to memorize the details. When he reached the entrance, he peeled off the trench coat, rolled it up and tossed it into a nearby fifty-five-gallon drum that was partially filled with garbage.

The soldier tried the knob and found it was locked. The door was secured with a dead bolt. Kneeling, Bolan reached into one of the slit pockets on his blacksuit and withdrew a set of lock picks. Within minutes, he'd opened the door.

Stepping across the threshold, the soldier blinked involuntarily at the light as he pulled the door shut behind him. As his eyes adjusted, he swept his gaze over the warehouse's interior. Overhead, catwalks crisscrossed the cavernous space. An overhead crane, presumably used for moving the large shipping containers, was suspended from the ceiling.

A half dozen or so palettes piled high with crates were scattered around the warehouse. He studied the crates and saw that they had markings that identified the contents as auto parts. The soldier crouched beside one of them. A padlock sealed the crate, telegraphing that it didn't contain auto parts regardless of the markings stenciled on the sides in French and German.

Bolan picked open the padlock and lifted the top. Digging his way through the shredded packing materials, his fingertips quickly struck something hard. As he cleared away the packing materials, the soldier found four rectangular steel cases piled on top of one another. Opening the top case, he found a Kalashnikov AK-47 and several curved magazines. He quickly shut the case, then sealed the crate, putting the padlock back in place.

The soldier uncoiled from his crouch and wound his way between the stacks, mentally cataloging more than a dozen similar crates. He headed toward the large bay doors, using parked forklifts and stacked pallets for cover.

When the murmur of voices reached him, he melted into the shadows provided by several larger shipping crates lined up along a wall.

Peering from the shadows, he saw five men standing in a semicircle. A forklift burdened with a single crate stood to one side. Bolan recognized two of the men as the exterior guards. The three other men each carried an AK-47.

One of the men, his complexion a deep brown, a long unkempt beard hanging from his chin, was waving his arms and speaking in a loud voice at the others. The man spoke English, and Bolan thought he detected a British accent.

"Something's going on," the man said. "You think we don't hear things on the street? The Americans are looking for Khan! If they're looking for him, that means they'll come looking for us, too."

The heavyset guard gestured for the other man to shut up. "You don't know what you're saying. Listen to you. You're like a child, scaring himself with silly stories."

"Silly? I heard what happened to Sharif. I know he was killed. He and his people all are dead!"

Bolan watched as the fat man's lips turned up in a humorless smile. "Sharif was a fool."

"Fool or not, he's dead. And he was killed by the Britisher."

"You don't know that."

"Bullshit, the Englishman killed Sharif, shot him in the head to silence him. He's supposed to be on our side, but he gunned down Sharif in cold blood. What the hell was that about?"

The fat man realized he was losing the argument. When he spoke again, Bolan noticed a hard edge had crept into his voice.

"Look, if you don't like the deal you're getting, maybe you'd like to join Sharif."

"Fuck you," the other man snapped. "Just give me the shipment and I'll move it out of here. You know I'll do it. It's not like I have any damn choice."

Something in the man's tone struck the soldier. Why didn't this guy have a choice? Was he being coerced in some way or just playing victim? Regardless, the guy seemed disgruntled and scared enough that Bolan probably could pump him for information.

But first, he had to deal with the situation at hand.

Moving in a crouch, the soldier came around the crates he'd used for cover. The bearded guy who a moment ago had been complaining glimpsed Bolan first. His eyes widened and locked on the big American.

The nervous guard on steroids noticed the change in the

guy's face. He wheeled around while his hand clawed at his sidearm. The MP-5 spoke first, chugging out a brutal burst that stitched the guard from left hip to right shoulder.

Pistol already freed, the heavyset guard pivoted toward Bolan. The guard's pistol cracked and a bullet sizzled just past the Executioner's temple. Before the guy could correct his aim, Bolan squeezed the H&K subgun's trigger and loosed a concentrated burst that shredded the man's torso. As the guard crumpled to the ground, Bolan trained the MP-5's barrel on the three men, all of whom stood frozen and stared at him.

Bolan ticked through the numbers in his head. He'd seen four guards enter at what seemed to be shift change. Two were done, leaving as many unaccounted for.

He wagged the MP-5's barrel.

"On the ground," he growled between clenched teeth. Two of the men, including the bearded man who'd been speaking a few minutes before, complied immediately. The third man, who looked no less terrified than the others, hesitated. When he glanced at the others and saw them going to ground, he mimicked their behavior. Bolan guessed the man didn't speak English.

The soldier's combat senses screamed for his attention. On instinct, Bolan spun to the left. In the same instant a gunshot registered with him and a bullet whistled past his head. He spotted a guard, pistol held in front of him in a two-handed grip, who had tried to sneak up on the soldier's flank. Bolan whipped the MP-5 around, triggered a blistering barrage of 9 mm slugs and dragged the weapon in a horizontal line. The gunfire cut the man down like a scythe slashing tall grass.

Bolan guessed that, if the fourth guard remained in the building, he'd seen the carnage unfolding either firsthand or via security monitor screens. The big American walked to the three men laying on the ground, all of whom were trying to sneak looks at the soldier.

"You two," he said to the men closest to him, "get the hell out of here."

The first man scrambled to his feet and put his hands in the air. The second man, the one who seemed to not understand English, saw that the first man was standing and followed suit.

"Go," he said. He gestured toward the doors with his submachine gun. Turning, they headed for the door. Bolan had no illusions. Just because they'd complied and left without a fight, didn't mean they wouldn't call Khan and alert him to the raid on his warehouse. It mattered little to him; he planned to be gone soon enough.

The Executioner walked up to the third man and nudged him in the thigh with the toe of his boot. The guy took a sharp intake of air, but turned his head and chanced a look up at the soldier.

"On your feet," Bolan said.

The man rose quickly to his feet and raised his hands above his head.

"Don't shoot," he said.

"I won't," Bolan replied.

The man shot the soldier a confused look. "You just killed three of Khan's guards. Why the sudden mercy?"

"You're an inquisitive SOB. I need you to send a message to Khan. Yeah, Khan. The big guy. You ready?"

The guy swallowed hard, but nodded.

"Tell him I'm just starting. I'm going to destroy every last piece of property, every business, every weapon he has. Then, when I'm done with that, I'm going to destroy him," Bolan said.

"Who are you?"

"Cooper. He'll know."

"He's not going to take this well."

"Good."

"Can I go?" the guy asked.

"Not yet," Bolan said. "A couple of minutes ago, you said you had no choice but to follow Khan's orders. Why is that?"

The man cast his eyes downward and studied the tops of his shoes for several seconds. When he looked back up at Bolan, all the fear had drained away, replaced by a steely anger.

"He has my half sister."

"Captive?"

"Might as well be."

Bolan knew he was running out of time, but he wanted to know more.

"Explain."

"She's a prostitute," the man said. "A whore, okay? Khan runs whores here in Dubai. He lures women, poor women like her, from Karachi and brings them here to have sex for money. Even if she could leave Khan's organization, she couldn't go home again. Not to Pakistan, anyway."

"And you got involved in this how?"

The guy shrugged and uttered a humorless laugh. "I came here to help her. I had a little money and thought I could pay Khan to let her go. Instead he has me driving a truck for him."

"And whenever you step out of line, someone threatens your sister," Bolan concluded.

"Yeah."

"You won't have to worry about Khan much longer," Bolan said.

Nodding, the guy turned and took a step toward the truck.

"Stop," the soldier said.

The guy halted in his tracks.

"You have cargo in there?" Bolan asked.

"Sure, we just loaded it."

"Is it your truck?"

"Like I could afford this," the man replied.

"Then leave it. Toss the keys and get the hell out of here."

The man did as he was told. He was gone within a minute.

Bolan searched the rest of the premises, checking the contents of shipping containers and planting explosive charges along the way. Inside one of the offices, he found a laptop resting on a desk, the power still on. He turned the machine off and stuffed it in his satchel, figuring that maybe Kurtzman could mine it for additional information.

After Bolan exited the warehouse, he walked around its perimeter one last time, making sure the area was clear of bystanders. With that accomplished, the soldier left the premises and put some distance between himself and the warehouse. He punched a couple of buttons on a detonator. A heartbeat later, thunder pealed from a block away. A sudden flash of daylight seemed to illuminate the sky before it winked out. Bolan glanced over his shoulder and saw black oily clouds boiling up from the blast site, choking the night sky. Debris from the pulverized warehouse rained to the ground.

He headed for his car, his mind already focused on his next target.

# CHAPTER ELEVEN

The Raptor was a strip club located a mile or so from Dubai International Airport, making it an easily accessible stop for businessmen and royalty flying into or out of the country. The place had been owned by a pair of Russian brothers who'd immigrated to Dubai a decade or so earlier. At first, it had provided them with a place to launder money on behalf of their uncle, a former Soviet Union bureaucrat who'd siphoned off millions of dollars from the remnants of the Communist state after it had fallen. After the uncle died in an airplane accident, the brothers had found themselves unable to operate it without their uncle's money and had sold it to Khan.

Bad for them, good for Khan. Propped up by proceeds from Khan's gunrunning, the club had exploded, becoming a go-to nightspot for Dubai's high rollers, of which there were plenty.

This night, Mack Bolan was among them.

Decked out head to toe in black—suit, gleaming Italian loafers, T-shirt—the soldier rolled up to the club.

Bolan entered the nightclub, a cigarette clenched between his teeth. The bouncer, a thickset man, head topped with bright red hair, stood next to the door. He glowered at Bolan and held out an open palm. Pulling a wad of bills from his pocket, the Executioner peeled off enough to pay the cover charge and to buy some extra goodwill from the guy.

Bolan nodded at the stage, a round platform ringed by barstools. "When's the next show?" he asked.

Stuffing the money into his shirt pocket, the guy glanced at his watch. "Twenty minutes, give or take. If you can't wait that long, you can buy a private show with one of the ladies."

The Executioner nodded and swaggered into the club. He stopped along the way and checked his briefcase at the coatroom, giving the buxom young woman behind the counter a hundred-dollar tip to keep the satchel safe.

The soldier was playing the part of a high roller, Michael Siloviki, a first-generation American, the child of Russian immigrants. If anyone bothered to check on his name, they'd also find that Michael had grown up in Brooklyn, where he'd managed to string together three convictions as a juvenile, all sealed. Additionally, he had bragging rights on one assault charge for smacking around a New York subway cop.

The club's interior was dark and Bolan peeled away his sunglasses from his face, folded them and stuffed them into the breast pocket of his jacket. He swept his gaze over the place like he owned it.

The club seemed to be the size of a college gymnasium, and now that he'd stepped inside Bolan could see that there were several smaller stages located throughout the club. On the farthest one, he saw a blonde dressed in a black bikini and pumps, the skin of her legs and stomach glistening with a light sheen of perspiration, gyrating on the stage. Two guys, their suit jackets draped over the backs of their chairs, the sleeves of their dress shirts rolled up, whooped with approval as she moved.

A network of brightly colored lights burned down on the place. Heavy metal music pounded from overhead speakers, the bass throbbing hard enough to shake loose a kidney. Bolan guessed the whole alcohol-and-strippers theme didn't sit well with the locals. He also guessed that Khan couldn't care less, any more than he cared about the scores of dead left by the weapons he sold around the world.

A young woman carrying a tray topped with a cash box and an empty glass approached him. Her jet-black hair was pulled back into a ponytail that looped around her neck, the tip dangling well past her collarbone. Her short white dress seemed to glow against her deeply tanned skin. Stepping close, she leaned in.

"You're new here, aren't you?"

"Is it obvious?"

She shrugged. "I know all the regulars. When I see a new face, it sticks out."

"My name's Michael," Bolan said.

"You're an American?"

"Last I checked."

"We get a lot of them here. Mostly business types. What business are you in, Michael?"

"I move money, among other things."

"Sounds mysterious."

"It is. Sometimes even I don't understand what I do."

She gave him a bigger laugh than the joke deserved. "I doubt that. You don't strike me as dumb. You seem like a smart guy."

"You seem pretty sure of that," Bolan said.

"Considering that we've been talking for all of—what?— two minutes. You haven't grabbed me or made a sleazy comment. You can't be all bad."

"Jet lag," Bolan said. "Otherwise, I'd be all over you. It'd be disgusting."

She laughed again. This time it sounded more sincere. "All right, Michael. I'll take your word for it. What are you drinking?"

"Scotch whiskey."

Nodding, she bustled away and Bolan allowed himself a chance to enjoy the sway of her hips as she moved. Once she'd disappeared into the crowd, Bolan turned his gaze back to his surroundings.

By the time a minute or so had passed, he had pegged at least a half dozen guys who he guessed were members of Khan's security team. The most obvious was a pair of bouncers, each of whom looked like he'd taken enough steroids to fuel a whole professional football team. Bolan tagged the other four because, even though they allegedly were operating under the radar, they looked tense and hyperalert compared to others in the crowd who were focused on the skin shows happening throughout the club. Plus, Bolan noticed that, other than a friendly wave, the strippers essentially ignored them to a degree they wouldn't ignore a paying customer.

The waitress returned. Bolan paid her for the drink and gave her a twenty-dollar tip.

"If there's anything else I can get you, let me know," she said.

Bolan nodded. "Thanks."

She gave him one more million-dollar smile before moving into the crowd.

Drink in hand, the soldier wove his way through the patrons, most of them togged in expensive suits and doused in gallons of cologne. The soldier brought the drink to his lips and took a small swallow. Setting the glass on a table, he looked the place over. A dancer stopped by and made small talk for a couple of minutes, then asked Bolan to buy her a drink. He handed her a twenty-dollar bill and told her he'd take a rain check on the drink.

Retrieving his glass, he started for a stairway located at the rear of the club. It led up to where Khan supposedly kept an office. A glance over his shoulder told him that three of the men he'd pegged as security types had broken away from the crowd. All were converging on him from different directions.

When Bolan reached the top step, he looked over his shoulder and saw a bouncer bounding up the stairs after him. Bolan flashed the guy his middle finger. If the guy understood what the gesture meant, the soldier hoped it would lead him to believe he was dealing with a belligerent customer, maybe a lovesick guy wanting to harass a dancer, or just another mean drunk. He saw no signs that the bouncers carried guns. If they did, they likely had them stowed in ankle holsters. Bolan guessed that the other security guards wouldn't show their weapons unless they had to because they wouldn't want to upset the customers. They'd want to keep everything as cool as possible. Maybe they'd try to push him around or intimidate him with sheer numbers, but they'd probably keep their guns put away as long as possible.

By the time they realized what they were into, it would be too late.

THE FIRST BOUNCER CAME at Bolan, his hands outstretched to grab the American. The soldier bent at the knees slightly and the bouncer's arms swiped empty air. In the same instant, Bolan drove a fist into the guy's solar plexus. The bouncer's eyes bulged, and his jaw went slack as he belched out the contents of his lungs. Pulling back his hand, Bolan made a fist and drove the little finger edge of it into the guy's temple. He pulled the punch so the blow wasn't fatal.

The man's knees buckled, and he dropped to the ground. Something registered in Bolan's peripheral vision, causing him to jerk his head back hard. A set of knuckles struck his jaw, shoving his head to the left. The force spun the rest of his body a quarter turn. By the time he caught his footing, he saw his attacker, the bouncer from the front door.

The guy obviously was used to relying on brute strength to win fights. He pulled back his right fist, ready to strike, his lip curled in a snarl. Bolan knew where the punch was coming from. He stepped left and his fist lashed out twice, striking the guy in the mouth and nose. The bouncer, his face a bloody mask, sagged and the Executioner drove him down with a final hard left to the jaw.

Two down, four to go.

A third bouncer raised his hand, in which he clutched something. Bolan recognized it as a stun gun. As the guy squeezed the trigger, wires snaked out in Bolan's direction. The soldier already was diving sideways. The implants from the stun gun buried into a fourth bouncer's overdeveloped pectorals as the guy had tried to sneak up on Bolan's six. The stricken bouncer jerked in place before he crashed to the ground.

Even as the gunner was still digesting what had just happened, Bolan was on the guy. He caught the man with an uppercut that staggered the bouncer before following up with a palm strike to the man's chin that knocked him off balance. Bolan gave the guy a hard shove that sent him crashing down the stairwell.

Two of the plainclothes guards were racing for the stairs, guns drawn. To Bolan's relief, he spotted a couple of other guards directing a crush of patrons, strippers and waitresses to the doors, presumably evacuating them in case any gunplay erupted.

Bolan spun on a heel and headed along the second-floor mezzanine to the club manager's door. From under his jacket, he pulled the Desert Eagle and thumbed back the hammer. When he reached the door, he drew down on the dead-bolt lock and fired. The single round punched through the lock and the door swung inward.

Whipping out of the doorway, Bolan just missed a volley of autofire that screamed out from the office. The shooters inside didn't stop there. Instead, they continued to hose down the wall with a vicious barrage that punched through the plasterboard, cutting a line toward Bolan and forcing him to give up some ground.

At the same time, from the corner of his eye, the Executioner spotted the two guards cresting the stairs, one just behind the other. Bolan dropped to one knee and drew down on the lead shooter. The guy, who had already been trying to get a bead on the Executioner, fired a couple of shots that screamed past the soldier's ear. The Desert Eagle thundered twice and the Magnum rounds pounded into the torso of Bolan's opponent. Geysers of blood erupted from the guy's chest and stomach, causing him to stagger before he crashed to the ground in a crumpled heap. The second shooter fared no better. Though he flattened himself against a nearby wall, trying to make himself as small a target as possible, Bolan managed to catch him in the face with a single Magnum slug, killing him.

Bolan reached under his jacket and yanked out a stun grenade, held in his belt with a special holster. He pulled the pin and tossed the bomb through the door of the office. The grenade erupted with a loud bang and a flash of light. The gunfire from inside suddenly ceased. He heard a panicked voice from inside the room calling for everyone to hold their fire.

Bolan holstered the Desert Eagle, exchanging it for the Beretta. He went around the door, the Beretta set for 3-round bursts. The room contained three people. Bolan recognized the manager, Zia Karmal, from pictures from a dossier that Stony Man Farm had provided. He pegged the other two, each armed with a Steyr AUG submachine gun, the barrels still smoking, as part of Karmal's security team. The hardman closest to Bolan, a rangy guy dressed in an expensive suit, was holding his Steyr with one hand, rubbing his eyes with the other. Bolan aimed the Beretta 93-R at the man and tapped the trigger. The pistol cut loose with a burst that cut a ragged vertical line along the guy's sternum. A pained cry erupted from the stricken guy's lips. His dying comrade's death cry spurred the other man to squeeze off an aimless burst from the Steyr. The gunfire punched through the glass of a recessed aquarium that ran the length of one wall. The glass burst and gallons of water, along with a dozen or so brightly colored exotic fish, spilled onto the floor.

The Executioner fired off another volley from the Beretta. The storm of 9 mm slugs caught the guy on the side of the head, stabbing into his ear and temple before blasting through the opposite side of his head. Even as the corpse crumpled to the floor, Bolan marched across the office. Shards of glass crunched beneath his shoes and he unconsciously avoided stepping on the fish flopping on the carpet.

Karmal by now seemed to have regained his senses. He yanked open the lap drawer on his desk and reached inside. The soldier took aim and fired a quick burst. The bullets chopped through the open desk drawer and Karmal pulled back his hand as though he'd been burned.

Bolan stepped into the guy's space and grabbed his necktie. He yanked it hard and Karmal pitched forward.

"Bad move, Zia," Bolan growled. He pulled up hard on the tie and forced Karmal to straighten. The soldier knew from Karmal's dossier that the guy spoke English, having worked as a translator and analyst for the ISI before joining Khan's organization.

"Who the hell are you?"

Bolan jerked the guy's tie again, then threw him up against a wall lined with bookshelves. The club manager's breath exploded from his lungs. The Executioner drove his forearm into Karmal's throat, pinning him against the wall.

"Here's the deal," Bolan said, the Beretta a few inches from Karmal's face. "I checked your record. You run a strip club for Khan. You run hookers in Dubai and are up to your neck in sexual slavery and human-trafficking rings. Now you've had the misfortune of meeting me."

"What do you want with me?"

Bolan gave a wicked smile. "You? I want nothing from you. You're barely on my radar screen."

"What do you want then?" Karmal asked.

"Your club."

"You can have it. Just let me go."

"Sure," Bolan said.

He let go of the guy's necktie and stepped back.

"It's all yours," Karmal said, holding up his hands, his palms forward, at shoulder height.

"Thanks," Bolan said, turning.

Karmal took a couple of steps toward the door. Bolan watched the guy's reflection in a pane of glass fixed in a liquor cabinet's door. Karmal chanced a look over his shoulder. When he saw Bolan's back was turned, he spun, raising a pistol at the same time. The soldier wheeled and let loose with a single burst from the Beretta that ripped into the man's midsection, punching him to the floor.

The soldier exited the room and headed down the stairs to the bar. He walked behind it, pulled up a couple of bottles and emptied the contents onto the bar. Grabbing a book of matches from a large glass bowl, he ignited the pack and tossed it onto the alcohol. A bluish-yellow flame rose up from the bar's top. Before leaving the now-empty club, Bolan stopped by the coatroom to make sure his satchel was still there. He located it tucked away in a corner of the small room lined on either side with rods laden with coats. Considering the briefcase's contents, he was grateful that the attendant hadn't taken off with it.

Satisfied, he found a back door, exited the club and put a couple of blocks between him and it. From inside his jacket, he pulled a detonator and thumbed the button that would trigger the thermite charges hidden inside the briefcase he'd checked at the coatroom.

# CHAPTER TWELVE

*Moscow, Russia*

Sasha Lebed balled his big hands into fists when he heard the report.

Lev Bria, the bearer of the bad news, was a young man, a Russian like Lebed, and had served as Lebed's intelligence expert. The younger man, dressed in an expensive suit, hair slicked back, reeked of cologne. In Moscow's underworld, Lebed knew that Bria enjoyed a reputation as an unholy terror, a killer. But right now the man's saucerlike eyes were locked on Lebed as he waited for his boss to say something. He licked his lips and fidgeted. Lebed savored the moment. He'd worked hard at getting people to be terrified of him, and it never hurt to enjoy the fruits of one's labor.

Lebed uncoiled from his seat and the young hit man flinched.

"Tell me again," Lebed said.

"The arms shipment planned for Kabul never left Dubai," he said. "Someone blew up the warehouse and everything in it. Millions of dollars in ordnance were lost."

"Khan told you this?"

"Yes," Bria replied.

"Did he tell you who did it?"

The young man shook his head. "No." He paused. "Well, he said he wasn't sure."

Lebed felt his face flush hot. "What do you mean, wasn't sure? How the hell does that happen?"

"Apparently someone had tapped into the phone system remotely and shut down the alarm system and any security cameras. We have nothing."

"They must have some idea," Lebed said, his voice sharp.

Bria nodded. "There's a federal agent. An American. He showed up after Khan killed the other man, Lang. Apparently he was investigating the disappearance."

"Apparently," Lebed said, "until he started blowing shit up. What kind of federal agent lands in a foreign country and starts blowing up warehouses?"

"I don't know," Bria stated.

"Of course you don't. You're an idiot, and it was a rhetorical question, besides."

Lebed watched, amused, as the other man's eyes narrowed and he set his jaw. He swallowed and in the silence between them the sound might as well have been a rock hitting the floor.

"Of course."

"Does this federal agent have a name?" Lebed asked.

"Matt Cooper."

Lebed rolled the name over in his mind, but it prompted no memories. It was a bland, common name. He'd never encountered the man before, that much he knew for certain. He leaned forward, set his fists on the desktop and stared at the hit man.

"Does this Cooper know what we're doing?"

"He knows about the weapons, obviously," Bria stated.

"Not us smuggling some shitty assault rifles to the world's mudholes, you idiot. I mean, does he know about the Red Mercury? Does he know about what we're planning for Mumbai?"

Bria shrugged. "I don't know."

"Seems like something you ought to know."

"You're right."

"Don't tell me I'm right, damn it. Tell me more about

Matt Cooper. I want to know who he is, what agency he works for, where he is staying. And I want to know if he knows about Mumbai. Understand?"

The other man nodded.

"Good, then get the hell out of here."

"What if Khan takes him out?" Bria asked.

"If he does, fine. But if not, we need to do it ourselves. If this son of a bitch gets in my way, I will hammer him. Do you understand me? I will pound him into meat. Now get the hell out of here and get me answers."

Bria turned on his heel and left. Khan walked around from behind his desk and swept his gaze over his luxuriously appointed office. He considered the situation and spit a curse. If Khan had told him ahead of time that he planned to kidnap an American—any American let alone a damn spook—he'd have told the Pakistani no. But Khan had— how did the Americans say it?—gone off the reservation. He'd done his own thing and had fucked things up. Now, they'd drawn the attention of the U.S. government.

Damn, damn, damn.

Lebed always had known that the Council of Seven's activities eventually would have attracted some kind of attention. Even the most clandestine organizations could remain submerged in the dark waters of espionage for only so long before time, carelessness or bad luck drove them to the surface. And not that he was scared of the Americans, of course. He'd given up on fear a long time ago, considered it the indulgence of lesser men, like his intelligence chief or Nawaz Khan.

No, Sasha Lebed had spent too much time and money, had spilled too much blood to indulge in fear now. Besides, no matter how much it pained him to admit it, he didn't cast the sole deciding vote on what missions the Council of Seven pursued. Even if he did, the goal was bigger than him, bigger than any single council member. He, like the other members of the group, wanted to see a resurgent Russia, one that stood toe to toe with the United States economically and militarily. It was a laudable goal and in his heart he knew it was the right thing. But he also knew it wouldn't come easily. It would take spending more time and money and spilling more blood, American blood, lots of it, if they were to achieve their goals.

He considered the carnage and violence that lay ahead. A yawn escaped his lips. More dead Americans? He could live with that.

It was the least of his concerns.

# CHAPTER THIRTEEN

Agent Potts slapped a wad of cash onto the tabletop and let the other man, Rajiv Yahya, get a good look at it before he snatched it back and stuffed it into his coat pocket.

"It's all there," Potts said.

"I want to count it."

"Sure, you can count it. Give me the information, I'll give you the money and you can count it, put it in the bank. Hell, you can wallpaper your bathroom with it, for all I care. But first tell me what I want to know."

The other man scowled at Potts and muttered an obscenity in Pashto.

"Rajiv," Potts said, "you're upset."

"You understand Pashto?"

"Just the nasty words," Potts said, grinning. He raised the teacup to his lips, took a sip and scowled. "Look, you called me here. I was at home, asleep, having nightmares about my divorce lawyer when you called. Now, either put up or shut up."

"You're looking for Nawaz Khan," Yahya said. He stared at Potts, apparently wanting to gauge his reaction. Potts made a conscious effort to keep his face impassive.

"Who says I'm looking for Nawaz Khan? I'm not even sure who Nawaz Khan is."

"You're full of it."

Potts leaned back in his chair and smiled. "Now you're just being mean."

"Do you want the information or not? I can sell it to someone else."

Potts rolled his eyes and pretended to stifle a yawn. "All right, high roller, what do you have?"

"So, you *are* looking for him."

"I didn't say that. But you never know what information will come in handy. Besides," he added, patting the breast pocket of his shirt, "I just love spending Uncle Sam's money. You know how many forms I have to fill out to pay a moron like you a little scratch?"

"Scratch?"

"Never mind. What've you got?"

"I have the cell phone number of Faquir Bajaur, Khan's number one lieutenant."

"Wow," Potts said, his voice bored.

Yahya leaned forward and hammered his fist on the table. "Damn it, Potts, listen to me."

"No, Rajiv you listen to me," Potts said, the index finger of his right hand stabbing the air between them. "You called me. You dragged me out of bed for a phone number? A fucking phone number? And you want me to pay you for it? I can get that with one call to Washington, assuming I ever wanted it in the first place, since it isn't even Khan's."

"It's his cell phone," Rajiv countered. "And you can get to Khan through Bajaur."

"Wow, I can barely contain myself."

Undeterred, Yahya continued. "You want the number or not?"

Potts sighed, retrieved the money and slapped it onto the tabletop. He pressed a palm over the money.

"I'll take it," the FBI man said. "My generosity is my curse."

Yahya recited the number and Potts slid the money to

him. The young man grabbed the cash, jammed it into the pocket of his blue jeans and rose to his feet.

"Pleasure doing business with you," Potts said.

The informant gestured at Potts with his middle finger and walked out of the restaurant. Potts allowed himself a grin. If the number worked out, this was very good news indeed. They could use it to trace the user. Potts weighed whether to call Cooper, but decided against it. He'd let Cooper know about the number eventually, of course. But it struck Potts as stupid not to do some preliminary checking before he passed on the information. He knew Washington had sent Cooper to Dubai, and Potts answered to Washington. Still, the last thing he wanted was to hold someone's coat while they waded into a fight. Besides, what if the information turned out wrong? He'd really feel like a horse's ass then and the last thing he needed was one more opportunity to feel that way.

To hell with it. He'd check it out.

YAHYA STROLLED THROUGH the open-air market and absentmindedly patted the pocket holding the cash from the FBI agent.

A grin tugged at his lips. Not bad for an hour's work, though certainly not worth all the bowing and scraping Potts required of his informants before the cheap American bastard would part with his cash. Stopping at a booth, he purchased a bottle of cola, twisted off the cap and guzzled some of the sweet liquid as he walked. He dragged the sleeve of his left forearm across his mouth and wiped away the cola's remnants.

Potts had paid him a thousand dollars for the information, not bad at all for a telephone number. The beauty of the deal was that the man who'd supplied him the phone number had promised to pay him five times that amount to pass the information to the FBI agent. Yahya had resisted the idea at first, of course. The last thing he needed was to piss off an American federal agent, particularly one who could be counted on to buy information on a regular basis.

But the man who'd supplied the phone number had assured Yahya that passing along the phone number was harmless, simply an effort to direct Potts and his fellow agents away from Nawaz Khan's trail. Once Potts found out the number was useless, Yahya would simply plead ignorance, tell Potts that he'd thought the information was good, that they both had been taken for fools. Potts would be angry with him, but he'd get over it. No informant passed along good information one hundred percent of the time. And, besides, if Potts wanted to be an ass about it, Dubai was a big damn place, and he could sell the bits and pieces he dug up to law enforcement and intelligence agencies from a dozen other countries.

He drained the last of his soda and tossed the bottle into a trash can. Walking a couple more blocks, he reached his destination, a glitzy fitness club that catered mostly to the Westerners who worked in the city as well as members of royal families from throughout the Middle East. Pushing through a pair of glass double doors, he stepped into the air-conditioned lobby, felt his cheeks and forehead suddenly turn cool as the climate-controlled air mixed with the perspiration on his skin.

When he reached the front desk, he showed them his membership ID, the one that had been dropped into his mailbox in a plain white envelope only hours before. He handed the card to a petite blonde woman who stood behind the counter. Taking the card, she studied it for a few seconds, handed it back to Yahya and gave him a wide smile.

"Have a good workout," she said.

Yahya thanked her and pocketed the card. A couple of

minutes later he was in the locker room where he went to a designated locker, worked the combination lock until the last tumbler fell into place and opened the door. He plucked a white envelope from the bottom of the locker, weighed it in his hand for a moment and smiled, satisfied that it probably contained the money he'd been promised. He pulled a second envelope from inside his pocket and shoved it into the locker and shut the door.

Message delivered, he thought. Time to go home.

"Did you get a location on that number?" Potts asked.

The guy seated in front of a PC nodded, but didn't break his gaze from the computer screen.

"Yeah," said Jake Restin, a member of the Dubai office's cybercrew. "We tapped into the cell phone provider's system and nailed it down by locating the signal."

Restin jotted something on a yellow message pad next to the computer, tore off the sheet and handed it to Potts. The FBI man studied the address, but it didn't strike a chord with him.

"Thanks, man," he said to Restin, and returned to his office. "Get me whatever other intel you can on this address and email it to me."

Picking up the receiver of his secure phone, he punched in Matt Cooper's number and waited for an answer. The phone rang several times before the call got switched over to voice mail. An automated voice told him to leave a message after the beep, which he did.

Hanging up the phone, he exited his office and marched into the bullpen area for the other agents. At that hour, he only found two agents working.

"Let's roll, girls," he said. "I've got something that needs our attention."

Both looked up from their work. Ed Russell, a fortyish agent with black hair and a tanned complexion honed on the golf course, sleeves of his white dress shirt rolled to just below his elbows, scowled. He had the contents of a folder—papers, fingerprint cards, photos—scattered over the top of his desk. He gestured at the papers and other items.

"Seriously, Potts?" Russell asked. "What the hell is it? Look at all this shit I have to do."

Potts pointed a finger at a secure briefing room located in the corner of the office.

"Asses and elbows," he said. "I'll explain in there."

POTTS STEPPED FROM THE revolving doors and into the sky-scraper's brightly lit lobby, Russell two steps behind him. Cam Timmons, whose stick-thin body and impossibly large head reminded most people of a lollipop, strode in a diagonal line across the lobby and positioned himself in a corner so he could watch people coming and going. He'd remain in the lobby and make sure the other agents weren't tailed upstairs.

Potts and Russell, in the meantime, rushed past the security desk and headed for a bank of elevators situated in the middle of the lobby. One of the guards fell in behind them, ordered them to halt but stopped short when Potts whirled and shoved his credentials in the guy's face. He let the guy study them for a couple of seconds and then stuffed them back in his pocket.

"If anyone asks, you never fucking saw us here," Potts said through clenched teeth. "If I hear otherwise, I'll arrest you and figure out what to charge you with later. Understand?"

The guard swallowed hard, but nodded and let the two men go.

"Smooth," Russell muttered as they stepped into the elevator.

OTHER THAN AN AIR conditioner's hum, the room was dead silent. Youssef Nadal knelt on the floor next to the office door, a handheld monitor unit lay close by. A thin, flexible tube stretched from the top of the unit and snaked through the space between the bottom of the door and the floor and into the hallway. The tube contained a camera lens that fed images from the hallway to the small television monitor on the floor. An Uzi with a sound suppressor threaded into the muzzle was within Nadal's reach as he watched the small screen.

Iranian-born Nadal stared at the monitor and remained perfectly still. He'd been a sniper for the Iranian Revolutionary Guard for years before he'd left the guard to work as an assassin, and a damn well-paid one. He could sit still for hours if the job demanded it.

An elevator dinged in the hallway and excitement fluttered in Nadal's stomach. He glanced at the monitor and saw a pair of men, both dressed in dark suits, moving down the hallway. One of the men was tall and had dark hair. He matched the general description Nadal had been given of the American, Cooper. A moment later his cell phone vibrated in his right pocket and stopped almost immediately. He withdrew the phone and saw a text message that simply read "Okay." It was a message from a pair of spotters positioned outside the building.

Another look at the monitor told him the two men had stopped at the door across the hallway. Nadal watched the dark-haired man draw a pistol from beneath his suit jacket, clutch it in a two-handed grip and flatten against the wall next to the door. The other man rapped on the door with his knuckles and announced that they were federal agents. The man who'd knocked on the door took a step back and kicked hard at the door, driving it inward.

Nadal monitored the two agents as they launched themselves through the door, disappearing from view. His heart began to pound as the adrenaline pulsed through his body in anticipation of the conflict. Pulling a black mask over his head to disguise his features, he grabbed the Uzi from the floor, got to his feet, popped open the door and darted across the hallway.

His 10 MM SMITH & WESSON raised in front of him, Potts bulled his way into the office. Blood thundered in his ears as his body began reacting to the stress. He swept the pistol's muzzle over the interior of the office, but found no targets. The outer room was a nicely appointed waiting area with a reception desk, a couch and two wooden chairs. Light streamed from underneath a door directly in front of him. Potts popped open the door, letting it swing inward. When nothing happened, he chanced a look around the doorjamb, but saw no one inside the room. Just plenty of furniture, a laptop open on a desktop covered in scattered papers, fax machines and other routine office items. He crept into the room and searched it more carefully, but found no one hiding underneath a desk or behind a filing cabinet.

"Clear," he yelled over his shoulder to Russell.

Moving to the desk, he studied the items on its top and spotted the lower half of a cell phone poking out from beneath some papers. He cursed. Holstering his weapon, he looked up at his partner.

"Did he know we were coming?" Russell asked.

Potts opened his mouth to reply, but stopped when Russell suddenly jerked forward, a groan escaping his lips. The man's midsection exploded in a spray of crimson and an unseen force shoved him forward. He crumpled to the floor in a boneless heap.

Potts dived to the floor and clawed at his sidearm. The weapon cleared its holster in the same moment that a black shadow filled the doorway. The FBI agent by now was operating on instinct and training. Everything had begun to move in slow motion for him, as though he were a detached observer rather than a man fighting desperately for his life.

The Uzi the shadow clutched chugged through the contents of its clip. Slugs tore into the floor, shredded carpet and cut a line toward Potts. He snap aimed his weapon and squeezed the trigger. Before he could track the shot, rounds seared his midsection, caused him to cry out involuntarily. He couldn't catch his breath or stop the force that jerked his body to and fro. A curse welled up from inside him, choking him. His vocal chords no longer functioning, his rage seeped out as a pitiful gurgle. Blinding pain lanced through his chest, his stomach, arms. His vision blurred.

Shoot! his mind screamed. Goddamn you, shoot!

The impulse prodded his finger, which jerked the trigger. The Smith & Wesson cracked once and a bullet drilled into a nearby leather couch. Potts, overtaken by blackness, never knew he'd squeezed off one last shot.

YAHYA SAUNTERED THROUGH the crowded market, his hands stuffed in the hip pockets of his blue jeans, and whistled. The wad of cash he'd just scored was crumpled into the bottom of his right hip pocket where his extended fingertips could brush against it. He smiled at his good fortune.

Money was nice, he thought. Scoring ass was even better. But getting laid with someone else's money? Who could ask for more?

He brushed past the hotel's doorman, who stared at him as he approached the front entrance. Yahya wasn't surprised. The place usually catered to well-dressed and well-heeled business travelers, not a local like him dressed in jeans and a T-shirt. But they all came looking for the same thing, he thought.

Yahya studied his reflection in the double glass doors, noticed that his hair was mussed and ran his fingers through it to bring it under control before entering the hotel. The young woman at the front desk, her pretty face framed by straight black hair that hung past her shoulders, brushing just above her breasts, smiled at him.

"Can I help you?"

"I'm here," he said, "for some company."

She nodded encouragingly, but said nothing. He leaned forward and muttered the code word to her.

"Of course," she said. "How long would you like?"

Yahya calculated what he believed to be the hourly rate against the wad of bills in his pocket. "Two hours," he said. "How much will that cost?"

She told him. He pulled out some cash, peeled off bills until he reached the right amount and slapped it onto the counter. Picking up the money, she counted it again and then stuffed it underneath the counter. Her smile undiminished, she thanked him and gestured toward the elevator. Yahya turned and headed for it.

"Enjoy," she called after him.

Count on it, he thought, his lips widening into a smile.

During the elevator ride, he thought for a moment about Potts and wished he could have seen that stupid prick's face when he'd learned the information was bogus. A pang of fear passed through him as he considered, not for the first time, that Potts likely would be angry at him for wasting his time with a bad tip. He shrugged away the thought. That'd be the extent of it. Yahya had provided too much good information over the years for Potts to cut him off entirely. The FBI agent needed what the young man had to sell if he wanted to operate in Dubai because Yahya was tapped in to the locals like no one else. So if Potts wanted to have a tantrum, let him.

By the time Yahya had reached his floor, he'd already forgotten about Potts and was thinking about what awaited him. He turned down a short corridor and spotted a big white guy decked out in a black suit, his thick arms crossed over an even thicker chest, standing next to the penthouse door. Yahya handed the man a gold-plated token that he'd been given at the front desk. The thug snatched it from his hand, pinched it between his thumb and index finger and studied it. After several seconds, the guy took the coin and dropped it into the pocket of his coat. He opened the door and gestured for Yahya to enter.

The contrast inside was striking. The lights were dim and some saxophone-heavy jazz music was piped in through the loudspeakers. Smoke—a mixture of tobacco and marijuana—hung heavily in the air.

A half dozen or so young women of various races and nationalities sat around the room on couches or overstuffed chairs. While a couple barely seemed to pay attention to him, the others made eye contact and smiled. He took his time and studied each one, allowing his eyes to linger over each curve. Finally, he pointed to a woman with kinked blond hair that spilled down to her shoulders. She smiled and stood. He admired her strong legs and heavy breasts, barely covered by a lacy white negligee.

Taking his hand, she led him from the living room to a small hallway.

She turned and looked over her shoulder at him.

"You like what you see?" she asked him in heavily accented English. Having met more than his share of Russians during his time in Dubai, he thought he recognized the woman's accent as Russian.

"Let's go," he snapped.

Her smile didn't waver, though he thought he saw anger flicker in her eyes before it quickly died. And for the money he was paying, Yahya couldn't have cared less whether she was angry. Instead he amused himself by admiring the sway of her hips and the soft ripple of her well-developed calf muscles as she led him down a corridor.

When they reached the room, she halted, rested a hand on the doorknob and flashed him a dazzling smile.

"Here we are," she said.

She swung the door inward and waved him inside. The room was clean, but nondescript—a bed, a nightstand, a wall clock, a couple of lamps, a table and chairs and a television. Several tumblers stood on the nightstand, along with small bottles of liquor, like those sold on airplanes, and a basket for the money to pay for alcohol or tips.

He turned and saw her still standing in the doorway.

"One moment, please," she said.

Before he could protest, she'd shut the door and disappeared. He glanced at the clock and noted the time in his head. As far as he was concerned, his time didn't start until she was in here, in the bed with him. Not a damn minute before. He turned his back to the door.

If her disappearing act was a way of squeezing a few extra bucks from him...

The rattle of the doorknob registered with him and snapped him from his thoughts. He wheeled around, expecting to see the beautiful woman. Instead he found himself face-to-face with a medium-height man, Caucasian, dressed head to toe in black—jeans, tennis shoes, shirt.

"Wrong room, asshole," Yahya growled.

As he uttered the last word, he spotted the small handgun the man clutched, the snout tracking in on the informant's midsection.

Reflexively, he put up his hands and opened his mouth to ask the guy what he wanted. Before Yahya could speak, something hammered against his stomach. He reeled a couple of steps back, his hands clutching his midsection, and fell to his knees. The shooter drew down on Yahya's chest and tapped the trigger once more.

A scream died in the informant's throat and his world went dark.

MASTERS TOOK AN ELEVATOR down two floors and slipped into a men's room. Checking to make sure the coast was clear, he pulled the top from a trash can that stood next to the sink. He sank a hand into the mess of sloppy wet discarded paper towels and fished around until his fingers struck fabric. He'd checked the janitor log posted on the door earlier and saw that they weren't due to clean the bathroom for another two hours. Nevertheless, he still was grateful to find the backpack where he'd left it.

Stepping inside a stall, he peeled off the short-sleeved blue dress shirt and turned it inside out, revealing a red lining. He slipped the now crimson shirt over his head and tucked it into the waist of his pants.

He yanked the black wig from his head and stuffed it into his backpack. After that, he wrapped his blood-splattered pants and loafers in a thin plastic bag, stuffed them into the backpack, exchanging them for a pair of blue jeans and three-hundred-dollar sneakers. One after the other he snatched the blue contacts from his eyes and flushed them down the toilet. He slid nonprescription wire-framed glasses onto his face.

Three minutes later he was walking down the sidewalk, putting some distance between himself and the hotel. A pair of police cars roared by him, lights flashing, sirens wailing. Feigning curiosity, he stopped, turned and stared after them for a moment, like several other passersby. Shrugging, he continued on.

Walking another block, he spotted a taxi parked along the curb. Approaching it, he double-checked the registration number painted on the side. Satisfied it was the right one, he popped open the passenger's rear door and slid into the backseat.

The driver was seated in the front. His left elbow jutted out the driver's window and a burning cigarette was clenched between his teeth. "I'm out of service," he said.

"Just a drop-off," Masters replied. "A small item."

The man nodded. "Of course."

Masters set the backpack and his spectacles on the backseat of the taxi. He exited the vehicle through the rear door on the driver's side and headed for his next destination.

## CHAPTER FOURTEEN

Bolan took the cell phone from his pants' pocket and thumbed the power button while he eased the black Mercedes into traffic in Dubai's financial district. A message flashed on the phone's screen, alerting him that he had voice mail. While he drove, he worked his way through a series of prompts by punching in digital security codes from memory with his thumb.

When he finally accessed his voice mail, he heard Potts's recorded voice. "Cooper? Potts. I have a location for Faquir Bajaur, Khan's top lieutenant." Potts recited the address and Bolan made a mental note of it. "I'll explain more later. Info comes from a good source. Guy's a piece of shit, but his stuff usually pans out okay." Bolan spun the wheel into a right-hand turn and goosed the accelerator.

Potts's message continued. "Look, I'll get a couple of my agents and roust Bajaur. Bring him to the office. You can question him here. No need to blow up more shit, okay? You're killing me here."

Bolan heard the weariness in Potts's voice, but also detected a hint of humor. The message ended and Bolan listened to two brief messages from Potts, where he identified himself and asked for a return call, exasperation increasingly audible in his voice with each message. The soldier scowled, punched in Potts's number and listened as the phone rang four times before putting him into voice mail. Scowling, the soldier disconnected and plugged the address he'd just been given into the dashboard GPS system.

In the meantime, he called Grimaldi.

"You heard from Potts?" Bolan asked.

"Nothing," the pilot replied. "You?"

Bolan told him about the multiple phone messages from the FBI agent.

"You want me to give you some backup?"

"Negative," Bolan replied. "Has our lady friend said or done anything useful?"

"Can't help you there, either, Striker. She went to her office and has been there for a couple of hours now. I have the Farm monitoring her internet and phone traffic remotely in case she actually says or writes something interesting. But so far nothing."

"She's no dummy," Bolan said. "She probably realizes she's being monitored, even if she doesn't know by whom. But the fact that she's refusing our protection—or FBI protection for that matter—after someone tried to kidnap her tells me something's not right with her."

"Any theories?" Grimaldi asked.

"Hard to say," Bolan replied. "Could be she doesn't trust us, pure and simple. Or it could be she has something to hide."

"Because she's on the wrong side."

The car's GPS system told Bolan to make a left turn at the light, which he did.

"Maybe she's on the wrong side," the soldier replied. "Or it could be out of some weird loyalty to Lang. Hell, maybe she's just scared. If she was working for Khan's group, you'd have to wonder why they are trying to kill her."

"Yeah," Grimaldi said. "Speaking of which, did we ever get IDs on the bodies at Gillen's apartment? I haven't heard one word from the Farm."

"Me, neither."

"What about Potts?"

"Negative. I'm heading his way right now. Let me know if you hear anything else in the meantime."

"Roger that," Grimaldi said.

GILLEN WORKED TWO HOURS in a vain attempt to forget about the events of the past two days. She combed through emails, opened what little snail mail she had and listened to a dozen or so voice messages from colleagues and competitors wanting to ask her questions about Lang or the shooting at her apartment building.

Occasionally her hands trembled as she tried opening envelopes or punching numbers on the keypad of her telephone. Even though she knew she was the only one in the room, she still looked around self-consciously whenever her hands shook.

For what seemed like the millionth time in the past two days, her mind wandered to thoughts of Lang. Sadness caused her throat to ache, and she worried that her eyes might well up. She swallowed hard and began to ask herself questions.

Who had killed him? Why? Who was this federal agent hunting the killers? If he *was* a federal agent. Gillen had already run his name through three internet search engines and found several Matt Coopers, but none who matched the man she'd met earlier.

She typed out a quick email to a friend in the newspaper's Washington bureau, asking whether he knew anything about Cooper. A second or two later, she deleted it.

Stroking her right cheek with her hand, she stared at the computer for several seconds. The bureau's Justice Department reporter was new to the business.

And if she asked him questions, he'd likely return the favor and want to know why she needed the information. The wires were already hot with stories about Lang's death. Smaller items about the shootings at her apartment building and other locations in Dubai also had popped up on various wire services. Local authorities and the U.S. Embassy were attributing the violence to competing organized crime gangs running loose in the city. A horseshit excuse for sure, but apparently one of her colleagues was willing to swallow and regurgitate to readers and viewers, at least for the moment. Not that she blamed them. If it came from official sources, they had to go with the best information they had, even if it was crap.

She shook her head. How long did she have before they came for her again? Probably not long. A pit of fear opened in her stomach. A yellow sticky note clung to her computer screen. She leaned forward and studied the phone number scrawled in black ink in her own handwriting.

It was Cooper's phone number. Maybe she should call him, tell him what she knew.

Maybe.

What would Terry think? a voice boomed in her head. Who the hell cared? another, calmer voice replied. Terry was dead. She was alive—for the moment—and she needed help.

Heaving a sigh, she reached for the telephone.

Footsteps thudded on the stairs outside the office. She froze in midreach.

BOLAN HAD PARKED THE Mercedes in a nearby parking garage and had entered the tower in which Bajaur's office was located. He pushed through the revolving doors, stepped into the lobby and flashed his credentials at the guard. The guy behind the desk studied them for several seconds, occasionally flicking his gaze up at Bolan before returning it to the ID card. He shot Bolan a quizzical look.

"What?" Bolan asked.

"You're the fourth guy tonight who's flashed U.S. government credentials at me. You mind telling me what the hell's going on?"

"Who else has been here?"

The guard exhaled. "Three guys," he said, holding up as many fingers. "Two of them went upstairs, left a third down here in the lobby. After a few minutes, he tried to raise them on his phone but couldn't."

A sense of dread washed over Bolan.

"What happened?"

The guard shrugged and gave Bolan a weak smile. "He got impatient and jumped in one of the elevators. I guess he wanted to find them."

"And you stayed here?"

"What, you think something's happening in this building that three—now four—federal agents couldn't handle? And what if it was? I'm a med student, not a police officer. If they can't handle it, I don't want to know about it."

"Fair enough," Bolan said. He turned and headed for the elevators.

"Hey, who said you could go up there?"

"Now you're going to assert yourself?" Bolan called over his shoulder. He didn't wait for a reply. Moving into an elevator car, he jabbed the button for the thirteenth floor.

# CHAPTER FIFTEEN

When the elevator reached the correct floor, Bolan stepped from the car onto the main floor. During the elevator ride, he'd tried Potts again and had gotten his voice mail. He considered contacting Stony Man Farm to see if they could pinpoint Potts's cell phone or that of one of the other agents, to see if they even were in the building anymore. He decided against it, at least for the moment. He had no time for that.

The soldier drew his Beretta and moved down the corridor, trying to keep the gun as close to his body as possible. Since the guard knew he was a federal agent, he wouldn't be surprised to see the Executioner wielding a handgun, if he was even watching him on a surveillance monitor. But if there were others on the floor, he didn't want to panic them or to attract undue attention to himself if he didn't have to.

It took a couple of minutes for him to locate the hallway in which Bajaur's office suite was located. He stood at the mouth of the corridor and stared down its length. All the doors were closed, and none of the agents was visible. The soldier heard no voices, no footsteps, no laughter. He couldn't imagine that if Potts were here, he was being this quiet.

When Bolan reached Bajaur's office door, he listened for a few heartbeats, but heard nothing from inside. He tried the doorknob and found it unlocked, which only made him more suspicious. The door swung inward.

Light filtered into the room, forming a long yellow rectangle. Something dark protruded from the darkness into the lighted area. Bolan recognized it as the tip of a shoe. He brought the Beretta to shoulder level in his right hand. With his left hand, he felt around for the light switch, found it and activated the recessed overhead lighting. The glow from the fluorescent bulbs cut through the darkness, and the soldier got a fuller picture of what had happened. A man lay sprawled facedown on the floor, one leg straight out, the other cocked at a ninety-degree angle.

His face was buried deep into the carpet, and the bloodied mess that had been the back of his skull gleamed crimson under the lights and had stained the back of his jacket from the collar to just between his shoulder blades. The upper portion of his right arm jutted straight out from his shoulder and his forearm was bent at a forty-five-degree angle, a 10 mm Smith & Wesson still clutched in his hand.

Bolan's heartbeat accelerated. Stifling the urge to curse, the soldier passed through the outermost room and into the larger office. He swept his weapon over the area to make sure whoever had waxed Potts no longer was present.

When he found no one, he stared down at Potts's corpse, his shirt and jacket darkened by large bloodstains. His service weapon lay a foot or so from the curled fingers of his right hand. Another man that Bolan didn't recognize lay to one side of the door, crumpled in a heap. While the soldier didn't recognize the two men with Potts, he assumed they both were FBI agents, though he couldn't be sure without checking their IDs.

A dull ache in his jaw registered with Bolan and he realized he was clenching his jaw, holding back the rage sparked by the carnage that surrounded him. Walking over to Potts, he knelt next to the Fed and searched through his pockets until he found the guy's cell phone, figuring that maybe its contents could provide some additional intelligence. He also pocketed the key card that would get him into the local FBI office, should he need to do so. He made a mental note to let

Brognola know that he'd removed both these items from the crime scene.

Returning to his full height, Bolan let his gaze linger over the three dead men for several seconds. He spun on his heel and exited the office.

GRIMALDI STUBBED OUT his fourth cigarette in the Cadillac Escalade's ashtray, tapped his foot impatiently and scanned the dashboard clock. Two minutes had passed since he'd last looked at the clock.

The pilot, all fast movements and explosive energy, hated sitting for long periods. Unless of course, he was in the cockpit of an aircraft. At least then he could shake things up by coaxing more speed from the plane, maybe wiggle the wings, or at least trade insults with his passengers, the other Stony Man Farm warriors.

Here, he was just developing sores on his backside.

When Bolan had asked him to keep an eye on Gillen, he'd agreed without giving it a second thought. When his old friend asked for something, Grimaldi did it, no questions asked. The two had been friends longer than either cared to admit, had survived campaigns in countless hellzones around the world. You built that kind of history together, and a request to tail a woman, especially an attractive one like the lady reporter, seemed like a small deal.

Until you burned 120 minutes on your butt, in a car, in Dubai's heat. Once that happened, a guy got a little antsy for some action.

Grimaldi was weighing whether to step out of the car to stretch his legs when his cell phone rang. Looking at the screen, he recognized the caller as Bolan. He flipped the phone open and brought it to his ear.

"This sucks," he said without preamble.

Bolan apparently knew what he meant. "Sorry to leave

you in the car by yourself. Maybe later I can scratch your ears and throw a ball for you. Listen, I've got bad news."

Grimaldi straightened a bit in his seat.

"Yeah?"

"They took out Potts," Bolan said, "and two of his guys."

Grimaldi swore. "What happened?"

He listened as Bolan shared the details of the shooting. Unconsciously he balled a fist in anger. Though he'd only barely met Potts, he hated to see one of the good guys take a bullet.

"Who did it?" the pilot asked.

"I can't say who specifically shot them. Whoever did it had already left by the time I arrived," Bolan said. "Hal's trying to get the surveillance video from the locals. And, if he can't get it through regular channels, he'll put the cyberteam on the case, see if they can steal the damn thing. My guess is the locals aren't feeling very charitable toward us right now, considering the body count I've left here."

"You tend to do that," Grimaldi said.

"Anyway, it's hard to say what I'd stand to gain from some video footage. Even if we could ID the assassin, it's likely to be a low-level guy. We know the guy we want now is Khan."

"We just need to find him."

"And kill him," Bolan added.

"If you don't, I will. What do you want from me?"

"Check on Gillen," Bolan said. "Take her back to the safehouse—regardless of whether she wants to go. I have a bad feeling about how things are going here."

"I'm on it," Grimaldi said.

The two men signed off. The Stony Man pilot slipped out of the Cadillac. With fast strides, he closed in on Gillen's place. As he moved, he felt the reassuring weight of the SIG-Sauer P-226 holstered in the small of his back. Extra clips for the weapon were in the pocket of his khaki pants along with the speedloaders for the .38 Llama Scorpio that rode in an ankle holster. A Colt Commando was sealed inside a steel carrying case inside the SUV.

He scanned his surroundings for anything unusual, but nothing stuck out as dangerous. Of course, he'd never been to this neighborhood until a couple of hours earlier, so he had no frame of reference for what constituted normal here. He was acting as much on gut instinct as anything. He hoped under the circumstances that it would be enough.

KELLOGG SHOVED THE .38-CALIBER Kimber into a leather holster and fitted it on his belt, in the small of his back.

He yanked his shirttails from inside his waistband, draping them over the holstered weapon. The exposed shirttails likely wouldn't arouse suspicion in Gillen, Kellogg guessed.

Like a lot of reporters, he dressed in different gradations of shabby, depending on whether he had a press conference to attend or maybe an interview with a high-level bureaucrat. Most days, he dressed just well enough to get by.

A long steel tube with threads machined into one end lay on his desktop, next to an open suitcase. He slipped the tube, a sound suppressor for the Kimber, into the briefcase. Shutting the lid, he sealed the case and exited his apartment.

Heading down the stairs, his mind flashed back to his conversation with Gillen several hours ago. Though she'd tried to play it down, the worry and strain in her voice had been audible, even through a faceless phone connection. She was scared. And, from Kellogg's perspective, rightfully so.

Through no fault of her own, she'd walked into the middle of something nasty, something in which she had no business.

Now, she needed to be eliminated, and Kellogg was the poor bastard tasked with killing her.

Stepping out from the building, he felt Dubai's heat press against him. Sweat broke out on his forehead almost immediately, and he scowled. These days, the heat seemed to bother him more than it once had. When he'd first come to the Middle East nearly twenty years ago, he'd enjoyed the relentless heat and the even more relentless sunlight. It had seemed like a gift after decades in London.

It had helped, of course, that he also was basking in the excitement of his first overseas posting with Britain's Secret Intelligence Service, or M-I6. Back then, he actually believed he'd been called for something great. The newness and excitement that had accompanied his first solo posting had been damn near intoxicating.

As with all good things, it had come to an end, though. He'd become dissatisfied with his civil servant's salary and the prospect of living on a modest pension in his native Wiltshire, England.

At that point, he'd opted to go freelance, leaving state service and selling the information he gathered to the highest bidder. Coincidentally, that was almost never the British, he thought sourly. He'd always found the Saudis, the Russians and the Americans more willing to cough up cash for good information. Invariably, the Brits had appealed to his patriotism rather than his greed.

So here he was in Dubai, sweating his butt off and pulling dirty tricks.

Unfortunately this day's trick was the dirtiest. Masters had couched the job as a request, though Kellogg knew better. If Masters briefed you on a job—laid out the targets, the times, the dates—you damn well agreed to do it. Otherwise he'd pop you once in the head, silencing you in the name of "operations security."

Kellogg had a lot of respect for Gillen. He'd been a reporter for several years before he'd been recruited into M-I6. And, even in the years since, as he'd led a dual life as a foreign correspondent and an agent, he'd tried to adhere to some level of journalistic ethics and standards wherever possible. He respected the press, even though he often found himself working at cross purposes with his supposed brethren. He'd found Gillen to be a tough, hardworking woman who'd stuck her neck out more than once to get the job done.

So, no, Kellogg didn't much relish the task of killing her. He guessed he'd spend the evening sulking in his apartment, sipping bourbon and listening to Rachmaninoff or Tchaikovsky. But he'd wake up tomorrow with a few more pounds in his account, which always had a way of snapping him out of his dark moods.

Slipping into a drugstore just a block or so from his apartment, Kellogg picked up a pack of cigarettes, a red disposable lighter and a plastic bottle of cola. While he didn't anticipate ever being tied to Gillen's impending murder, they did have offices in the same building. He anticipated questions. He wanted to establish an alibi that he'd been out running errands at around the time she was killed.

Taking a sideways glance, he saw stacked copies of the *Near East Gazette,* a locally produced English-language newspaper. In the right-hand column, above the fold, a picture of Terry Lang—the one that usually accompanied his weekly column—stared out from the front page. Reporter Dies in Plane Crash, the headline read.

A cynical smile played over Kellogg's lips. Plane crash? Proof positive that a person shouldn't believe everything he or she read, he thought. He grabbed a copy of the newspaper and held it up so the clerk could see it. The man nodded and rang it in along with the other items. Kellogg paid for everything and left the store, making sure to slip the receipt into his pocket so he had it later.

As he walked he read the story about Lang, all the time knowing the truth about what had happened.

Whereas Kellogg liked and respected Gillen, he'd never acquired a taste for Lang. The man was brave and tough and one hell of a reporter. But he'd also been brash, sneaky and, frankly, had kicked Kellogg's ass on more than one story.

Lang had many admirers, especially in the journalism world, but Kellogg didn't count himself among them. And then there'd been all the rumors that Lang was a spy on top of it all, which had only compounded Kellogg's distrust of him.

So given a choice, he'd much rather be walking into a news bureau to put a bullet into Lang's head. Unfortunately, that wasn't the way things had worked out for him.

Reaching Gillen's office building, he sneaked around to the rear. As expected, he found the back door propped open by a jagged chunk of concrete, a common practice by the maintenance men.

He had a security card that would open the front door, but it also would keep a record of his arrival, and he was trying not to leave a trail.

Once inside, he moved quickly through the maintenance offices to a flight of stairs and he started up them, ready to take out his target.

YAKOV BERLIX RARELY GARNERED anyone's attention.

It was by design.

In his tan slacks, sky-blue shirt and brown moccasins, he seemed to blend into the background, as though rendered invisible by some urban camouflage. The woman who walked with him, Kiska Chernikova, was similarly unremarkable. Her mouse-brown hair was wound into a tight bun. Her clothes fit, but not well enough to accentuate her figure. Sunglasses hid her most remarkable feature: she had one blue eye and one green one. They'd arrived at the building that housed Gillen's office ten minutes before. She had sat in a chair in the lobby, leafing through a magazine. He'd remained standing, staring at a series of abstract paintings that lined the walls.

Berlix's phone rang. He pulled it from his pocket and stuck to his ear.

"Yes?" he said.

He paused and listened. "Okay, good."

Ending the connection, he returned the phone to his pocket. He walked over to Chernikova and put a hand on her shoulder.

"He's here. It's time."

The woman nodded.

GRIMALDI SAW A MAN STANDING outside the door to Gillen's office, his hand resting on the handle. The pilot didn't recognize the man and saw no sign of a weapon hidden on his hips, which were obscured by his shirttails. Grimaldi knew better than to take comfort in that. The guy could have a gun strapped on his ankle or at the small of his back. And until he identified the man, the Stony Man warrior planned to treat him as a potential enemy.

Hugging the wall, Grimaldi moved quickly, silently, upon the guy. It wasn't until the two men were about twenty feet away that the guy realized Grimaldi was moving in on him.

When the man saw Grimaldi, his hand darted behind his back. Grimaldi, who'd already grabbed the SIG-Sauer, raised the weapon.

"Stop!" the pilot ordered.

The man did, hands freezing in midreach. In the same instant the office door swung open and Gillen stood in the doorway.

"Mike, what are you doing here?" she asked.

Instead of responding, the man's hand snaked out. He grabbed a handful of the sleeve of her blouse and yanked hard, trying to put her between himself and Grimaldi.

Her own hand stabbing out, she grabbed the door frame and resisted his pull.

Grimaldi stepped forward and whipped the SIG-Sauer

across the guy's face. "Mike" yelped in pain, released Gillen's sleeve and took a step back.

Grimaldi stepped in and landed a hard left on the man's jaw. The blow caused him to spin away, his body colliding with a wall. With a hard push, he used the wall to launch himself at Grimaldi, his hand freeing the pistol he carried on his belt.

The pilot struck him again in the head with the pistol's barrel, this time opening a large gash on his temple. He dropped like a sack of stones. His grip loosened and the gun fell, clattering across the floor.

Grimaldi knelt next to the guy and scooped up the pistol.

"What are you doing?" Gillen asked, her voice just below a yell. "I know this man. His name's Mike Kellogg. He's a reporter."

Grimaldi straightened.

"Nice guy," he said. "If you know him so well, can you explain why he grabbed you and tried to pull you between us?"

She thought about it for a second, then shook her head.

"No," she replied, her voice quiet.

Grimaldi held up Kellogg's gun. "Is this standard issue? A little something to keep his notepad and pens company?"

As she stared at the gun, she bit her lower lip and crossed her arms over her chest. She looked down at Kellogg, then back up at Grimaldi.

"I don't understand this," she said. "I've known him for years."

Grimaldi put a hand on her shoulder. She looked up at him, confusion etched on her features. The pilot felt sorry for her. He could tell that in a matter of hours, her world had been turned upside down through her association with Terry Lang. Now someone she knew had turned on her. The pilot guessed her mind was on overload.

"Maybe you should go into your office," Grimaldi said.

"Why? What's going to happen to Mike?"

Grimaldi shook his head. "Nothing. I'll bring him in with me. Just go in there and take a breath. We'll figure this all out together, okay?"

She nodded her agreement. Grimaldi picked up Kellogg's briefcase and held it out to her. Gillen took it, her movements wooden as she disappeared into her office.

Holstering the SIG-Sauer, Grimaldi reached into his pocket and produced a set of wrist restraints. He knelt next to the injured man and secured his hands behind his back. The movement caused Kellogg to stir and he let out a moan.

Grabbing Kellogg by the arm, Grimaldi hoisted him a couple of feet off the floor, ready to drag him into Gillen's office.

Simultaneously he saw a man and a woman step out from the stairwell. Their gazes immediately locked in on him. Grimaldi opened his mouth, ready to utter some bullshit about being a federal agent, when they silenced him by bringing up their hands, each of which held a gun.

Fueled by adrenaline, Grimaldi lifted Kellogg up just us as the new arrivals began shooting. The crackle of gunfire reverberated throughout the hallway. The bullets pounded into Kellogg's torso, penetrating his body and jerking him violently.

Grimaldi simultaneously released Kellogg's body and grabbed at the SIG-Sauer. He darted sideways and moved through Gillen's open office door. Using the door frame for protection, he double tapped the handgun's trigger.

The bullets drilled into the man's torso. Sprays of crimson erupted from his chest, wheeling him around violently. The woman stood her ground and continued firing. The spray of bullets lanced through the air within inches of Grimaldi's face and partially exposed shoulder, ripping through the fabric of his shirt. Two more shots exploded from the SIG-Sauer's barrel and pounded one after another into the woman's chest, the force shoving her off her feet.

Grimaldi raced over to the fallen assassins and made sure they were dead. He then marched double time to Gillen's office, where he found her crouched behind her desk.

He held out a hand to her. "It's okay to come out," the pilot said.

It was then that Grimaldi spotted a rectangular object about the size of a pack of gum on the floor next to her. Numbers were counting on a liquid crystal display screen.

He clenched his fist.

"Damn it, are you recording? What the hell?"

"What do you expect me to do?" Gillen asked.

Grimaldi brought up his foot and stomped down hard on the recorder. Small, jagged pieces of plastic shot out from beneath the sole of his boot.

Gillen shot up to her feet. "Why did you do that?"

"For a lot of reasons," the pilot snapped. "Not the least of which is my friend and I don't like being recorded or filmed. Or written about."

"But there are gunshots right outside my office," she said. "I can't not write about it."

"Trust me, you won't write about this," Grimaldi growled.

"Later, maybe."

"Try never. Now, c'mon. Let's go."

"Where's Mike?"

"Dead," the Stony Man pilot stated.

Her skin paled and her hand flew to her mouth.

"Fuck," she muttered.

"Yeah, fuck. Let's go."

# CHAPTER SIXTEEN

Grimaldi held Gillen's hand and led her up the street to the Escalade. He fisted the SIG-Sauer, but had slipped his other weapons into a duffel bag, which was slung over his shoulder. When they reached his vehicle, he opened the door and Gillen climbed into the passenger's side. He went around to the front of the vehicle, scrambled into the driver's seat and was inserting the key in the ignition as he shut the door. When the SUV started, he put it into gear and whipped into traffic.

After less than a minute he glanced at Gillen and saw her rubbing her hands together, as though she was washing them. She chewed on her lower lip and stared out her window.

"You all right?" Grimaldi asked.

"No," she said. "I thought Mike was a friend."

"You need a better class of friends," Grimaldi said.

She turned toward him and glared. "Like you and your partner? People didn't start dying until the two of you showed up!"

Grimaldi knew he shouldn't take the bait. But he was tired and his adrenaline still was pumping from the confrontation a few minutes earlier.

"Look, if it wasn't for us, you'd be dead."

"So you say."

"How many people have tried to kill you today?" Grimaldi asked.

She crossed her arms over her chest and stared straight ahead.

After a couple of minutes, she spoke again. "Did Kellogg kill Terry?"

The pilot knew who had killed Lang and how he'd died. But he also wasn't about to tell Gillen. He shook his head no.

"Kellogg didn't have the juice," he said. "He was just a sneaky bastard—"

"Hey!"

"—who'd kill someone from behind. He wasn't in Lang's league."

"Which was?" Gillen prompted.

"Never mind."

"That's bull."

"Seriously, the less you know about him, the better. This time, ignorance truly is bliss," Grimaldi told her.

"Why?"

"Jesus, are you persistent or stupid? I can't tell."

"I want answers," the reporter stated.

Grimaldi snorted derisively. "No," he said, "you don't."

He cut the wheel right, turned down a boulevard and passed a gleaming hotel. Two men in loud pants and flowered shirts were unloading their golf clubs from the back of a blue BMW convertible. Apparently money really couldn't buy taste, Grimaldi thought sourly.

"Why not answer my questions?" Gillen asked.

Grimaldi sighed. "Because it will only lead to more."

"So?"

"So, questions will get you killed. Are you not listening?"

"I'm listening," Gillen said. "I just don't believe what I'm hearing. I need to know what happened to Terry. I need to know why Mike came after me. I deserve to know these things."

Grimaldi shook his head again. "You know all you need to know."

"Did Mike know too much?"

"I doubt it," the Stony Man pilot replied.

"Now he's dead."

"Mess with the best, die like the rest."

Gillen slapped an open palm down on her armrest. "Damn it, I'm serious!"

"Sorry," he muttered.

From the corner of his eye the pilot could see the woman staring at him, probably trying to gauge his sincerity. He knew he was sorry that Gillen had gotten pulled into this mess. Lang apparently hadn't been thinking with his brain when he involved her in all of this. That made Grimaldi question the guy's judgment.

"I wish Terry was here," she said. "I have a lot to ask him."

"Did you care about this idiot?"

"Excuse me?" she responded, her voice sharp.

"Lang. Did you care about him?" Grimaldi asked.

"I didn't love him."

"I didn't ask whether you did."

She sighed and nodded. "I cared about him."

"You think he cared about you?"

She hesitated. "Yes," she said.

He thought he detected more doubt in her answer to that question.

"Then go home. Hop on a plane and get out of here," Grimaldi told her.

He saw her start to blink quickly, and she wiped at the corner of her eye with her index finger.

"Getting answers won't help," the pilot continued. "Trust me. You think it will. But if you really cared about him, knowing the ins and outs of his death won't make you feel better. It's cliché as hell to say it, but it won't bring him back. It won't."

"Maybe I can help you get the people who killed him," she said. "I can help track them down."

"Lady, have you seen anyone using handcuffs and reading people their Miranda rights? In case you haven't realized it, we don't arrest people. We're going to find the people who killed Terry Lang and we're going to deal with them, permanently."

"By *deal,* you mean kill them."

"No comment," he said.

From the corner of his eye he saw her staring expectantly at him. He turned and flashed her what he hoped would be his most disarming grin. Though she didn't return the smile, he saw something in her eyes soften.

"Funny," she said. She turned her head and stared out the window again.

"You're leaving Dubai," he said. "End of discussion."

"You're an ass."

"Look, I want to get you home safely. I can't take you to the airport myself. I'm going to call a couple of guys from the U.S. Embassy to take you to the airport. You get there in one piece and all's right with the world."

"You're transparent as glass, you know that? You want me escorted to the airport to make sure I get on the plane and leave. You're not worried about my safety."

"Tamara, if I had the energy, I'd argue that point with you. As it is, think what you want. I can't protect you and be nice all at the same time."

By now, they'd reached the safehouse. Grimaldi guided the SUV into the driveway. He switched off the ignition, exited the vehicle and entered the house. With the SIG-Sauer in hand, he ran a quick check of the building's interior, but found nothing amiss. With that completed, he unloaded the weapons from the Escalade and set the duffel bag with a metallic clank on the kitchen table.

"Do you always travel like that?" Gillen asked. "I mean, with all those guns?"

"Sometimes I carry a bazooka, too."

She scowled. "I'm serious. Do you?"

"You ask a lot of questions."

"I'm a reporter. Hello?"

Grimaldi thought about it. Like the other Stony Man warriors, he was so used to traveling with guns, explosives and high-tech communications and surveillance gadgets, he never thought about how odd or threatening it might seem to an outsider.

"Yeah, I travel like this all the time," he admitted.

"That must be difficult."

"Draws unwanted attention at airports," he said, grinning.

She rolled her eyes. "You know what I mean. Living in danger all the time. Today, all the things I've seen, all the blood, it's been horrible. How do you wake up in the morning, knowing it's going to be another fight?"

Grimaldi shrugged. "I just do."

"Do you have a family? Don't you get lonely?" Gillen asked.

"Lonely? Hey, is this where you seduce me?"

Another roll of the eyes. "Dream on, tough guy. Just because you saved my life doesn't mean I'm going to sleep with you."

"Glad I didn't waste time on dinner and flowers then," Grimaldi said.

She crossed her arms over her chest and stared at the floor. "You're not making this easier."

"Sorry," the pilot replied, not sure where she was leading with all the questions.

"My point is, you and Cooper did something for me,

twice. You saved my life and I've been a combative shit in return."

Grimaldi just nodded.

"I have no idea what Terry was into." She held up a hand, her palm facing forward. "Don't say anything. I'm not asking to know this time. But a couple of us had an inkling there was something more to him. He knew some pretty shady people. And some of the stories he was able to get were incredible. Things a lot of us couldn't come up with after months of reporting, he'd churn out regularly. He understood WMDs in a way most of us couldn't touch. We were are all generalists. I wrote that off to his military background, but his knowledge seemed pretty up-to-date."

She brushed her hair from her eyes, but with her head turned downward, it immediately cascaded back across her face. She looked up at Grimaldi, her eyes red and moist. "What I'm saying is, we—I—had a feeling there was more to him than I knew, like he was hiding something. At the back of my mind, I guess I figured it was all the womanizing. Or maybe he was plagiarizing or making stuff up. Wouldn't be the first time in my profession."

"Sure."

If she heard Grimaldi, she gave no outward indication.

"What I'm saying is, I have a better idea now that he was trying to do some good."

"He was," Grimaldi replied, figuring he could give the woman that much.

"I think you and Cooper are trying to do some good, too. The least I could do is help you. We had dinner out one night. Terry got drunk, like he usually did, and passed out at his apartment. I'd had a few, too. Not as many has him, but enough to lower my inhibitions. When he fell asleep, I went through his drawers and his financial records. That's when I found the key. I lied. Terry never gave it to me. I took it."

"Why?"

"Put yourself in my place. I knew Terry's reputation. Not as a reporter, but as a man. I found a key."

"You assumed he had a love nest somewhere."

"I thought it was possible. It also could have been a key to a gym locker. But I was jealous and scared, so I took it. As if that would stop him from screwing other women."

"What does it go to?"

"When I woke up the next morning, I was hungover and too embarrassed to say anything. I just took it with me. If he had another woman on the side, I figured he'd never say anything about it. He never did. After he disappeared, it had been maybe thirty-six hours without a phone call or email, I guessed he was with another woman. What else could it have been, right? I went back to his apartment, I had a key and the password for his alarm system, and rooted through his stuff again. I found some receipts for a small office a few blocks away from his bureau."

"The key goes to the office."

She shrugged. "I never tried the key. I went into the building, walked up to the door, but never went inside. Not that I didn't want to. But I guess by that point even I had hit a limit as to how willing I was to humiliate myself. I waited around until it became obvious he wasn't there and he wasn't coming. I went to my office and, later, went home. Then I waited to hear from him. Needless to say, the call never came."

# CHAPTER SEVENTEEN

Lang's office was little more than a closet with a nameplate that read Ambrose and Cronin Inc. screwed to the door. Grimaldi assumed the name meant nothing, but figured he'd send it to Stony Man's cyberteam to see what they could come up with.

An hour before, Grimaldi had dropped Gillen at the airport. Brognola had arranged to have a couple of agents from the Diplomatic Security Service assigned to the American Embassy in the United Arab Emirates put her on a plane to London. He'd then had the cyberteam working remotely from Stony Man, tap into the local fiber-optic network and bypass the alarms on the door.

He extracted the key that had once belonged to Lang. He slid the blade of the key into the dead bolt, turned it and the bolt slid back easily. The same key worked on the doorknob. He gave the knob a twist and the door swung silently open. He proceeded through the entrance slowly, looking for sensors or even trip wires. He hoped that when the cyberteam shut down the alarm, they also had successfully turned off any other sensors. But he wasn't going to take such a thing for granted.

A desk, its front pushed up against one of the longer walls of the rectangular room, took up a third of the small space. A secure satellite phone sat on one corner of the desktop. Grimaldi picked up the receiver, punched in a couple digits and the liquid crystal display flashed the number at him.

Setting aside the satellite phone, he took out his own phone and punched in a series of numbers. He waited as the call clicked through a series of cutout numbers before it started ringing.

After two rings, someone answered. "Hello?" It was Aaron Kurtzman at Stony Man Farm.

"I have a number for you to check out."

"Your wish is my command."

Grimaldi recited the number. On the other end of the line, he could hear keys clicking, accompanied by Kurtzman whistling a classic rock melody.

"Interesting," the computer wizard said.

"Yeah?"

"Yeah. Phone's registered to a William Ambrose, a principal with Ambrose and Cronin."

The pilot ran his gaze over the interior of the small office.

"Makes sense," he said. "I'm standing in Ambrose and Cronin's spacious offices. You couldn't fit two rats in here with me. This is where I found the phone."

"Well, Ambrose and Cronin is a front company."

"Okay, Aaron, no offense, but so far you're giving me a lot of the Earth-is-round kind of information. No one's going to confuse this with a Fortune 500 headquarters."

"No, listen, it's a front company for the CIA. And, before you say it, I know Lang was with the CIA, so spare me the witty asides. The point is that it's a front company that's fronting for another front company."

"I think my head just exploded."

"Let me slow it down for you. The company's listed in the commercial business databases as an import-export company. It has its home shop in Washington, D.C., but it also has offices sprinkled throughout the Middle East and Asia."

Grimaldi's brow furrowed. "Interesting."

"What did I say? Anyway, according to the intel I have

here, the company acts as a technology broker, mostly in the nuclear sphere. They acquire stuff they shouldn't have, like parts for centrifuges and nuclear triggers, and then sell them to countries that shouldn't have them."

"So Lang was mixed up in something illegal?" Grimaldi queried.

More clicking of keys on the other end. The excitement was audible in Kurtzman's voice. "Well, here's where it gets a little screwy. See, what they do is illegal, technically."

"Technically?"

"Let me put it this way. Ambrose and Cronin isn't getting away with anything. The U.S. government knows everything they do," Kurtzman said.

"Because the U.S. government is running them."

"Bingo. Essentially, they sell bad stuff to bad people, or at least promise to do so, because it lets us watch what they're doing."

"Pretty smart. But why would Lang come here? His cover had nothing to do with this company, right?" Grimaldi asked.

"Sure. There are a lot of possible scenarios. But you want to hear my theory?"

"Let it rip."

"According to Ambrose and Cronin's website, the company has no Dubai office," the computer wizard stated.

"Right, it has a closet."

"Seriously, my guess is they're using the name just to make it seem legitimate. If someone sees the nameplate and gets curious, they can look it up on the internet, call an office in another city and confirm the company really exists."

"So what's the purpose of having it here?" Grimaldi asked.

"It's a letter drop. Figuratively speaking, anyway. Lang and some of the other locals probably drop off information there, someone else collects it and sends it back to Washington or wherever."

"Okay," Grimaldi said. "I'd better give it the once-over."

Thirty minutes later he was seated behind the desk, still rifling through the drawers. He glanced through the door and into the hallway, where he saw a shadow moving along the wall in his direction. He slid his hand beneath his windbreaker and rested his palm on the butt of his SIG-Sauer. Craning his neck, he peered through the door and got a better look at the form moving toward him and recognized the man's confident gait. It was Mack Bolan.

Bolan filled the doorway. His lips were pressed into a tight line and his eyebrows were arched.

"Hey," Grimaldi said.

The soldier nodded at him. "Find anything?"

"Not much," Grimaldi said. The pilot briefed Bolan on the background about Ambrose and Cronin and Kurtzman's theory about the office. The soldier listened, but said nothing. The pilot then nodded toward a flash drive that sat on the desktop, along with a book.

"The book's a flight log," Grimaldi said. "The guy kept meticulous records, if they're real. Lots of information about refueling and maintenance. But he's been making quite a few trips to Russia and Pakistan over the last six months."

"That can't be good," Bolan replied.

"You okay?"

"Better than Potts," the soldier said.

"Poor bastard," Grimaldi said. "Hell of a way to go."

"Yeah."

Grimaldi shifted in his chair. "You think they were after you?"

Bolan nodded. "Most likely."

"You've really gotten under Khan's skin," Grimaldi said. "Or someone's skin."

"And I'm not done yet," Bolan said, a cold undercurrent audible in his voice.

"Thank God I'm on your side," Grimaldi said. The pilot then nodded at a computer and the scanner hooked to it. "I scanned the most recent entries in Lang's book," he said, "and sent them to Aaron. He said he'd sort through them, see if he could cross-reference the other planes landing at those same airports and find some kind of a pattern."

Bolan nodded at the flash drive. "What about that?"

"I plugged it into the computer and Aaron copied the contents remotely. We'll see if he and his crew find anything."

The soldier nodded his approval. A couple of minutes later Grimaldi's phone rang. Kurtzman was on the other end of the line. The Stony Man pilot switched the phone to speaker mode and set it on the desk. In the meantime, Bolan closed the door behind him.

"What did you find?" the soldier asked.

"Lang's been busy," Kurtzman said. "The guy made more trips to Karachi in two months than he did in the year before that. At least a dozen by my tally. I applied a little of my data-mining magic and found that we have a few overlaps here. Our good friend Nawaz Khan, who travels between Dubai and Pakistan regularly, was in town at the same time. The guy has houses in Karachi and Rawalpindi, so it's not that surprising. But here's the interesting part. On at least six of those occasions, Sasha Lebed was also in Karachi. Name sound familiar?"

"Yeah, I've heard of him. Do we have any other intel?" Bolan asked. "Something that tells us why any of these guys actually were in town?"

"We have Lang's own reports. If they're accurate, he's suggesting that he was checking on the Khan-Lebed meetings, essentially doing what you'd expect a CIA agent to do. He had a couple of assets on the ground, guys in Khan's inner circle who were feeding him information. According to the reports he was filing, he considered the information good."

"He didn't think they were feeding him false info?" Bolan queried.

"He gives no indication he suspected them of being doubles. That doesn't mean they weren't, of course."

Grimaldi spoke up. "What were they discussing?"

"It gets a little fuzzy there," Kurtzman said. "All Lang was able to find out was that they were working some kind of deal with a third party. An arms deal. But he didn't have a name for the purchaser or the exact nature of the weapons."

"Clear as mud," Grimaldi said.

"Judging by these narratives, Lang was worried about it, too. The reasoning he lays out here is that, if the weapons were AK-47s or even rocket launchers, Khan wouldn't be so tight-lipped about it. I mean, a lot of these guys operate in the open when it comes to conventional arms, particularly small arms. They don't care if they get admonished by the United Nations for it. As long as they don't sell the big stuff to guys like al-Qaeda, these guys can do their thing for years without getting dinged for it."

"So Lang was worried about what they were selling," Bolan said.

"Not just that," Kurtzman replied. "He'd been trying to infiltrate Khan's organization for a year or more. He'd been doing it under his guise as a reporter. Just the same, though, he was getting the vibe that some of Khan's people, including Khan himself, had an eye on Lang. They didn't trust him. Surprisingly, though, about six months ago, Khan gave Lang an interview where he denied any involvement in gunrunning as well as any connections to Pakistani intelligence."

"In other words, he lied," Grimaldi said.

"Now you're just being ugly," Kurtzman said, amusement audible in his voice. "But, yeah, he lied like a politician busted with a dead hooker in his bed. Said he'd been unfairly targeted by the Western media. Said he was an innocent businessman who used his logistics network to move food and clothing to the poor. He claimed that any arms shipments he did make were to the militaries of sovereign governments. I'm not a journalist, but the piece seems pretty fluffy to me. My guess is Lang was trying to ingratiate himself with Khan."

"It was a risky play," Bolan said.

"Seems like it worked for a while, though," Kurtzman said.

"What do we have on Lebed?" Bolan asked.

"You already know some of the basics," Kurtzman said. "His family made their fortune in the energy business after the Soviet Union collapsed. Sasha was the oldest of three sons, apparently the most ambitious of the lot, too. He studied economics at MIT. Got his bachelor's degree from there, but had to quit while he was in graduate school. Apparently his parents were killed in a hotel fire in Madrid, where they were vacationing. He came back to run the family business. Rumor has it that he was also tied in pretty closely with a cadre of former KGB agents."

"Does that theory hold water?" Bolan asked.

"Yeah," Kurtzman replied. "I'll spare you the details over the phone. But, having pored over these files, there's a small group that he's kept in close contact with. All are members of Russia's elite, either in business or politics, or the offspring of such people. They all have some kind of ties to the Kremlin. Barb actually worked up a dossier to send you, along with photos. But the bottom line is, it's not only possible, but probable that these individuals were either with the KGB or have ties with Russia's current intelligence apparatus."

Grimaldi looked at Bolan. "You think the Russians are giving the orders here?"

Bolan rubbed the stubble on his chin with his thumb and forefinger for a few seconds and mulled the question. "It's possible," he said finally. "Whether it's coming straight from the Kremlin or some splinter group within the Russian government probably is something we need to nail down. If it's small arms sales, I sort of doubt it, especially if the customer is a terrorist. It doesn't seem like something that would benefit the government."

"Though it might help a small group of rogue players," Grimaldi said.

"Exactly."

# CHAPTER EIGHTEEN

"Sorry to hear about Potts," Brognola said. The big Fed was speaking to Bolan from Washington via a secure com link. "He was a good agent."

"He took a bullet meant for me," Bolan replied. He was pacing in the living room of the Stony Man safehouse.

"How do you figure?"

"He said in his message that he'd gotten a tip from a source," Bolan said. "He went to check it out for himself. I can only assume that the whole thing was a setup, a trap for me. Bajaur's a trusted lieutenant to Khan, supposedly. Potts gets a tip on where to find Bajaur and he ends up dead. Do the math and see what you come up with."

"You're probably right, Striker," Brognola said. "But if it's any consolation, Potts knew the risks when he inserted himself into the case. Otherwise, why take two other agents with him?"

"You're probably right. I'm probably right. None of it makes me feel any damn better."

"Understood." Bolan heard papers being shuffled. "We do have some information that might be of interest to you, though."

"Let's hear it."

"Bear's been scouring Potts's laptop remotely, hunting for some clues. Fortunately for us, Potts keeps pretty meticulous notes on the people he meets with, including a lead on Potts's informant."

"He have any record of me?"

"One step ahead of you, soldier," Brognola countered. "The cyberteam checked his computer from stem to stern and found nothing on you. He knew you were the type of visitor who never existed and he played it right.

"Anyway," Brognola continued, "his informant was a young guy named Rajiv Yahya. Not much of a prize. In fact, he's basically a hustler, a con artist."

"Was?"

"He was found dead in an upscale brothel. It was a messy death carried out by person unknown."

"So that lead is a literal dead end."

"Yeah," Brognola said. "I'll let you know when Aaron comes up with something else."

THE SEA BREEZE, WARM and briny, blew across the deck of the 120-foot yacht moored in the seaport. His hands gripping the yacht's railing, Bajaur stared at the water, a churning oily blackness interrupted by occasional whitecaps and the lights from other neighboring boats.

He heaved a sigh, but it did little to calm the nervousness roiling his insides. Only a fool would think he could work for a major crime figure like Nawaz Khan and not piss people off, maybe even become a target. But the whole notion that Bajaur had been the pawn in a plot to kill a federal agent? It was almost too much to imagine, but he did know nothing good could come of it.

What if the crazy SOB survived and came looking for him? Bajaur thought. It was obvious the man wouldn't hesitate to put a bullet in his head. And even if he did die, it was possible that another American agent or agents may come looking for him. Even the state police, a group that normally gave Khan's organization a wide berth, might come after him either out of a misplaced sense of justice or just to placate the United States.

Regardless, he wanted nothing to do with it. He was

Khan's right-hand man, but he was also his money man, a bean counter, as the Americans would say. His specialty was taking cash and hiding it. Not all of this cloak-and-dagger stuff.

The sound of footsteps to his right startled him, and he whipped his head toward the noise. Instantly he recognized his bodyguard, Qadeer, a Pakistani man who stood well over six feet tall and was sheathed in thick pads of muscle generated by steroids. The man noticed Bajaur's agitation and smirked at him.

"What do you want?" Bajaur snapped.

"We got the call," Qadeer said. "Three Americans were shot dead in your office. All three were FBI agents."

"Cooper?"

Qadeer shook his head.

"Fuck! How did that happen? I thought the whole point was to get Cooper."

"Apparently, it didn't work."

"Apparently," Bajaur snapped back.

"Cooper's still out there," Qadeer said. "We should get you belowdecks. You're too vulnerable up here."

The word *vulnerable* hit Bajaur like a sledgehammer. He nodded. "You're right."

Qadeer stepped aside and gestured at a nearby door. After Bajaur took a couple of steps toward the door, Qadeer fell in behind him and the two men disappeared inside the yacht.

Seconds later, a figure clad in a black wet suit climbed over the side of the yacht and onto the deck.

BOLAN SET HIS WATERPROOF weapons bag on the deck and slid his diving mask from his face, which was followed by the rebreather strapped onto his back. He stowed both items, along with his swim fins, underneath a nearby stairwell. Most likely it would only be a matter of time before the items were found, he thought. But it didn't matter; he didn't need much time.

He guessed that within minutes everyone on the boat would know of the intruder in their midst.

With fast, precise moves, Bolan took the MP-5 SD from the weapons bag, followed by the .44-caliber Desert Eagle, which he strapped to his right hip, and the Beretta 93-R, which he stowed in a nylon shoulder rig. Finally he strapped several grenades—a mixture of HE, fragmentation and flash-bang rounds—to his web gear. He also carried a large combat knife and several garrotes.

The soldier slipped through the door Bajaur had passed through a few minutes earlier. The MP-5 at hip level, the soldier glided down the corridor of the luxury craft. The intel the soldier had received from Stony Man Farm had indicated the yacht was owned by Khan through one of a dozen of his shell companies. The interior was luxurious—wide corridors, floors covered with thick red carpeting, huge chandeliers suspended from the ceiling. According to research conducted by the Farm's cyberteam, the craft had circled the world several times and Bolan guessed it had been used to carry contraband and not just for pleasure cruises.

A door several yards ahead opened and the sound caused Bolan to freeze. A heartbeat later one of Khan's men stepped into view, an AK-47 strapped over one shoulder, the barrel canted at a forty-five-degree angle. It took a full second for the guy to spot Bolan and even longer than that to react. By the time the AK's barrel started an upward swing, Bolan already had his subgun positioned for the kill. The MP-5 chugged out a punishing burst that chewed into the man's midsection, punching him into a mad death dance that ended only when the soldier eased off the trigger.

Before Bolan completed his second step forward, two more gunners sprang from the door. The first covered his mad dash with a sustained burst of autofire. The fusillade slashed through the air around the Executioner and buzzed inches from his cheek.

The second man wrapped himself around the door frame, an arm, a leg and half his face exposed. Muzzle-flashes blossomed from the man's handgun.

The soldier dived forward. A swarm of 9 mm stingers spit from the MP-5's barrel. The initial burst chewed into the floor just in front of the guy with the handgun, causing him to lose his nerve and disappear inside.

The Executioner, in the meantime, landed on his belly and the impact jarred his shooting hand. The barrel jerked and a burst from the H&K subgun lanced up at an angle that shredded several ceiling tiles.

Even as Bolan readjusted his aim, the other shooter kept his cool and returned fire. Bullets from his assault rifle struck the floor several feet ahead of the soldier and began to saw a path toward the big American.

The MP-5 in Bolan's hand flared to life again. This time the subgun delivered a gut-shredding volley of slugs that spun the man and sent him hurtling to the floor like a limp sack of laundry.

The soldier uncoiled from the floor. He let the MP-5 fall on its strap. He drew the Desert Eagle from the hip holster, thumbed back the hammer in a fluid motion and bore down on the third gunner. His arm outstretched at shoulder level, Bolan let the hand cannon lead the way.

Driven by fear, stupidity or perceived opportunity, the last shooter popped out from his hiding place. He bent himself around the door frame, but only allowed his arm to protrude from the doorway and part of his face to come into view.

Bolan drew a bead on the guy and tapped the Desert Eagle's trigger. A peal of thunder erupted from the hand cannon's barrel. The .44 Magnum slug that rocketed forth drilled into the shooter's eye, tunneling through his brain before it punched through the back of the shooter's skull in an explosion of blood and flesh.

The thudding of footsteps to his six caused Bolan to whirl. Instead of confronting another attacker, the soldier spotted a man dressed head to toe in the gleaming white duds of a sailor. The soldier guessed the guy was a member of the ship's crew, maybe even the captain.

"Freeze," Bolan ordered. "Or I'll drop you."

The man froze suddenly, as if snagged by a tractor beam. His hands automatically went up.

"Wise choice," Bolan growled.

The Executioner strode forward and grabbed the guy by the scruff of the neck. The sailor gasped, but said nothing. Bolan spun him ninety degrees and shoved him face-first into the nearest wall. A quick search told the soldier that the man had no weapons.

"You the captain?" Bolan asked.

The sailor shook his head. "First mate," he said.

Bolan thought he detected a trace of an English accent in the man's quavering voice.

He turned the man so that they were facing each other. "Where's Bajaur?"

The man shrugged. "I don't know."

"Bullshit," Bolan snapped.

The man stared at his captor for a couple of beats, his lips pressed in a tight line. "He's in the security center. Along with Qadeer."

Bolan's mind ran through several names from the Stony Man Farm dossier on Khan's organization. "Khan's security chief."

The man nodded vigorously, apparently eager to please the human wraith that stood in front of him.

"How many people are in the crew?"

The guy told him.

"Are they all in uniform?"

The man nodded. "Most of them are on the bridge," he added.

Bolan gently nudged the man's right cheekbone with the Desert Eagle's barrel. "Get up on the bridge," the soldier said, "and tell everyone on the crew to keep their heads down. Consider this fair warning. I'm here for Bajaur and any gunners he may have on hand, not the crew. As long as you don't cross my path, that is." He nodded at the trio of corpses littering the hallway. "If any of you decides to play hero and draw down on me, well, you can see how well that worked for them."

The man, the collar and armpits of his white shirt darkened with sweat, nodded again. Bolan asked for directions to the security room. The first mate gave them up easily, and the soldier sent him packing.

Bolan stared after the man for several seconds until he disappeared from view. Satisfied that the guy had no plans to make a hero play, the soldier headed for the security room.

The way Bolan saw it, he'd come here for Bajaur. Any of Khan's gunners that he could take out likely would benefit him down the road. He had no problem with the crew as long as they stayed out of his way. In the strictest sense, many of them could be considered accessories to Khan's murderous crimes, including his spreading weapons and misery to some of the worst hellzones on the planet. In the strictest sense, yeah, they were guilty of something. But the soldier knew that didn't mean they deserved to die. He didn't kill cops, even if they drew down on him first, though he had taken out a couple of rogue cops in his day. And he'd abort a mission before he'd involve innocent bystanders. These were simple rules, though occasionally hard to live up to in the midst of combat. But it was this code that allowed Bolan to keep his perspective and his humanity, prevented him from becoming a killing machine, as bad as the savages he hunted.

According to the first mate the security room was in the bowels of the ship, so Bolan headed that way. In the process, he took out two more guards. The first was DOA after a head-on collision with a slug from the Desert Eagle. Bolan dropped the second thug with a swipe of a knife blade across the man's throat.

The soldier grabbed the MP-5 and snapped a fresh clip into the weapon and burrowed deeper into the yacht until he reached his destination. He eyed his surroundings. Unlike the over-the-top luxury of the upper decks, this level was all about utility. From the ceiling to midway from the floor, a glaring white paint covered the walls, while the lower half was covered with a thick gray. Bundles of thick cables ran overhead in a wire-mesh platform that stretched overhead. Gray-painted plumbing was visible. A portal stood about one hundred feet ahead and, if the first mate's information had been correct, a second corridor and the security room lay beyond that door.

From what Bolan could tell, getting to the door presented no problems.

Getting through it would be another story.

# CHAPTER NINETEEN

Bajaur stared at the security monitors and watched as the black-clad intruder burned down three of his trained killers, seemingly without breaking a sweat. Sealed in the security room, he felt an icy fist bury itself in his gut as the American moved around the yacht, looking for him.

What had he gotten himself into? he thought. He needed to talk to Khan, to figure out what to do. He picked up his cell phone, punched in Khan's number and got nothing for his trouble but silence. Canceling the call, he tried the process again and got the same result. His throat went dry, his breathing became shallow. He slammed the phone hard on the console.

He whipped his head around in Qadeer's direction.

"Can they jam our cell phones?"

The security chief, who was staring at another of the monitors, shrugged. When he spoke, he was clearly distracted and irritated. He didn't bother to turn to look at Bajaur. "I guess, yeah."

The icy fear that had seized Bajaur began to thaw as anger overtook him. "What the hell do you mean, you guess?" he snapped. "What kind of answer is that?"

Qadeer twisted in his seat and glared at Bajaur. "The only fucking answer I owe you. Can they jam our cell phones? Yes. How are they doing it? Who knows. Let's get one thing straight, though—I'm guarding you because it's my damn job. Because you're the money guy and Khan doesn't want anything to happen to you. I'm following his orders. But if you want to stay alive, you will shut up and do as I say. Otherwise, I can't guarantee a damn thing."

Bajaur opened his mouth to protest, but checked himself. He was in the weak position here. He knew numbers, knew every nook and cranny that Khan's cash had been stuffed in, knew all the passwords. But he wasn't worth a damn in a gunfight. He hated taking crap from Qadeer. Not surprisingly, he hated the notion of dying even worse. Discretion being the better part of valor, he decided to shut his mouth.

He watched as Qadeer hefted a two-way radio from the console and spoke into it. The guy's voice was cool as he ordered the remaining guards to double time it to the lower levels and put a buffer between Bajaur and the big American tearing his way through the yacht.

Qadeer shrugged on his suit jacket, stuffed his radio inside the jacket and fitted the earpiece into his ear. He picked up the Uzi, chambered a round and shot Bajaur a look. "Stay here," he said. "Don't open the door for anyone but me."

Bajaur nodded. "Sure."

And if that black-suited SOB isn't dead when you come back, don't expect me to open the door for you, either, he thought.

He turned back to the monitors and watched as the American crept along the corridor. Suddenly the guy halted and looked up at the surveillance camera's lens. The feeling that the icy-eyed killer was looking directly at him acted like a nerve toxin, seemingly paralyzing every muscle in Bajaur's body. Fists clenched, he drew his arms up to his chest and crossed them protectively at the wrists. Terror seized his throat muscles. He swore cold, invisible fingers of terror encircled his throat, choking him.

Then the screen went black and Bajaur really got scared.

THE MP-5 SNUGLY HELD at shoulder level, the soldier was on the move for the security room. He peered up at the surveillance cameras that tracked his every move. Up until now he'd left them intact and allowed them to track his progress. It had been by design. He wanted Bajaur to know someone was coming, wanted him to realize Death was coming for him. Allowing the guy's level of distress to peak could only help the soldier as he interrogated Bajaur. Besides, as much as Bolan tried to keep emotion out of the equation, he knew Bajaur had been part of the plot that ended up costing Potts his life. As much as he hated to admit it, that burned at the back of the soldier's mind, too.

Flipping the MP-5's selector switch to single shot, the soldier drilled a couple of rounds into a surveillance camera fixed to a wall several yards away. The body of the camera cracked open and sparks shot out from inside it. Bolan took out two more cameras with well-placed shots from the MP-5.

Switching the subgun back to full-auto mode, he was on the move again.

QADEER FOUND THREE MEMBERS of his security force waiting for him when he left Bajaur.

Qadeer, a former lieutenant in Pakistan's ISI, knew the trio well. All three men had run paramilitary operations against Indian forces in the disputed Kashmir. They'd not only trained local Islamic fighters in the art, science and craft of warfare, but had also participated in more than one off-the-books operation during their time there. All were skilled warriors, battle-tested and courageous. More than a match for the intruder.

Or at least Qadeer hoped they were. If they got steamrolled, if something happened to Bajaur, Khan would string Qadeer up, literally, and treat him to a very horrible and public death. Make an example of him. Qadeer knew this because he'd seen that ruthless bastard Khan do it to others in his employ. When someone failed and Khan had his ring of "advisers" torture them by administering shocks from a car battery, Khan didn't see it as torture, he viewed it as a way to keep the troops focused. And compliant. Qadeer was on board with that, as long as he was the one meting out the punishment and not the one receiving it.

But he wouldn't be on the receiving end of it, he assured himself. The American had showed himself to be a formidable adversary. But he still was just human, and Qadeer had killed more than his fair share of those along the way. This time would be no different, he vowed.

He ordered the two men closest two him to head to the front of the corridor, making up the first line of defense, while he and the third guard hung farther back where they could lay down a punishing barrage of gunfire from a standing position.

A voice buzzed in his earpiece. "Sir?"

Qadeer recognized the speaker, another of his security team. "Yes?"

"We're almost in position."

"How long?"

"Less than twenty seconds and we'll be behind him."

"Good."

"Looks like he's taken out the rest of the team," the man said, an undercurrent of anxiety in his voice.

"That's because we were scattered and unprepared," Qadeer snapped. "He took us out one by one. Now we're working as a unit. Focus on the job at hand and shut up."

"Yes, sir."

One of the men in the corridor with Qadeer gestured for his attention. The security chief nodded and the man pointed at the door, indicating that their target was closing in on them. Qadeer returned the nod and drew a bead on the door with the Uzi.

The sound of gunshots erupted from behind the door and

a grim smile tugged at the corners of Qadeer's lips. They'd caught the intruder unawares, and now it was time to finish him off.

DOWN!

Bolan's combat senses had shouted for him to drop into a crouch. The soldier had learned long ago not to ignore his instincts when in combat, and that lesson had kept him alive in some of the worst conditions imaginable.

The soldier dived forward, hit the ground and rolled. Bullets sizzled through the air above him and slammed into walls. Geysers of dust erupted as autofire pierced plasterboard.

On his back, the soldier spotted the source of the gunfire. A pair of hardmen emerged from a doorway, jagged flames flaring from the muzzles of their submachine guns as they doused the corridor with a punishing barrage of autofire.

Still lying on his back, his head raised from the floor, Bolan loosed a blistering sustained burst, firing it in a figure-eight pattern. The barrage scythed down Bolan's attackers, but also emptied the weapon's clip. The soldier ejected the spent magazine from the SMG. His fingers scrambled for another one as he rolled into a sitting position. Just as he slammed the new clip home and chambered a round in the weapon, the door he'd been heading to flew open and another guard emerged, his arm raised over his head and something clutched in his hand.

The MP-5 whispered its silent message of death. Bullets pierced the man's midsection and caused him to jerk in place for a stretched second before Bolan eased off the trigger and the guy crumpled to the ground. His fingers loosened and the metallic object he'd clutched in his hands came loose and struck the floor.

Bolan recognized the object as a flash-bang grenade. He averted his gaze and, letting the MP-5 fall free on its strap, clapped his palms over his ears to shield them from the noise.

Even with his eyes screwed shut, the flash still penetrated the lids and the crack, though audible, was muffled.

The soldier knew what was coming next.

As his eyes popped open, he freed the Beretta from the shoulder holster and twisted at the waist. He locked the 93-R's muzzle on the doorway and, through the white haze of acrid smoke, spotted a silhouetted form, the shadow of a long gun visible, coming into view. The soldier tapped the Beretta's trigger and unleashed a triburst of subsonic ammunition that pounded into the approaching gunner. The man howled with pain, spun and disappeared from view.

Wide arcs of autofire sprayed through the door and forced Bolan back.

Dropping into a crouch, the soldier reached for an M-68 fragmentation grenade. Yanking the pin, he tossed the explosive through the door and rolled off the firing line. The blast had rent the wallboard, causing it to bow and triggering a heavy rain of dust and debris, covering Bolan and his surroundings in a heavy film.

The soldier got to his feet. He leathered the Beretta and took up the MP-5. Stepping through the door, he peered through the eye-stinging haze of smoke and dust. Four bodies were arrayed in front of him, flesh rent by the small slivers of steel driven from the grenades. Bolan checked each of the bodies to confirm that the men were dead. He found a key card clipped to the first corpse's belt, pulled the card free and pocketed it.

Bolan rolled up on a steel door that he guessed led into the security room. The blast had left black burn marks on the door, but it seemed otherwise unfazed by the explosion. Likewise, the security card reader had been chipped in a few places, but seemed to be in one piece. The Executioner slid the card through a groove on the side of the machine. A small red light next to the keypad winked out and the steel barrier slid open with a hiss.

Inside, Bolan found Bajaur crouched in a corner, trying to work the slide on a small Walther handgun.

The big American sighted down the Beretta's barrel and locked it on the guy's forehead.

"Drop it," the soldier said.

Bajaur stared at Bolan for a stretched second before he tossed the weapon to the floor.

"You're going to kill me," Bajaur said.

"Probably."

"I can help you. I know things."

"I know things, too," Bolan said. "Like that you helped set up Carl Potts for assassination. Him and two other FBI agents. Two of them were husbands and fathers. I also understand that you were trying to kill me. And that for years you've helped Khan run his murderous enterprise. Run it and prosper."

"I was just following orders," Bajaur protested.

"Sure, you're just a victim," Bolan said. "My heart bleeds for you."

"I can help," Bajaur repeated.

"I heard you the first time," Bolan said. "You sound like you want to make a deal."

Bajaur nodded enthusiastically. "Absolutely. I will tell you everything I know. Just don't kill me."

"Seems fair," Bolan said. "Where's the safe?"

The Pakistani blinked at him. "What?"

"You're an accountant. You do know what a safe is, right?"

"Of course I do."

"Then show me where it is."

He gave Bolan a hard stare. When he spoke, the soldier detected a hint of disbelief in the guy's voice. "You came here to rob us? All of this just to steal money?"

Bolan gave him a grim smile. "Not even close. Even if I took every dime you and your pack of thieves and murderers had, I wouldn't consider it stealing, I'd consider it justice. But this is about sending a message to Khan."

"And that message is?"

"Get up," Bolan said. The soldier waved the Beretta for emphasis. Bajaur got to his feet and, at least for the moment, seemed to have given up on arguing. Instead he exited the security room with Bolan two steps behind him. The big American heard Bajaur inhale sharply when he saw the carnage outside the security room, the blood-splattered walls and the flesh rent by the grenade blast.

Bajaur turned and looked at Bolan. The fear in his eyes was evident. "You killed them all."

"And I'm just getting started. Now show me to the safe."

The accountant led Bolan to another stairwell secured by a thick steel door, one that reminded the soldier of the interior doors found inside naval vessels. Unlike the other parts of the ship, opening this door required a much more complex security regime. Bajaur first pressed his face up against a retinal scanner until it emitted a soft beep. After that, he punched a numerical code onto a keypad and finally swiped a card through a reader. The locks released with a metallic click. Bajaur pushed against the door with his fingertips and it swung inward. He motioned for Bolan to go inside, but the soldier shook his head.

"You first," the Executioner said. "The last thing I need is for you to slam the door behind me and lock me inside."

Bajaur scowled and Bolan guessed it wasn't because his feelings were hurt. He went inside with the soldier, a couple of steps behind him. Bolan had called it a safe, but the room really was more of a vault. Small drawers that reminded him of safe-deposit boxes found in banks lined one of the walls. Large rectangular drawers were stacked one on top of the other on two other walls. He guessed at least some of the drawers contained weapons or other contraband. He'd let someone else sort that out later; right now, he was here for a very specific reason.

"I want the cash," he said.

Bajaur scowled, but he opened two of the large drawers and stepped aside. Bolan peered inside and saw bundles of U.S. dollars as well as a few stacks of assorted foreign currency.

"This it?" Bolan asked.

Bajaur nodded. "There's a small fortune here. More than a million dollars."

"But the emphasis is on small," Bolan replied. "Khan's worth a hell of a lot more than this."

"He is. But it doesn't make sense for him to store too much money on the boat. It could get stolen. Or seized. Or the boat could sink."

"That'd be too damn bad."

Bajaur shot Bolan an irritated look. "How much do you plan to take?"

"Every last dime," the soldier replied. "You tell Khan who took it. Tell him it's just the start of what I plan to take from him."

Bolan thought he saw hope flicker in Bajaur's eyes. "So you are going to let me live?"

"For now," Bolan said. "Of course, once Khan finds out you gave up all this money, he'll likely kill you himself. Enjoy the reprieve, but I wouldn't start making long-term plans."

"You're a son of a bitch."

"So they say."

## CHAPTER TWENTY

Though it had been years since he'd lived in Pakistan, Nawaz Khan had kept a home in Karachi for occasional visits. It had been several hours since he'd parted company with Haqqani. Khan was in his study, seated in a high-backed leather chair, a book fanned open on his lap. A cup of coffee stood cooling on a table next to him, and a cigarette burned in an ashtray.

He felt strangely unsettled, even though he'd been able to accomplish his part of the mission against what had been difficult circumstances, namely the intervention by the American, Matt Cooper.

Picking up the coffee, he brought the cup to his lips and sipped. Despite the unease that roiled inside him, all the problems of the past few days, the magnitude of what he'd done, he still was glad to be in Karachi, his homeland, even if only for the night.

A two-way radio buzzed in the background. He only half listened to the members of his security team as they spoke back and forth. More than a dozen men patrolled the grounds or prowled the inside of the sprawling home. They were his absolute best, veterans of the ISI or soldiers who'd retired from the Pakistani army. All had been tested in battles in Kashmir, and Khan knew they were loyal enough to take a bullet for him.

Under normal circumstances he traveled with a smaller security contingent, maybe two-thirds the size of his current team. But with Cooper cutting a bloody swath through his organization, he'd decided some extra muscle couldn't hurt.

He also kept an Uzi submachine gun tilted next to his chair, within easy reach.

Staring up at the ceiling, he watched as the fan churned through slow revolutions. In spite of the coffee, he had begun to feel drowsy and his eyes itched from a lack of sleep. Finally he dozed. He still held the coffee cup in both hands on his lap. The ringing of the phone startled him awake. Some of the coffee sloshed over the side of the cup and onto his lap. He swore bitterly. Apparently, though, he'd been asleep for several minutes as the coffee that soaked through his trouser leg was warm but not steaming hot.

He slammed the coffee cup on a table. Grabbing the cell phone, he brought it to his ear.

"What?" he barked into the phone.

"Thanks," a graveyard voice replied.

Though he hadn't heard the voice before, Khan instinctively knew who it was. His lips suddenly felt dry and his heart slammed hard in his rib cage.

"Who is this?" he demanded.

"You know who it is."

"Cooper."

"Bingo."

"What do you want?" Khan demanded.

"Like I said before, thank you."

"For what?"

"For the two-million-dollar gift you just gave me. Very generous."

"You're not making sense."

"From the yacht. I'm taking money from your boat," Bolan stated.

Khan swallowed hard and his grip on the phone tightened. He was on the yacht? What the hell had happened to Bajaur?

He decided to keep the American talking. "So you're a thief. I thought you were a Justice Department agent."

"Who says I'll keep the money? The important thing is that you won't have it. Hell, I'd rather feed it to the fish than let you see it again."

Khan's heart continued to race, though the fear had morphed into rage.

"I have other money," he said. "Plenty of money in places where you'll never get it."

"Maybe," Bolan said. "But don't bet on it."

"What do you mean? Quit talking in riddles!" Khan was yelling now.

His outburst was greeted by silence. The bastard had hung up on him! Khan realized.

Cursing, he threw the phone across the room. It struck a wall, the body exploding into multiple pieces that rained to the floor.

How did Cooper do it? How had the American been able to get his number?

A tentative knock sounded on his door.

He spun toward it.

"What?" he yelled.

One of his guards, an Afghan named Jalaluddin, entered. Arm extended, he offered Khan his phone.

"You have a call," Jalaluddin said.

Khan snatched the phone from his hand. If this was Cooper—

"What?" he demanded.

"Khan?" It was a man's voice, sounding strained.

"Bajaur? Is that you?"

"Yes."

"What happened?"

"He took the money," Bajaur stated.

"The American?"

"Yes."

Khan pressed his lips into a hard line as he tried to contain his rage.

"What happened?" he asked.

"Cooper hit the boat. He climbed aboard while we were a couple of miles out from the coast and burned through everyone. I'm the only survivor."

How convenient, Khan thought. Immediately he felt suspicion overtake his anger, but he kept it to himself for the moment. He didn't want Bajaur to shut down on him.

"Did he take anything else?"

Silence greeted Khan's question. He waited a couple of seconds, then said, "What else did he take?"

"He took my laptop." Bajaur's voice sounded small.

Khan's chest suddenly grew tight, and he found himself taking a sharp inhale to get enough air.

"It contains all my accounts."

"Most of them," Bajaur admitted.

"Fuck!" Khan raged. "How does that happen? How does that fucking happen? That has—what?—seventy-five percent of my bank account numbers. Tons of passwords. And now he has it!"

"It's all encrypted," Bajaur said. "There's no way he can crack the passwords. We can change everything before he does."

"You'll never get it all."

"You're right. But we can get part of it," Bajaur said. "Give me a couple of our best computer guys and a few hours. I'll secure as much of the information as I can. I can transfer the money through some cutout accounts, and at least we can keep some of it. Trust me."

"That's worked so well so far," Khan said.

"I can fix this, Nawaz."

Khan exhaled. What choice did he have?

"Fix it. Or you're dead."

Bajaur said nothing. Khan heard him breathing on the

other end of the phone and sensed he was thinking of something.

"What," Khan said finally. "What is it?"

"The American said something."

"What? Thank you?"

"No, he said he's coming. For you."

Another chill raced down Khan's spine, causing him to shiver. His world suddenly seemed very small and dark.

# CHAPTER TWENTY-ONE

Bolan was back in the safehouse. He'd plugged Khan's laptop into a broadband connection and several windows were popping up on the screen, carrying messages the soldier only vaguely understood.

Kurtzman was on the other end of the line, the excitement audible in his voice.

"This is too sweet, Striker," the leader of the cyberteam was saying. "We're downloading the contents of the machine right now to see what kinds of information we can get from it."

"How secure is it?" Bolan asked.

He heard the sound of keys clicking on the other end of the line.

"Lots of encryption. Just how clever it is, it's too soon to say. Anywhere you want me to focus?"

Bolan didn't hesitate. "The money," he said. "I want to get every last dime that we can from Khan."

"You have a car payment coming up?"

"Funny guy. I just know that if anything will break him, it's taking away his money. If we dismantle what he's built, he'll get sloppy, get distracted. It gets easier to screw with his head. There's more than one way to drain the life out of someone."

Kurtzman let out a low whistle. "Shit, Striker. Remind me not to piss you off, ever."

"Don't piss me off, ever."

"Thanks for the reminder," Kurtzman said with a laugh.

"Next, if one of you can start combing through the shipping manifests, that'd be good. Maybe we can circumvent some of his shipments. Also, look for any references to Terry Lang." Bolan thought for a minute. "Or Tamara Gillen."

"Will do."

SASHA LEBED SAT ON THE edge of the front of his desk, the sleeves of his white dress shirt rolled up to the middle of his thick forearms. He was staring at the screen of a laptop and the image of Konstantin Zhukov, a former Kremlin defense official, stared back.

Zhukov had a wide face that reminded Lebed of the head of a shovel. His white hair was thick and perfectly combed. The bridge of his nose was wide, the tip bulbous and deeply crimson. Red splotches mottled the skin of his cheeks and neck, telegraphing his anger.

The two men were speaking via secure satellite link.

"This is completely, utterly out of control." Zhukov's voice was thunderous.

The corners of Lebed's lips turned up in a slight smile. "Out of control or out of your control?"

"Out of anyone's control," Zhukov said. He was jabbing a finger at the camera. "You've handed Red Mercury to a group of terrorists."

"One man's terrorist is another man's freedom fighter," Lebed said offhandedly.

"What were you thinking?"

"I was thinking that they paid us millions of dollars for the Red Mercury," Lebed said, shrugging. "Then I thought about how happy I was to have that money. Understand?"

"Bullshit. You didn't do this for the money. We both know better than that. Not for a few million dollars. You make and lose that much with your stock market investments. We can make that much selling spark-gap detonators or some other technology to some backwater country. This isn't about money."

Lebed's smile widened a bit, pleased.

"Very astute," he said. "You're right. At least to a point. It's not just about money, though I won't ever turn away such easy cash. It benefits us all, you know."

"Then why do this?"

"This is so much bigger than you and me. So much bigger than the Seven."

"Let me guess," Zhukov said. "You did this for Mother Russia." The older man let loose with a loud, derisive laugh, and it was Lebed's turn to flush with anger.

"It is about our homeland," he said. "It's about keeping her strong. We both know that, though I'm starting to doubt whether you share my level of commitment."

"You sanctimonious son of a bitch!" Zhukov roared, his face moving closer to the camera. "I served Russia, the USSR, back when you were still a boy. I ran operations in Cuba and Central America, spent months at a time in jungle hellholes all over the world. Don't you dare question my patriotism!"

"You did all that," Lebed countered. "But now you're a grandfather. You spend six months of the year in Tel Aviv or Paris, playing with those little brats."

"So?"

"You're comfortable. Your commitment's soft," Lebed stated.

"My commitment is fine. What you need to understand is that my commitment doesn't mean blind faith in you or other members of the Seven. And it certainly doesn't mean blind faith in your moronic plan, particularly when it entails giving radioactive material to terrorists. What can you hope to gain with this?"

"I explained this before."

"Then explain it again," Zhukov said, the challenge evident in his voice.

"It's a white-knight play. We hand this material over to Haqqani and his crew through a third party. Then we swoop in and take it back," Lebed replied.

"Which accomplishes what exactly?"

"To the outside world, it puts us on the map, establishes us as a global player among security companies. We stop a massive disaster from happening."

"One we created," Zhukov said.

Lebed shrugged. "By the time I'm done with this, there will be no one to share that information."

"Meaning?"

"Meaning that Haqqani and his men won't be long for this world."

"What about Nawaz Khan?" Zhukov demanded.

"What about him? The way the American has been chewing through the landscape, I have grave concerns about Mr. Khan's future."

"Someone will talk," Zhukov growled. "They always do."

"Then they talk," Lebed said. "Let them. But let me ask you this—who will the authorities believe? A gunrunner, an Islamic terrorist or a group of well-heeled Russians. I've taken steps all along the way to keep our fingerprints off this."

"And you plan to kill any witnesses?"

Lebed allowed himself a smile. "A little dramatic, I guess, but necessary, nonetheless. I'd kill one hundred Nawaz Khans if it meant reaching our goals."

"I see how this benefits Paradigm Systems, and how it benefits you. But I fail to understand how this helps Russia."

"Your lack of vision surprises me, Konstantin. I won't lie to you. Making money is important to me. The more the better. But there's much more to it than that."

By now, the anger had drained from Zhukov, replaced by genuine curiosity.

"I don't understand," the older Russian said.

"This is about the Seven," Lebed said, an edge of irritation creeping into his own voice. "The important thing is that we have to do only a little to get what we want. Not just you and me, but all the members of our group, as well as our benefactors in the Kremlin. That's what this really is about."

"I still don't—"

Lebed cut off the other man.

"It's simple. A group of Pakistanis, ones with ties to the Pakistani government, sneak into India to detonate a nuclear explosion. Suddenly the tensions between the two countries skyrocket again, possibly pushing us to the edge of a nuclear conflict. Pakistan suddenly finds itself having to move as many of its troops and equipment as possible to the Indian border. They'll be of no help in Afghanistan or the border areas. In the meantime, we continue selling weapons to the Taliban. It's a one-two punch for the Americans. We undercut one of their most important foreign policy initiatives, and we weaken their standing in the region."

Zhukov nodded encouragingly and Lebed continued.

"And we also link the sale of the nuclear materials back to the Americans, putting them at odds with India. We'll do irreparable harm to them in the process."

"But what if Haqqani and his people succeed in detonating the substance?"

"Then they do. I can live with that."

*Karachi, Pakistan*

BOLAN DROVE THE VAN TO within a couple of blocks of Khan's estate and parked the vehicle on the street. The vehicle was black and, other than on the driver's and passenger's-side doors, had no side windows. It was registered, fraudulently, to the French embassy, a status that might not repel thieves, but that Bolan hoped would at least keep the police from bothering it.

The soldier wore his combat blacksuit underneath military webbing. An overcoat a couple of sizes too large, plenty big enough to hide weapons and equipment, lay nearby on the floor.

It was Bolan's second trip to the neighborhood; he'd driven through it once before a few hours earlier, dressed in nondescript street clothes and driving a small green hatchback borrowed from an employee of the U.S. Consulate. That brief recon—paired with information gathered by a local CIA team—had given him necessary intel for the mission. A twelve-foot-high concrete wall surrounded the property's perimeter, broken only in one spot by a gate. A guardhouse populated by one or two guards stood next to the gate. Two more gunners saddled up on motorcycles buzzed around the estate. Cameras positioned at the gate and at other strategic positions throughout the property also kept watch. Brognola had requested a flyover by a Predator UAV to snap up additional visuals of the property's layout and had fed the information to Bolan via a secure internet connection.

Bolan trusted the CIA station chief and her inner circle had kept her mouth shut. They'd also taken great pains to keep the information from the local U.S. ambassador so he could claim, truthfully, the following morning not to know a thing about the raid.

Still, Khan knew he was coming. For starters, Bolan had called the guy and told him as much, a decision he didn't regret. The soldier knew the call had tipped his hand a little bit. But he'd wanted Khan to stew, to get worked up so he wouldn't be thinking clearly. The guy was a pro, but he also was a jackal who trafficked in human misery and death, the kind of man who always thought first of saving himself. The kind of man who was much more comfortable putting a target on someone else's back than his own. Bolan guessed the guy was sweating, and that gave him a bigger emotional stake in the outcome. Therefore, no matter how hard he tried, he likely wouldn't be thinking right. His fear would give Bolan the advantage.

That was the working theory, anyway, which meant it would fall apart once the first shots were fired, Bolan thought ruefully.

The soldier popped open the door and climbed down from the van, grabbing a handful of the overcoat as he did. He shrugged on the coat, reached back inside for a duffel bag filled with an M-16/M-203 combo and additional clips for the weapon. The Beretta was stowed in its shoulder rig and the Desert Eagle rode on Bolan's hip.

Locking the van, he slung the duffel bag's strap over one shoulder and started down the street toward Khan's estate. Even with the additional weight of the weapons and other gear, the soldier moved silently, easily, over the pavement. When he reached the estate, he huddled in the shadows along a security wall that ran the perimeter of Khan's property. Unzipping the bag, he extracted a twenty-foot rope tipped with a grappling hook and got to his feet. He tossed the grappling hook up and over the wall. It caught. Giving the rope a hard tug to make sure the hook had set, he scrambled first up the side of the wall and then onto the top of it.

Perched atop the wall, Bolan broke open the grenade launcher and thumbed in a high-explosive round. Snapping the breech shut, he scanned his surroundings. He spotted one member of the motorcycle patrol guards walking away from a cycle that was parked on the winding driveway.

Bringing the M-16/M-203 combo to his shoulder, the Executioner drew down on the bike and stroked the launcher's trigger. The HE round sizzled through the air and punched into the motorcycle. A thunderclap followed, immediately reverberating throughout the compound. The force of the explosion yanked the bike into the air, engulfing it in flames. A second or two later it crashed back to the earth, a twisted mass of flaming metal. The burning wreckage pumped out oily black smoke.

The guard initially had thrown himself to the ground when the explosion had rent the air. Now he was climbing back to his feet, a weapon of some kind in his grip. With the M-16 set for single-shot mode, the soldier squeezed its trigger and cored a round into the guy's chest. The force of the shot spun him a quarter turn. The gun fell from his hands and he grabbed at his wounded chest, his mind likely still not grasping that he'd just taken a bullet. His legs suddenly gave out on him and he dropped to the ground.

The Executioner flicked the M-16 to full automatic, then slung the weapon over his shoulder and scurried down the wall. He hit the ground of Khan's estate in a crouch. By the time his boots had hit the ground, three more gunners had materialized from somewhere, presumably in response to the explosion.

Bolan took up the M-16 just as one of the guards spotted him and shouted a warning to his comrades. The three gunners moved in a ragged line toward the soldier. He triggered the assault rifle, jagged flames blossomed from the weapon's barrel. The Executioner maneuvered the weapon in a figure eight, the spray of bullets punching through flesh and bone, knocking the gunners down in quick succession.

Hot lead sizzled just past Bolan's left ear. The report from his assailant's weapon told him that the shot was coming from behind. Acting on instinct, the soldier dived forward onto his stomach and rolled. A barrage of bullets tore through the air where he'd stood just a heartbeat earlier.

Lying on his back, the soldier fired with one hand. He dragged the chugging assault rifle in a long sweep, hosing down the gunner's position with a merciless barrage. Bolan rattled through the rest of the clip, the onslaught of 5.56 mm stingers smacking into the shadows, jerking the hardmen around wildly as they wilted under the blazing autofire.

Bolan ejected the spent clip and shoved in a new one.

In the next instant the soldier heard the growl of another engine. Bringing himself to his full height, the big American wheeled in time to see a motorcycle bearing down on him. A second figure was seated behind the first, a small submachine gun spitting flames and hot lead at Bolan.

The Executioner stood his ground. The M-16 flared to life, the muzzle-flashes illuminating the grim-as-hell expression on his face. Bullets sparked off the vehicle's handlebars, ripped through the face shield of the driver's helmet. The guy's dead hands released the handlebars. The rider had dropped his weapon and was trying to reach around the dead man in the driver's seat, gain some control over the careening motorcycle. Another burst from the M-16 took out the rider.

Just what the bike's front tire hit, Bolan would never know, but the impact caused the front wheel to stop suddenly. The back end of the bike rose from the ground and was launched into the air, the vehicle pinwheeling through the air at Bolan.

KHAN WONDERED HOW LONG the American could keep going.

Fists clenched in rage, he watched on a series of security monitors as the blacksuited wraith cut through his people like a scythe cutting down wheat.

Even as he watched the man, Khan weighed his options and found them all terrible. He could try to escape. He had a secret tunnel, cramped and cold, that would lead from the house into the sewers below Karachi. He'd had the escape hatch installed years ago, back when he'd still been with the ISI. At the time Khan had kept it primarily as an escape route should the Indians decide it was time to sneak into the country and take him out. Or, for that matter, it was always possible that his ISI comrades could come looking for him. A sudden change in military dictators or civilian leadership was hardly unheard-of in Pakistan. And if he had found himself on the wrong side of an internal struggle for control of the country? It never hurt to have a contingency plan.

So, yeah, he could crawl through the sewers like some kind of vermin. Maybe he'd get the chance to return to Dubai or try somewhere new, like Morocco.

But in a few days he'd be back in the same damn position. Cooper would be gunning for him, relentless, focused. Maybe he could wear the guy out. After all, no one could keep up that kind of pace forever. Eventually, Khan knew from personal experience, fatigue would cause Cooper to get sloppy and screw up, perhaps fatally so.

Maybe.

More likely, though, Cooper would find him when he least expected it. Maybe the damn American would put a bullet through his head as he drank coffee or while he was with a prostitute. Khan scowled at the thought. There was no way he was going to let the American take him out. He couldn't just sit and wait to take a bullet in the head as he ran away. The way he saw it, such an ending didn't suit him. He'd face up to the American. He'd either take the bastard out or vice versa.

Khan hefted the Uzi from where it was tilted against his chair. He looped the strap over his head and clipped an arm through so the strap cut across his chest diagonally. In long strides, he crossed the room, stopping at the couch. He grabbed the back of the couch and, with a grunt, slid it a couple of feet. Dropping to one knee, he knelt next to a wall safe that had been hidden behind the couch.

He punched in a code on the keypad. The locking mechanism emitted a small beep followed by a loud click that indicated that the lock had disengaged. He pulled open the door and reached inside, where he found several more clips for the Uzi. He stuffed the 20-round clips into his pockets. Next he withdrew a Browning Hi-Power handgun from inside the safe and he stuck that into his belt.

Returning to his full height, he exited the study. In the room outside, he found three of his men—all guards dressed in civilian clothes—waiting. Judging by the firepower the three carried, they'd already broken into the on-site armory and snatched up AK-47s. Khan nodded his approval.

"This ends now," he said.

The oldest of the three, a former commander with Pakistan's Frontier Corps, nodded his agreement. Khan knew the man to be a stone-cold killer. The youngest of the three—Khan couldn't recall the guy's name—looked nervous, his eyes wide and a sheen of perspiration filming his forehead. Like the other man, he nodded his agreement.

Khan had no idea whether the young man had even an iota of combat experience, but was willing to bet the guy didn't. Still, he'd come in handy, even if it was drawing fire away from the others.

The third man was a Pashtun, a big man with his skin turned leathery from too many hours in Wazirastan's sun. He had less formal training than the other two, though he'd also spent years fighting the Soviets after they'd invaded Afghanistan. Once the Russians had turned tail and run, he'd turned mercenary and offered his services to whichever Afghan warlord seemed to be winning at the time. He'd spilled more blood than any ten men Khan had known.

Khan nodded his satisfaction as he started for the door, motioning the others to follow. Not a bad crew. Surely, they'd at least give him enough muscle to take out one man, even one as deadly as Matt Cooper.

# CHAPTER TWENTY-TWO

The motorcycle arrowed toward Bolan like a flying tomahawk. The soldier thrust himself sideways and hit the ground, rolling as the cycle punched into his former position.

Then Bolan was back on his feet, reloading the assault rifle on the run, his eyes sweeping the area for a new target. A check of his watch told him that less than two minutes had passed since the first shots had been fired. If he was lucky, he had maybe another two to three minutes before local police or a military unit stormed the place.

If that came to pass, his best-case scenario was that he'd spend the night in jail. One night if he was lucky. Maybe more if Brognola or the local station chief couldn't talk the locals into letting him go.

The house lay just ahead. Bolan moved toward it in a crouch, the M-16 held at hip level. The soldier scrutinized the three-story home as he moved up on it, searching for any sign of a threat.

Gunfire erupted from one of the first-floor windows, the glass pane disintegrating under the onslaught of fire and lead. Remnants of the window cascaded to the ground. The shooter came into view, his AK-47 unloading a stream of bullets in the Executioner's direction.

Slugs slammed into the ground several feet in front of the Executioner, kicking up geysers of concrete dust or dirt.

Bolan dropped into a crouch, chattering the M-16 with a line of 5.56 mm slugs. The first volley from the assault rifle lanced through the window, but flew high enough to pass harmlessly over the other man's head.

The shooter disappeared from view. The M-16 now snug against his shoulder, Bolan stepped to the left and tried to refine his aim on the window. The way he figured it, the shooter likely would make another run at him and it would be best to be in a new spot, make the guy adjust his aim.

Sure enough, the guy popped around the window frame, his AK-47 churning out a murderous barrage. The first rounds lanced into the spot where Bolan had been standing. The guy started to correct himself, swinging barrel in his adversary's direction. Bolan tapped the rifle's trigger and the autofire caught the guy in the right side of his stomach, stitching a diagonal line to his opposite shoulder.

The soldier's sixth sense clamored for his attention. He spun and found two more shooters, still a dozen or so yards away, trying to sneak up on his six. The assault rifle flared to life as Bolan swept it in a horizontal line. The punishing swarm of slugs unleashed from the weapon punched the two shooters to the ground.

Another reload and Bolan ascended the trio of steps leading to Khan's house. The thick double doors hung open, daring the Executioner to enter.

THE ENTRYWAY WAS ROUND, like the hub of a wheel, with hallways jutting from it like spokes; marble covered the floors; a circular staircase twisted its way up from the ground to the second and third floors; chandeliers glittered overhead.

The soldier hugged the nearest wall and eased his way along it until he reached one of the corridors. He slipped into the hallway. A quick check of that area turned up the body of the guy who'd fired on him from the window, now sprawled on the floor in a pool of blood littered with shell casings. A couple of other rooms were stuffed with expensive furniture, but no people. The dead guy looked young, maybe early twenties, and he was big, but otherwise nondescript and certainly not Khan.

The soldier kept moving, checking two more corridors, but found nothing for his efforts.

A figure at the top of the stairs registered in his peripheral vision. He wheeled in that direction and spotted another of Khan's gunners staring down on him. The guy grinned, held out his hand and uncurled his fingers. A steel orb plummeted to the ground.

Bolan spun on his heel and hurled himself into the nearest corridor. He threw himself flat on the floor and let his momentum carry him forward, the M-16 slipping from his grasp. He cupped his hands over his ears and pulled his knees to his chest in a protective move. His eyes were squeezed shut.

His hands only slightly muffled the sound of the blast. Dust shook loose from the walls and the ceiling and rained down on him. Small bits of razor-sharp steel sliced into the wood-paneled walls at the mouth of the corridor, but didn't travel far enough to strike Bolan. He rode out the blast and waited several seconds to see whether the guy would drop a second grenade. Smoke had begun to stream in from the entryway, filling the soldier's nostrils. He guessed the grenade blast had set walls or curtains afire. While he waited, he reached over and retrieved his M-16.

After several seconds, he stood and flattened his body against the corridor wall. He glided up to the door leading back into the entryway and chanced a look. Flames were chewing through a paneled wall, the fire pumping out an oily black smoke.

Bolan surmised that the grenade had probably hit the ground and bounced away from him, a bit of dumb luck that had saved his life. He couldn't expect to get that sort of reprieve from death twice in one night.

FOOTSTEPS TO THE RIGHT snagged Bolan's attention. He whipped his head in the direction of the noise and spotted Khan darting through a doorway at the end of the corridor. The soldier tried to draw a bead on his quarry, but Khan already had disappeared.

The Executioner moved forward silently, ready to take the other man out once and for all. He slipped through the door that only seconds before had swallowed Khan, moving quickly so his silhouetted body didn't present a target, then swept the assault rifle's barrel over the interior of the room. It was empty. Another door on the other side of the room stood open.

The soldier took a couple of steps forward. Alarm bells began to ring in his head and he sensed someone else's presence.

Whirling, he caught sight of a big shadow towering over him.

The man's arm was raised high, a knife in his hand. The blade fell toward Bolan.

The M-16 flared to life and stuttered out a short burst. The image of his attacker, a large man with a long black beard, flickered under the strobelike effect of the muzzle-flashes from the assault rifle.

The onslaught of 5.56 mm bullets chewed into the man's midsection and caused geysers of blood to erupt from his torso. His body went slack and he crumpled to the ground with a hard thud.

Bolan spun and continued his pursuit of Khan.

KHAN FELT HIS HEART SLAM in his chest as he slipped through the house. Blood thundered in his ears. He fought to bring his breathing under control even while sprinting away from the house to put as much distance between himself and Cooper as possible.

He still carried the Uzi in his right hand. Sweat gathered

between his palm and the weapon's pistol grip. He hadn't expected the man to get this far, frankly. Considering the number of guards he had on-site, the chance of the American burning his way through Khan's guards seemed impossible.

But he had churned his way through them. Now Khan found himself once again on the run. When he reached a door, he rested his palm on the knob and paused for a couple of seconds, listening.

The house's interior had again fallen silent. The absence of sound, though, did nothing to quiet his nerves. Rather it only heightened his anxiety.

Cooper had to be on his trail, moving through the darkness like a wraith.

Twisting the knob, Khan pushed through the doorway. Cool air pressed against the skin of his face and immediately seemed to clear his head.

He needed to get to the garage.

Veering left, he sprinted for the four-bay garage. Inside was a black SUV. It didn't have armoring, like some of the other vehicles in his fleet. But once he reached it, it would get him off the property fast enough. Cooper wouldn't get to him—unless the guy could stand up to thousands of pounds of speeding metal, which Khan seriously doubted.

It was his best chance.

When he reached the garage, Khan slipped through a side door into the building. He left the lights off to keep from attracting Cooper's attention. Sliding behind the wheel, he pulled down the sun visor and the key dropped into his hand. He stabbed the key into the ignition.

BOLAN EXITED THE HOUSE and dropped into a crouch.

The sound of labored breathing registered with him. Turning his head toward the sound, he glimpsed Khan heading toward a low-slung building.

The Pakistani quickly melted into the shadows around the building. The soldier, still in a crouch, fell in behind the other man. When he heard a car door slam inside the building, he picked up the pace. By the time he reached the building, he heard an engine growl as it turned over.

The door jerked into motion and haltingly began to roll upward. As the door reached its halfway point, the soldier stepped forward.

Bolan heard the driver rev the engine, followed by the squealing of tires and a thud.

The garage door nearest Bolan exploded, the wood breaking apart and whizzing through the air. The SUV, its headlights blazing, rolled out of the garage in reverse. Bolan stepped from the shadows and onto the concrete driveway. The vehicle's lights fell on him and the 4x4 suddenly shuddered to a halt.

Bolan knew Khan had spotted him. For a stretched second the SUV stood there, plumes of exhaust rising up from behind the vehicle. He guessed the other man was weighing whether to make good on his escape or to slam the vehicle into Drive, gun the engine and mow down his adversary.

The big American squeezed the M-16's trigger.

Jagged muzzle-flashes erupted from the barrel of the weapon. The volley of rounds pounded into the SUV, sparked off the hood and shattered the headlights. Bullets punched through the windshield, their entry points marked by spiderwebs on the glass. The vehicle's engine revved. It lurched forward and cut a path toward the Executioner, who dived from the vehicle's path. He hit the ground, the impact causing him to grunt, and rolled over the wet grass.

The SUV's front end hammered into the concrete-block exterior of the garage. The impact crumpled the vehicle's front end, causing the hood to bow upward.

Already on his feet, Bolan slung the now-empty M-16 and drew the Desert Eagle. He thumbed back the hand cannon's hammer and marched toward the SUV. Even from a distance, he could see Khan slumped forward, his head resting on the steering wheel.

Orange-yellow flames curled up from within the SUV's engine compartment.

The Desert Eagle's muzzle aimed through the window on Khan's still form, the soldier yanked open the door. By now the plumes of smoke rolling from the engine compartment reached Bolan, stung his eyes enough that he had to force them through sheer will to stay open.

Reaching inside, Bolan released Khan's safety restraints. With one hand, he grabbed a handful of the man's jacket, the fabric just behind his neck, and yanked him from the driver's seat. With the Desert Eagle still in his grip, he scanned his surroundings for further threats, but found none.

Once he had dragged Khan a safe distance from the vehicle, he stretched him out on the ground. The soldier pulled a small flashlight from a pocket, clicked it on and ran it over Khan's blood-soaked form. At least three bullet holes had pierced the man's chest.

Khan's eyes fluttered open. Bolan noticed that the former ISI agent's gaze looked unfocused. His breath came in shallow pulls. After a second Bolan's presence registered with him, and he turned his head slightly to look at the big American.

"Cooper," Khan said.

The American said nothing.

"Not over," Khan told him.

"It is for you," Bolan said.

"Not you. Not close. Daniel Masters is a tough son of a bitch. You're finished."

Khan turned his head and stared skyward. A shudder passed through his body and he let go with a death rattle.

# CHAPTER TWENTY-THREE

Bolan had returned to the hotel. He'd taken a shower, finished two cups of coffee and was eating a dish of spicy rice with chicken when the laptop on a nearby table pinged. The soldier picked up his coffee mug, moved across the room and seated himself at the table.

He tapped the space bar and the screen lit up. David McCarter's image stared back at him. A small camera embedded in Bolan's laptop beamed his image back to Virginia.

"Well, aren't you a vision?" McCarter said, smirking. "The Bear mentioned that you had a busy night."

"You could say that," Bolan replied.

"He asked me to talk to a couple of my mates in the Special Air Service to get some details about Daniel Masters."

"Yeah. What'd they say?"

"That you'll have your hands full with him," the Phoenix Force leader replied.

"That's what Khan said."

"Look, I knew his papa. He was a stand-up guy, a colonel in the SAS himself. When the Iranians seized the embassy in London and the SAS took it back, he helped coordinate that. Taught us a lot of our counterterrorism chops back in the day. The guy was a damn genius."

"Until?"

McCarter gave a wry grin. "My stories never have a bloody happy ending, do they? Yeah, the old boy had a hell of a rise followed by an even grander fall. Damn pity."

Bolan nodded and McCarter continued.

"Daddy Masters—first name Lionel—had a bit of a drinking problem. Not the end of the world. He was a good bloke. But it caused him some serious financial setbacks. He got in the hole for several thousand dollars, well more than he'd ever pay back on a military salary. He was indebted to the Mob. Deeper than he cared to tell anyone."

"What'd he do? Sell secrets?"

"After a fashion, but not what you're thinking. He didn't have a lot of access to technology, such as it was in the 1980s. Wasn't really his bag. He didn't know a lot about satellites and he didn't have the names of M-I6's assets behind the iron curtain. He did have training and expertise, which he happily sold to the highest bidder, though."

"He sell to the Russians?"

McCarter shook his head. "No, not them. It was the cold war. I guess even a treasonous arse like him had some rules. He always saw a difference between selling out his country to Arab terrorists like the PLO instead of the big guys, the ones who actually had the ability to wipe merry olde England off the map."

"Difference without a distinction, if you ask me."

"Guess that's how the old man slept at night. I'm sure the psychologists have a nice term for the ability to compartmentalize behavior like that. Me? Like I said, I think he was a treasonous arse."

"What happened to him?"

"The British government kept the whole thing quiet. He was neutralized, as we like to say in the trade. A female agent from M-I6 lured him to her hotel room in the French Riviera, injected Lionel full of a paralysis drug that eventually shut down his heart and lungs. She left him for the maid service to clean up. We even had him buried with full military honors, if you can believe it."

"Where does junior fit into all of this?"

McCarter rolled his eyes. "He's a bloody treat, that one.

He came into the SAS several years ago, all full of piss and vinegar, says he's going to make up for all Daddy's shortcomings."

Bolan set down his coffee mug. "Seems like a security breech waiting to happen."

"You think? That's what a couple of old cynics like us would think. But the brass thought otherwise. Even after the old man got busted, he still had his fans. Yeah, I know it's crazy. But you have to remember he was a legend before all this came down. The fact that he pulled all this crap right under everyone's nose embarrassed a lot of powerful people who don't like to admit they fucked up. And some folks genuinely liked and respected the guy. Hell, I did before I found at that he was—"

"A treasonous arse. Got it."

"Hey, am I getting predictable? If you want witty repartee that costs extra. Anyway, some of the bigwigs decided it was a good idea to bring junior on board. Figured maybe they could make something of him, assuage their guilt for letting the old man sell out the country and for their having to kill him."

"Touching," Bolan said.

"And a damn good move," McCarter said, his voice dripping with sarcasm. "See, Junior, it turns out, was even worse than Daddy. He was a hell of a student, though. He took to the weapons training, the hand-to-hand combat stuff right away. Burned through all the classroom stuff. Guy's a sociopath, but he has an IQ that's off the bleeding charts. It was like he was born with his stuff, which in a sense, I guess he was."

"Still, it went wrong."

"Very. Problem with Danny was, well, he's crazy. Where Daddy had some rules to keep himself in line, Junior had no such limits. He had all his father's skills and aptitude with no moral compass. The old man, he was a straight arrow for years. It was only when his back was against the wall that he turned bad. And even then he had to put some kind of rules in place to make it palatable." McCarter paused and took a swig from a can of Coke.

"Not Junior. According to my sources, the bastard played bloody havoc during his brief time in the military."

"Got in trouble a lot?"

McCarter shook his head. "No, not like you're thinking. He just wasn't wired right. It was like he had all this crazy in his head and it'd build up and have to come out somehow. They tell me he was a damn killing machine. Never turned it on his own guys. No fights, no insubordination. But he had a habit of accidentally—" McCarter made air quotes around the word accidentally "—killing civilians in the heat of combat when he served in Basra, Iraq. His mates covered for him a couple of times. But, after a while, who needed the damn headache, right? Eventually the crazy started to bleed out in other areas, too. He drank like a fish and started getting into fistfights, first with civilians, then with other soldiers."

"So they tossed him."

"Like an empty soda can," McCarter said. "Of course, the same geniuses who wanted him in the military so bad also did their best to cover his trail, keep all this shit from getting out of hand. The top brass responsible for all this has been drummed out of the SAS, by the way, and are living out their golden years in the English countryside with their prune juice and their pensions. But young Danny finally did himself in, really screwed the pooch, as it were. Seems that he had a commanding officer he didn't much like, and the feeling was mutual. Their team was sent to Basra to wax an al-Qaeda cell that'd been churning out roadside bombs. It was right up his alley, lots of scorched earth and blood. And the Brits wanted it very visible to send those al-Qaeda bastards a message. Again it should have been perfect for the crazy bastard—a few grenades, a little spray-and-pray gunfire and then buy everyone some rounds at the officer's club."

McCarter scowled. "Yeah, it should've been easy," he said. "Long story short, he performed brilliantly at first. The al-Qaeda fighters had been making the bombs in an automotive garage. The SAS boys killed the bad guys and recovered all kinds of bad ordnance and electronics. But that's where it went wrong. When his commander came in to give the place a final inspection, it blew up. There was nothing left but a crater."

Bolan felt a cold sensation race down his spine. "Then how come he's still walking the streets?"

McCarter shrugged. He tapped his forefinger against his temple. "The lad's smart, smart enough that they never could totally pin the thing on him. The ordnance guys swore they'd deactivated any live explosives before the explosion, but their documentation, including some handheld video cameras, were destroyed in the blast. Masters had been missing before the blast happened, but no one saw him in the building. They had no proof."

"I assume he denied it."

"Of course. And I'll take it a step further. Not only did he deny it, but he showed no signs of lying. He was interrogated by some of the best, hooked up to polygraph machines, the whole bit. He sat there as cool as could be, and they never tripped him up on anything."

"It's possible he didn't do it," Bolan said.

"Sure, and it's possible I'm the damn tooth fairy. But it's not very possible. My sources chalk it up to him being a grade-A psychopath and not to his being innocent. He gave no signs of guilt because he did it and doesn't care that he did it."

Bolan nodded. He'd dealt with enough murderous savages during his War Everlasting to know it was possible for men to commit treason and to kill without guilt or remorse.

"Since they couldn't prove it," McCarter continued, "the military didn't press charges. They had an inquiry, of course. But without proof all they could do was suggest that he pack his gear and get the hell out of town. He did that."

"Which was when he decided to go solo."

McCarter nodded. "Yeah, he went solo, sort of. There are rumors that he did a little wet work for British Intelligence in Iraq and Afghanistan. But that's all they are—rumors, maybe even ones he started himself. He's obviously not above doing such a thing. My guess is, if you want to nail that stuff down, you'll have to knock on a few doors over at 10 Downing Street. That's a little above my pay grade, though, and I don't much like the notion of sidling up to bureaucrats, anyway. They rather make my skin crawl."

Bolan laughed. "Shocking, you being such a diplomatic guy."

McCarter, who'd just stuck a cigarette in his mouth, grinned around it. "I'm very diplomatic," he said, lighting the cigarette. "I tell people what to do, and they damn well better do it or suffer a boot to the arse."

The Englishman pocketed his lighter. "Look, when I said he doesn't have his father's morals and ethics, here's what I meant. His daddy was selective about who he sold his time and talents to. Junior's a whore, and a murderous one at that. He'll offer his expertise to anyone willing to sign the check. His client list reads like a damn rogues' gallery of the world's worst dictators and terrorists. He trained Sunni militants in Iraq, the same ones who were killing American and British soldiers. From what the intelligence types could surmise, he shared very dangerous information on the SAS and U.S. special operations forces—troop strength numbers, tactics, mission objectives, their whole battlefield playbook so to speak. He's consorted with the Russian mafia. I take it that, since you inquired about him, you plan to take him out of commission."

Bolan nodded.

"If you need any help—"

"I appreciate that, David. But hopefully he'll be dead and gone long before you could make the trip from Virginia to Mumbai."

"Understood. You take this guy out and you likely will be granted knighthood. There's more than a few blokes who'd like to put one between his eyes."

*Washington, D.C.*

MARTIN GREEN PULLED THE handkerchief from inside his sport jacket and, without unfolding it, patted it against his forehead, sopping up the perspiration that had collected there. He folded the cloth over once, so the damp part would face inward, and stuffed it back into his jacket pocket. A glance at his watch told him his guest now was ten minutes late, only heightening the volatile mix of irritation and anxiety that roiled inside him.

What in the hell? The crazy woman asked him to lunch, then stood him up? When she got here, he would—

Do what? His shoulders sagged just a bit as he reminded himself that he could do nothing to her at all. Raising a glass of ice water to his lips, he drained about a quarter of it and set the glass back on the table.

As he waited, Green looked around and studied the other diners. A few of them he recognized. They were among Washington's power players. Not necessarily cabinet secretaries and certainly not senators, but there were several high-ranking bureaucrats here, the people who actually made things happen in this godforsaken town. They were people like him, an analyst with the Central Intelligence Agency, who actually worked for a living. Not the ones with the expensive suits who mugged shamelessly for the cameras on the Sunday-morning news shows or on C-SPAN. Not the punks who spent two years as a press secretary only to leave and write tell-all memoirs that put bundles of money in their pocket.

Not that it did him or any of the other workhorses any good. The ones with dirt on their hands always got tossed under the bus first, always ended up with tire tracks on their backs.

He was considering whether to order himself a cognac when a voice interrupted his thoughts.

"May I sit?"

He stared up at the woman who'd spoken the words. She'd told him her name was Jennifer Birch, though the longer he knew her, the more he guessed it was an alias.

Her fiery red hair fell in loose waves well past her shoulders. Her green eyes beamed confidence, as did the wide smile she gave him. Her tailored green business suit accentuated the curves of her hips and the swell of her breasts.

As he looked at her, Green felt desire stir inside, followed by self-disgust. How could you still want this woman after all she's done? he wondered. What the hell's the matter with you?

"Sit," he said. He gestured at a seat on the other side of the table.

She ignored the gesture and dropped into a seat next to him. She crossed her legs and the hem of her skirt hiked several inches above the knee.

"Did you already order, Martin?" she asked, her voice bright.

"Of course," he replied. "You're not here to eat are you?"

"Well, it is lunch."

"Look, I don't know what kind of crap you're trying to pull here," Green stated.

"I just want to talk."

"Talk? About what?"

"Business," Birch replied.

"I didn't realize the business you did involved talking," he replied.

"Don't be like that."

"Like what? You fucked me, then you threatened to tell my wife, unless I gave you information. Now you want to have lunch like we're best buddies. You're crazy."

A server appeared and Green caught himself. The woman ordered an expensive white wine and Green winced inside, knowing he'd get stuck with this bill, too. He decided the hell with it and ordered himself a cognac. Maybe it would calm his frazzled nerves, he decided, allow him to think a little more clearly.

"You were saying?" Birch asked, her voice pleasant.

"I was saying, what the hell do you want from me? I did everything you asked."

"That makes two of us. And I have the pictures to prove it. All of it. And video footage, too," Birch stated.

It felt like his stomach clenched into the size of a marble.

"I gave you what I had on Lang. I told you everything you wanted to know. Do you understand? I committed treason," Green said. "I could hang for that."

Smiling, she patted him on the hand. "It's not that I don't appreciate that. I do."

"My point is, we're free and clear. Hear me? I did as you asked. Now a guy is dead and I have to live with that. Why the hell can't you leave me alone?"

She leaned toward him. "What's the fun in that, Martin? You know things, things you're willing to tell me. Because you don't want these passed around."

Opening her small handbag, she took a half dozen or so photos from within it and set them on the table. Each depicted them having sex at different hotels located throughout Alexandria. In the light of day, Green looked at the photographic proof of his indiscretions and felt sick.

The server returned with their drinks and he quickly placed an open hand over the photos to hide them. When the woman walked away, Green nodded at the pictures.

"Go ahead and take them," she said. "I have plenty."

He swept them into a single pile and shoved them into his pants' pocket.

"You can't keep pushing me like this," he said. "I do have a breaking point."

"Of course you do, but we're nowhere near it yet."

"I could just take these and show them to my wife," he said, patting the pocket where his photos were stored. "Once she knows, you have no power over me. It's game over and you can go to hell."

Birch shook her head.

"As if I was the only one," she said. "As if you haven't stuck your dick into anything with a pulse for years. Don't look at me like that. You think I just showed up in your life one day and took a chance that you'd stray from the arms of your loving wife? Please, we were watching you for more than a year before I ever even stepped into the same neighborhood as you. Sweetie, you know that's how the game is played."

Birch took a sip of wine, then set the glass back on the table. She kept the stem of the glass pinched between her thumb and forefinger. He noticed that her nails were lacquered with bright red polish.

"Does your wife know about all the others, Martin? Does she? Because I do, Martin. And so do the people I work for."

He opened his mouth to speak, and she silenced him with a gesture. "Don't bother trying to deny it, you lying, stupid bastard," she said. "I know you don't care about your wife, but how about those kids of yours? What are there names?

Oliver and Joanie? It would be a shame if something happened to them. A big shame."

Pulling away from him, she brushed a tendril of hair from her face, smiled and took a sip of wine.

"You wouldn't hurt my kids," he said without conviction.

"No, honey, I wouldn't. But the people I work for? Oh, they'd do it in a fucking heartbeat. Hurt them in ways you can't imagine and enjoy every last minute of it."

Green's chest felt tight, and he found it tough to catch his breath.

He looked down at the table. "What do you want?"

She told him.

"Okay," he said.

"You'll do this for me?" Birch asked.

He nodded his agreement without looking at her.

She stroked his forearm. "Thank you," she said. "You're such a help." Her tone was upbeat, light, as though he'd agreed to give her a lift home instead of committing treason.

Draining her wineglass, Birch stood and left. Her departure only vaguely registered with Green. He emptied his cognac, buried his face in his hands and tried not to sob.

# CHAPTER TWENTY-FOUR

*Washington, D.C.*

The black limousine hurtled along the highway, sunlight glinting off its bulletproof, tinted windows. Hal Brognola was seated in back. The big Fed chewed on an unlit stogie and gripped a white foam cup of flavored coffee.

The driver, Calvin Hayden, glanced over his shoulder. "You like the coffee, Chief?"

"Tastes like my deodorant smells," Brognola grumbled.

Hayden and the other two in the limousine—a man and a woman—laughed. A former Navy SEAL, Hayden had served in Iraq and Afghanistan, winning multiple commendations for his exploits in those conflicts. When he'd returned to the United States, he was handpicked to serve as one of the blacksuits who provided security at Stony Man Farm. When necessary, he pulled double duty as the big Fed's personal driver and part of his security team. Two other blacksuits, Darrell Woodward and Jennifer Taylor, were seated on the bench seat across from Brognola. Woodward previously had been a U.S. Army Ranger and later a sergeant on the New York Police Department's SWAT team before the Farm tapped him to work as one of its blacksuits. Taylor had spent a decade as a special agent for the Drug Enforcement Administration, chasing drug smugglers and cartels in Afghanistan and Mexico, before Brognola's Justice Department contacts had encouraged him to recruit her for security and analysis work at the Farm.

Brognola liked the group. Hell, the kids. He had neckties older than these people. But he hated being carted around like a damn rock star. Having to depend on someone else for security was an even bigger loser in his book. Sure, he'd had his butt pulled from the fire more than once by Bolan and the other Stony Man warriors. Still, he hated the idea of being followed around by an actual bodyguard or a security detail. It made him feel old, tired and helpless.

The reality was, though, he had found himself a target on more than one occasion. And he needed his hands free to work while someone else navigated the traffic leading into Washington, D.C. So he had babysitters and he was being driven around.

Suck it up.

"Are you comfortable, sir?" Taylor asked.

"Lovely," Brognola replied. "I've always wanted my own limo. It's like a dream come true."

All three members of his detail wore civilian clothes, but they kept Uzi submachine guns within easy reach and also carried 9 mm SIG-Sauer pistols.

"Another five minutes," the driver said.

"I'll strap on my parachute," the big Fed growled. He leafed through a handful of intelligence reports that had crossed his desk in the past twenty-four hours. None was related to Bolan's current mission, but instead included high-level information forwarded to him by the Director of National Intelligence or the President. He scanned one of the reports, a narrative about a rogue unit of the Mexican army that was negotiating a weapons-for-drugs trade with Hezbollah thugs in South America. For the moment the intelligence pros were keeping the situation under watch. They hoped to glean more information before they shut the operation down and Brognola, after reading the report twice, grudgingly agreed with their assessment.

He'd been called away by the White House. The stress

in the President's voice had been obvious during their brief phone conversation. He'd asked Brognola to meet with someone. When the big Fed had pressed for details, the Man had asked Brognola to trust him and had passed along an address.

Brognola felt the car turn and he looked up from his paperwork. A glance through the window offered a fleeting glimpse of a sign, Revere Lane Commercial Park. The name meant nothing to him. It seemed an odd destination for a meeting set up by the President.

"This is the place?" he asked.

"According to the directions," Hayden said. "Another right and two lefts, and we're there. You want me to check the directions again?"

Brognola shook his head. "Forget it."

Packing his papers into his briefcase, he stared at the pristine office buildings that lined the streets. After the second left, the driver stepped lightly on the brake and the limo slowed in front of a two-story, brown brick building. The vehicle nosed into a driveway and wound its way to the rear of the building. An American flag whipping at the top of a flagpole, a trio of parked cars and a sign that read Cassidy-Levine LLC provided the only signs of life at the building.

The driver stopped the vehicle outside a hunter-green garage door and let it idle. Brognola pulled his cell phone from inside his jacket and punched in an arranged number.

A woman, her voice bright and pleasant, answered. "Cassidy-Levine," she said.

"I want to see Mr. Cassidy," Brognola said.

"Your name?"

Brognola told her his name. As per his instructions, he provided not only his first and last name, but also his middle name.

"May I tell him what this is in regard to?" the woman asked.

"Overseas stocks," Brognola replied. "I want to invest in Asia."

A pause on the other end. "He'll see you right away," she said, and hung up.

Brognola clicked off his own phone. "Aren't I a lucky son of a bitch?" he said.

The garage door jerked into motion, retracting into the building. The driver tapped a drumbeat on the steering wheel with the balls of his thumbs while he waited for the door to open. Once the way was clear, he guided the limo into the garage and the door immediately started to close behind them.

"I guess we're staying," he said to no one in particular.

A PAIR OF MEN IN SUITS stood on either side of the limousine, each cradling an MP-5. By now Brognola and his team had disembarked from the limo. For his part, Brognola carried a .38-caliber Kimber autoloader beneath his suit jacket in a nylon shoulder holster. He sensed the tension from his people and knew he needed to defuse it.

A door to Brognola's left opened and a man came through it. A black business suit hung loosely on his small frame. His bald pate caught the gleam from the overhead fluorescent lights, reflecting it.

"Don Cassidy," the man announced. As he approached Brognola, he extended a hand. The big Fed ignored it.

"Tell your monkeys to put away their guns," Brognola said. "I'm not a prisoner here."

Something flickered in Cassidy's eyes. "They're just following security protocol. The security's quite necessary."

"Guns away," Brognola said. He jerked a thumb over his shoulder. "Or me and my people climb back into the car and we leave."

"We won't open the door."

"We'll ram it."

"It's reinforced steel," Cassidy said.

"Then we'll leave the car and go through the front door. You want to shoot a high-ranking Justice Department official in the back in front of my security team? It's your funeral." Brognola paused. "Professionally speaking, of course."

Cassidy's eyes narrowed. Brognola knew he'd put the guy in a bad position. He'd have to back down in front of his people. But the big Fed also knew he wasn't going to be herded around like a prisoner.

"The security's necessary," he repeated. "We have a lot of highly sensitive information here."

"I had top security clearance back when you were still in diapers. Guns away or we walk."

"The President wants you here."

Brognola looked left, then right. "I don't see the President. Do you?"

The younger man's narrow shoulders sagged.

"Shoulder your weapons," he called to the others.

Cassidy turned and headed for the door. Brognola fell in behind him.

"The President's going to hear about this," he said.

"Bet your ass he is," Brognola replied.

A LARGE, OVAL-SHAPED table stood in the center of the conference room. A single laptop rested on the tabletop, and a screen hung from one wall. Brognola dropped himself into a wing-backed chair and reached for a sweating pitcher of cold water.

Cassidy shot him an irritated look. "Have a seat. Make yourself at home."

"Thanks," Brognola said, nodding.

He turned to his team and shot them a wink. Taylor pressed her lips together hard, suppressing a grin. Hayden gave Brognola an almost imperceptible nod of approval.

The big Fed wasn't naturally given to unleashing the Alpha dog routine on someone else's territory, but he didn't like being pulled away from the Farm while he had operatives in the field, particularly with no explanation. And from the outset he read Cassidy as a bureaucratic tyrant bent on swinging his Johnson around. He had no patience for that and even less for being herded around by some gun-toting morons, as though he posed a threat. He wanted to find out what the guy knew and get back to the case at hand.

Brognola pulled a fresh cigar from the breast pocket of his suit coat and began to unwrap it.

Cassidy, who had seated himself, cleared his throat and held up a hand.

"This is a no-smoking facility," he said.

"Do you see a lighter?" Brognola asked while he peeled away the plastic wrapper. Wadding it, he set it on the table and popped the cigar in his mouth.

"Let me brief you so you can get the hell out of here."

Brognola nodded. "Finally, we agree on something."

"My unit tracks the shipment of radiological materials, with an eye toward interdicting illegal transfers of nuclear weapons and materials. We're a multiagency project, similar to the Counter Terrorism Center. I have people here from the CIA, the Department of Energy, the Department of Defense and several other agencies. Our particular operation is completely off the books. I was once with one of those agencies, but I'd prefer not to divulge which one."

Brognola tried not to roll his eyes.

"Anyway, within the last several hours, we received a report from one of our people in Moscow that there's been a transfer of Red Mercury."

"Red Mercury?"

"It's a radioactive substance created by the Russians during the cold war. It's tremendously concentrated, and it takes only a small amount to trigger a hellish nuclear explosion."

"I thought we'd been working with the Russians to secure loose nuclear materials?"

"This is different. Privately, we've pressed them to let us secure this particular substance for them. We even offered to leave it in their country."

"And?"

"They won't even acknowledge its existence. My guess is they think it gives them some kind of strategic advantage."

"Is it possible they're telling the truth?" Brognola asked.

Cassidy shook his head. "I wish they were. But we have good information on this. We're sure they have it."

"Okay," Brognola said. "Let's say for the sake of argument it exists."

"It does."

"Sure, fine. So what did they do with it?"

"They transferred it," Cassidy said.

"Heard that part the first time, Junior. I need specific details."

"We're a little sketchy on details."

"Jesus," Brognola stated.

"But we do know it was handed over to a man named Haqqani. A Russian man named Yuri Sokolov flew the Red Mercury to Karachi and handed it off to Haqqani. You ever heard of him?"

Brognola nodded slowly. "Sokolov, no. Haqqani, yes. Any idea where he took this stuff?"

"No, not yet."

"Did we get the Russian, Sokolov? Maybe he can tell us something," Brognola suggested.

"Good luck talking to him. He's dead."

"How?"

"The plane he took to Karachi apparently crashed on its way back home," Cassidy explained.

"Home being where? Moscow?"

Cassidy nodded. "Yeah. And before you ask, the plane went down over Russia, crashed into some farmland there. We made some inquiries, but we don't have access to it."

"Are the Russians cooperating at all?" Brognola asked.

"Not really. Sure, they're making all the right noises, assuring they'll share information as they get it. But they really aren't telling us anything right now. And why should they? A plane carrying a bunch of Russians crashed in Russia. They have no incentive to say anything."

"Do they know why we're curious?"

"No, and that's part of the problem," Cassidy stated. "We can't tell them why we want to know about the plane without also telling them what we know about the substance. We told them we thought the plane was smuggling weapons to the Taliban. They said they were sympathetic, but they wouldn't give us access to the wreckage. At least not until they have a chance to look it over first."

"Which will take how long?" Brognola queried.

"They said a week."

"We don't have a week."

"Why is that?"

Brognola scowled. The big Fed was willing to bet Cassidy already knew the score, but he wanted to hear Brognola say it. "We're hearing that Haqqani's on the move. If they've transferred this stuff to Haqqani, we have a very big problem."

"Yes, we do."

"Look, Junior," Brognola said. "I'm all for interagency cooperation. But you guys can just stand down on this one. We have one of our top operatives on it. The situation is well in hand."

Cassidy held up his hands in a placating gesture. "Look," he said, "maybe the heavy security here has confused you. But you have the wrong idea about us. We just want to decommission the stuff once your guys get hold of it. We don't kick in doors. If your guys can secure it, we'll take it off your hands. Otherwise, how will your guys get it out of the country? Would you rather hand it over to the Indians?"

Brognola let out a long sigh. "I think we both know the answer to that," he said.

"Good, then we have a deal," Cassidy said.

"Yeah, I guess we do. Get your team up in the air."

"We already have one en route. I assumed you'd say yes."

Brognola did his best to hide his irritation. "Well, aren't you something?"

The big Fed decided to send someone to Mumbai to brief Bolan on Red Mercury—as soon as Kurtzman could come up with some intel.

# CHAPTER TWENTY-FIVE

*Mumbai, India*

Someone knocked on the door of the apartment. Bolan, who'd just hit the Brew button the coffeemaker, looked at the screen of his laptop PC. A surveillance camera hidden in one of the smoke detectors in the corridor beamed back an image of Leo Turrin standing outside the apartment.

Bolan opened the door and Turrin grinned at him.

"Happy to see me? Let me in."

One of Bolan's oldest allies in his War Everlasting, Turrin was a small but sturdily built man who was decked out in a two-thousand-dollar gray suit. In his left hand, he carried a leather briefcase. He extended his right hand to Bolan, and they gave one another a warm handshake.

Once inside the apartment, Turrin set down his briefcase, cocked his fists on his hips and gave the Executioner's latest digs a hard look. The soldier was registered as Lou Antoniotti, a New York hedge fund manager. The apartment—decked out as it was with an indoor pool, five bedrooms, granite countertops and marble floors—was opulent enough to fit with Bolan's cover.

From what Brognola had told Bolan, the CIA occasionally used the apartment as a cover address for one of its agents who'd been playing a high roller.

Turrin swept his gaze over the place and let out a long, low whistle.

"Sweet digs," he said. "You must be doing pretty well for yourself these days."

"Lou Antoniotti's doing well for himself," the soldier said.

"What happened to the Matt Cooper alias?"

"Things were getting a little too hot for that," Bolan said. "I thought it might be a little easier to knock on doors here if I had a different identity. If Ahmed Haqqani has a network operating here, and I'm assuming he does, checking under the Matt Cooper name could raise some alarm bells."

"Won't they recognize your face?"

"Maybe," Bolan said, shrugging. "I have some tinted contacts if I need them. And before I left Karachi I had my hair cut shorter and can part it differently, if necessary. And I have a wardrobe of high-dollar suits."

"You do look dapper. Are my tax dollars paying for those clothes?"

Bolan laughed. "First, I didn't realize that semiretired wise guys were so scrupulous about their taxes. Second, I bought these with Nawaz Khan's money."

"He would have wanted that."

"It's recycling," Bolan said.

"On another topic, Sarge, you're the world's crappiest host. You fly me halfway across the world, make me take a taxi from the damn airport. Now you don't even offer me coffee."

"My bad," Bolan said. "C'mon, I'll fix you up."

Bolan poured Turrin a cup of coffee. The little Fed seated himself in a plush armchair and, his index finger looped through the ring on the coffee cup, balanced the drink on his right thigh.

Bolan exited the kitchen and made his way toward a couch.

"What have you got for me?" the soldier asked.

"Hal told me we've got Islamists armed with enough nuclear firepower to level a city," Turrin replied. "Something called Red Mercury. I'm sure you've read Hal's files."

"And?"

"He said you might need some help. Just back-office intelligence collection. No dangerous stuff now that I'm retired, kind of."

"And you went for it."

"Hell no, I didn't go for it," Turrin said. "I told Hal to get bent. Just because I don't work full-time doesn't mean I'm ready for the damn home."

"Deftly handled," Bolan said.

The soldier lowered himself onto the couch, perching on the edge of the seat cushion, his body tensed. His eyes burned from lack of sleep. He'd had the chance to sleep on the flight over, but instead he had decided to pore over new intelligence reports that Brognola had forwarded to him. He'd hoped to find something he'd missed or that the army of intelligence analysts already poring over the stuff hadn't yet found. He'd failed. That told him either he needed to dig up new information or wait until it presented itself, the latter of which wasn't Bolan's style.

"Do we know where Ahmed Haqqani's hanging his hat?" Turrin asked.

Bolan shook his head. "Nothing of the sort. We have tons of information on his Pakistani operations, but little or nothing here. We don't know who he meets with, who supports him, who moves his money."

"Does Indian intelligence have anything?"

"Barb Price is checking on that. We're guessing so, but it's a tough play. We need to get the information without initiating a massive manhunt that sends the guy packing back to his homeland."

"Would that be so bad? I mean, if he just left?"

"Not if he leaves the Red Mercury here and drops a dime to let us know its location," Turrin said.

"So it would be a bad thing if he left."

"That's the working theory."

Turrin sipped at his coffee. "Not to worry," he said. "I thought about this on the plane ride over, which, by the way, was freaking brutal. Anyway, I have a guy we can talk to."

*Moscow, Russia*

KONSTANTIN ZHUKOV POUNDED the flat edge of his clenched fist against the desktop, rattling the liquor glass that stood on it.

Rising from his chair, he paced the floor of his office for several minutes and ruminated over his conversation with Sasha Lebed. Zhukov knew he couldn't let the other man go through with this crazy idea. Zhukov liked to make money as much as the next man. This was sheer craziness, though. You couldn't put the destructive powers of a god into the hands of extremists, not without unleashing hell on earth. He imagined the destruction wrought by detonating Red Mercury in the middle of a crowded city such as Mumbai, and he shuddered.

As he walked back to his desk, a plan began to form in his mind. He knew a way to stop the whole thing with a couple of phone calls.

*Mumbai, India*

HAQQANI HATED INDIA, every last inch of it. Standing on the deck of a fishing trawler, he stared at the city's skyline as the boat nosed toward the docks.

The Pakistani particularly hated Mumbai with its crowded slums, its gleaming financial district and its debauchery. He hated that his brothers, Muslims like him, had to live in such cramped quarters and in such close proximity to the Hindus. He could only imagine the humiliation of living in a city, a country, controlled by unbelievers. It had to be an all-consuming, oppressive presence that clung to them as they tried to carry on as good Muslims.

The captain guided the boat toward the docks. Two men from the crew busied themselves unpacking ropes and making preparations to dock the craft. The diesel engine sputtered and belched out plumes of exhaust. Staring into the water, Haqqani noticed a sheen of oil floating on the surface.

An old man with an easygoing charm, the captain had been only too happy to take Haqqani's money in exchange for quiet passage into the country. Haqqani had told the old man that he was coming to India to look for work so he could send money home to his family in Bangladesh. The story, as thin as it was, had been more than enough for the old man once Haqqani had handed over enough rupees to cover the fare, plus a little extra for the captain. Smiling, the old man had taken the money and promised to get them to India safely.

And he had done just that.

Twinges of fear and anticipation warred with each other inside Haqqani. He stared at the assortment of warehouses, boat-motor repair shops and gas stations that lined the dock. The enormity of what he planned to do hit him, causing his heart to hammer in his chest.

He was crawling into the belly of the beast, inserting himself among those he most hated and who, if they knew the true purpose of his visit, likely would rip him limb from limb. At the same time, if he succeeded, it would be that very closeness to the enemy, his ability to blend in among them and draw blood, that would incite all the more fear in this nation of cowards.

And he would succeed, he assured himself. God willing.

Footfalls from behind prompted him to turn. Ishaq Mehta,

an old friend and a veteran of the Pakistani army, was approaching.

"We have arrived," Mehta said. "It won't be long now. God be praised."

Haqqani nodded in agreement. "The materials are safe?" he asked.

"Yes."

Haqqani turned back toward the dock. "We will make history today. You understand that, don't you, brother? God willing, we will strike a blow for Muslims everywhere, show the world which faithful truly enjoy God's blessings. You understand this, yes?"

"Of course," Mehta replied, nodding.

"Good," Haqqani said. "What lies before us, the task at hand, will not be easy. It will not be popular, even among other believers. Some of our brothers may criticize us for killing women and children, those they call innocents."

"There are no innocents among the unfaithful," Mehta replied. "You know that. I know that. We cannot delude ourselves into thinking otherwise."

"You are right. This must be done and it must be done for all to see. It will be bloody, but it must happen this way."

"It must," Mehta agreed.

## CHAPTER TWENTY-SIX

Ben Richards's office was stuffed away in the top floor of a sprawling warehouse that fronted the Arabian Sea. The walls were freshly painted, and Bolan could detect the smell of new carpet in the air, mingling with freshly brewed coffee. A large map of Asia was pinned to one wall, with red pins jabbed in several points in Afghanistan, Pakistan and India. Stacks of papers and folders were arrayed around the room.

Richards's secretary, an Indian woman who Bolan guessed was in her twenties, escorted them into his office. Richards rose from behind his desk and offered the soldier his right hand. It was then that Bolan noticed the man's left shirtsleeve hung empty from his shoulder.

Richards noticed Bolan looking and nodded at the sleeve. "Lost it in Dubai," he said. "Last I heard, they still haven't found it. Makes for some real hell when I get a mosquito bite on the back."

"Sorry," Bolan said.

Richards nodded. "No worries," he said. "It jars people first time they meet me." He turned and shook Turrin's hand. "Well, if you're here with Leo, it must be a big deal."

"Huge," Turrin said, grinning. "That's why they called in the big guns."

"I feel safer already," Richards said.

He turned to Bolan. "Leo and I go back a ways. He tell you that?"

"He was a little sparse on the details," Bolan said. "But he said you guys have some history."

"You could say that. Buy me a beer sometime and I'll tell you the story. Deal?"

The Executioner nodded. "If you're a friend of Leo's, we'll make it two beers."

Richards gestured at a pair of seats, both covered with more files and loose paper. "Have a seat," he said. "Sorry about the mess. I was trying to pull up everything I knew about Haqqani."

Turrin hefted one of the stacks from one of the chairs. "All these files have information on Haqqani?"

"Oh, hell no," Richards said. "Just one. The trick was figuring out which one. Organization's not exactly my specialty."

"Thanks for the heads up," Turrin replied as he sat.

By now, Bolan was also sitting. Richards dropped into a chair and nodded at a coffeemaker that stood on a nearby table. "Coffee's shit here, but it's free. Help yourself."

Bolan sized Richards up, guessing the man was in his mid-fifties. Except for a few wisps of hair, he was bald on top, with salt-and-pepper hair ringing the sides and back of his skull. He had a wide face, with deep wrinkles at the corners of his eyes. His skin was tanned deep brown and had the yellowish tinge of a man who smoked a lot of cigarettes. The toes of his black wingtip shoes were scuffed, and his necktie hung loose from an open shirt collar. A holstered pistol was clipped to his left hip, the gun's butt facing forward in a cross-draw position. Despite Richards's easygoing manner, the weariness in his eyes told Bolan the guy had seen plenty of bad things.

"Leo tells me you're here to hunt down Haqqani."

Bolan nodded.

"Just the two of you? You realize how dangerous he is?"

"Yeah," the soldier replied.

Richards stared at Bolan. After a few seconds the right side of his mouth turned up in a lopsided grin.

"You don't care, right? I figured as much just by looking at you. You spend a couple of decades on the street, you get a pretty good sense of people. I can tell you can handle yourself. Thought I should say something, just the same."

Bolan nodded his understanding. "What can you tell us? I mean, we know his biography. What we really need is some good intelligence on how to find the guy."

The smile disappeared from Richards's face, and his forehead creased as he apparently considered Bolan's request.

"He's got all kinds of links here in the city," Richards said. "He's a different animal than Khan was. Khan sold everything—guns, women, alcohol. He was a businessman, a professional criminal. He was a Muslim, but he wasn't a jihadist. Just a jerk out to make a buck. Haqqani has limits. He'll sell guns and he'll smuggle cigarettes. But for him it's not about making money. Not directly, anyway. He does it to further a cause."

"Kashmir?" Turrin asked.

Richards gestured dismissively. "He'll make noise about Kashmir, and I think he means it. He's a devout son of a bitch. He'd love to see a caliphate sprout up. He'd love to see India walk away from Kashmir. I think he even believes those are his primary motives."

"But you think there's something else driving him?" the Executioner asked.

Richards nodded. "Yeah, he wants revenge. Pure and simple. All the pious shit is just that, shit. Indian soldiers killed his father. He wants them to pay for that."

"Who's them?" Turrin asked.

"All of them, Leo. Every last person in India, if he had his way. He doesn't care which ones he kills or whether it makes sense. He's too far gone for that. He just wants blood, and he's not too particular as to whose hide he extracts it from."

"As long as they're Indian," Turrin said.

"Yeah, truth be told, though he'd be just as happy to kill some Americans if he had the chance. We're sort of a close second on his hate list. Like I said, the guy's a barely contained bundle of rage and he's found himself a like-minded bunch of psychos to hang with."

"What else can you tell us?" Bolan asked.

"Look, my thing is cigarette smuggling. This guy has his own fleet of trucks and he moves tons of cigarettes across Asia every year. The counterfeiters make millions of dollars. He makes a pretty tidy sum himself. He smuggles for the Taliban, when it suits his needs. Hell, he used to run guns, too. He ran them for Nawaz Khan before someone popped that poor bastard in the head."

Richards gave Bolan a pointed look. "I'm guessing that someone was you."

Bolan grinned. "No comment."

Richards rolled his eyes. "Now I know you're a damn Fed. Anyway, Haqqani smuggles, so I track him." The former federal agent leaned forward. "But to be honest, that's a secondary concern to me. I don't give a flying fuck whether some cigarette company loses a few bucks because someone buys a counterfeit or a name-brand cancer stick. What I do care about is how these smugglers use their money. If Haqqani funnels his money to jihadists, or if he uses it to kill people himself—either way, I'm not okay with that."

He stopped and sipped some coffee. A drop trailed down his chin, and he wiped it away with the back of his hand.

"I've gathered enough evidence to convict that piece of shit a dozen times," he said. "I've got dossiers on his top five guys here in this country. Every last one of them is a stone-cold killer."

"Let me guess," Bolan said, "the locals don't care."

"Not a lick. Maybe they're getting bribes. Maybe it's just a low priority for them. Maybe they hand all the information over to Indian intelligence, which then stores it away in a warehouse just like this one. All I know is I collect and offer up tons of data. All that work falls down a rat hole, never to be seen again. About the only reaction I get is from Haqqani's guys, some death threats. The usual crap. At least I get some attention from somebody, right? Nothing I can't handle. But the point is, I can't put them away. I don't have the authority. I send the information to corporate, I slip some to Washington. I'm sure it gets looked at, but nothing comes of it. The long and short of it is, I'd give you the information anyway because I used to be with the FBI. But even if I hadn't, I'd still give it to you because my guess is you'll do something about it."

"I'm not going to bring him to trial," Bolan said.

"No shit? Wow, I really misread you," Richards said, the sarcasm evident in his voice. "Look, I was born at night, but not last night. I know in my gut why you're here. I don't want to kill him outright myself, not unless he draws on me first. But I also don't want him around anymore. Get my drift?"

"I don't think you'll need to worry about that," Turrin said.

A smile ghosted Richards's lips. "I hope you understand. I've killed guys before, but it was always in self-defense. I can't just gun a man down. It doesn't sit right with me."

Bolan nodded. "Understood. I have rules, too. They're just different from yours."

"Here's a rule," Turrin interjected. "Don't drink coffee with chunks in it. What the hell is this stuff, Richards? You still mad about New York? You trying to poison me?"

"Nice, Leo," Richards said. "Okay, apparently the children are getting restless. Let's get down to cases."

Leaning back in his chair, his arm snaked out and he

grabbed an envelope from the top of his desk. He tossed it to Bolan. "That's the condensed version of Haqqani's life. It has names and address for a couple of his lieutenants. The guy has a pretty extensive network of sympathizers in the city. Most are Muslims living in the slums, but he also has a few money people in town, too. Guys who run an Islamic charity. Another who runs an import-export business. One of the most important is a banker. He makes Haqqani's money appear and disappear at will."

"Are these true believers?" Bolan asked. "Or can they be turned against Haqqani?"

Richards shook his head. "They're all devout, except for the banker. I think he just believes in the five-percent cut he takes off the top of Haqqani's cash flow."

"Sounds like a good place to start," the Executioner said.

DANIEL MASTERS COULD raise a small army with just a few phone calls. This day, he'd done precisely that.

Mumbai had in recent years become a magnet for mercenaries, former soldiers and intelligence agents, all looking to make a buck. That had made it a fertile recruiting ground for men like him, who ran all kinds of operations on behalf of both nations and private groups that wanted some level of plausible deniability.

Rarely did Masters deal with the West's major powers, of course. Neither his homeland of Britain nor the United States wanted anything to do with him, and vice versa. But he found second- and third-tier nations still had plenty of money to spend when it came to freelance espionage, especially Middle Eastern nations that were flush with oil money, like Saudi Arabia. Asia's major powers were also willing to throw some work his way. The downside, of course, was that these nations would be happy to turn on him if it meant saving face with the United States, Britain or some other entity of significant influence. He always walked a fine line between betraying someone and being betrayed by someone. He thrived on the uncertainty.

The day's agenda included treachery.

A group of six hard-looking men stood in the cellar of Masters's home in the suburbs of Mumbai. All wore street clothes, mostly jeans and short-sleeved casual shirts. None was older than forty, and all were highly trained and experienced mercenaries who'd been drummed out of the military for a litany of offenses ranging from theft to rape to murder.

Masters had always found these men to be perfect soldiers. They had plenty of deadly skills. They had no job prospects and, if they got killed in action, or if Masters decided after a mission to put one between their eyes, either out of necessity or to fatten his paycheck, he could do it and no one would miss them.

This particular group was weighted heavily toward former Serbian soldiers. Their weapons and equipment were situated throughout the basement floor in six piles. All the weapons—a mix of AK-74s, Mossberg shotguns and Glock .40-caliber pistols—had been acquired illegally and any identifying marks had been removed.

Masters always kept the weapons once the action concluded and personally made sure they were destroyed. He didn't want a gun that he provided ending up as a murder weapon in a bar shooting or some other situation where it would get traced back to one of his operations.

The men had been eyeing the weapons like ravenous dogs staring at freshly killed meat. Experience told Masters that some of the men thirsted to kill while others just wanted a chance to ply their skills. But their motivations mattered little to him as long as they did their jobs and kept their mouths shut.

He nodded toward the gear.

"Claim what's yours, gents," he said. "We've got lots of work to do today."

BOLAN AND TURRIN WALKED through Mumbai's financial district. It was lunchtime in this city of more than eighteen million. Bolan caught sight of numerous men pulling carts overstuffed with brightly colored containers. The air was thick with the smell of food. He guessed the men were dhaba-wallas, people who delivered hot lunches made in the suburbs to office workers in the city. Double-decker buses and black-and-yellow taxis choked the streets, filling the air with exhaust fumes and noise.

"Richards is a hell of a guy," Turrin said.

He had donned sunglasses and stared straight ahead as he spoke. "He'd never tell you this, but it was Haqqani's crew that took his arm. Back when Richards was with the FBI, he started nosing around in Dubai. He was looking into the nexus between tobacco smuggling and terrorist financing."

"Did you just say 'nexus'?" Bolan asked, grinning.

The little Fed shrugged. "Hey, I'm semiretired now. I have nothing better to do than read books and play shuffleboard. Anyway, Richards came over here, acting like he always does—easygoing on the outside, intense as hell on the inside. He starts rattling Haqqani's cage. Rolls up a couple of Haqqani's sidemen and squeezes them for information. Then he leads a raid that snags a few tons of counterfeit cigarettes."

"Pissed Haqqani off, I'd imagine," Bolan said.

"Pissed him right off," Turrin replied.

"What happened?"

"Haqqani puts a contract on Richards." Turrin stopped at a street vendor who was selling canned soda. He pointed to a can of cola pictured on the sign and held up two fingers. The vendor nodded, reached into a cooler and pulled out two cans, icy water dripping from both. Turrin dropped a wad of rupees into the guy's outstretched hand and took the drinks in return. Handing one to Bolan, he eased back into the crowd and started walking.

"I way overpaid that guy," Turrin said.

"You're a high roller," Bolan replied.

"Bet your ass. Anyway, what the hell was I talking about?"

"Richards."

"Right. Retirement's turning my brain to mush. So some moron plants a bomb in Richards's apartment. Fortunately it blew prematurely and a wall protected Richards from the blast enough to keep him alive. But it did take his arm. It also cost him his family."

Bolan's eyes narrowed. "They were killed in the blast?"

Turrin shook his head. "No, wife and kids were back in the States visiting relatives. That was the good news. But once that happened, the Bureau offered him a desk job and his wife wanted him to take it. He said hell no. He wasn't going to walk away from a fight and let Haqqani win. But he also wanted to take him down legally. That's never going to happen. I think Richards realizes that. Handing Haqqani over to you to deal with is probably the closest thing to surrender you'll ever get out of the guy. He knows you'll take Haqqani out for good."

"What was all the talk about how you two met?" Bolan asked.

Turrin shrugged. "Cue the flashback. I was running broads—"

"Broads?"

Turrin's cheeks reddened. "Sorry, ladies of the night. And some drugs, too. Pot, mostly. Anyway, I was making my bones as an undercover guy in the Mob. It was after you and I had met in the early days. There I was, overseeing a big shipment of marijuana that had come into the East Coast. I was supposed to be in New York when the grass came into the port, make sure it got to where it could be cut, bagged and shipped. Well, I arrive in the Big Apple, ready to work my undercover mojo. I stop at my hotel, grab a shower and open the door to leave. Guess who's standing there?"

"Richards?"

"Yeah, big Ben and a couple of his Bureau buddies. Apparently an informant, one who didn't like me, had dropped a dime on me and told Benzilla that I was in town to pull a hit on a federal judge. Since he wasn't working organized crime at the time, he didn't know me from George Steinbrenner. Next thing I know, he's dragging me into the federal building, putting me under the lightbulb, all that crap. Four hours later—yeah, I said four hours later—the U.S. Attorney shows up at the office, all red-faced and perturbed. He's screaming at Richards. Richards gave as good as he got, but eventually realized he was in the wrong, that he'd busted an undercover guy, and he released me."

"So you lost the chance to gather information on the drugs."

"Yeah, big freaking disaster, right? Except not. Apparently, another Family got wind that my people were hauling dope into New York. Even though we weren't going to sell a leaf of it in the city, they still wanted their cut. And they weren't going to ask nicely, either. They descended on my people, killed every last one of them and took the pot. It was brutal. Place looked like a damn slaughterhouse when it was all said and done."

"You could've been one of them."

"Could've been," Turrin said. "You never know for certain. But I think it's a better than average chance my ticket would have been punched that night if I hadn't gotten arrested. The guy who dropped the bum tip on me, by the way? Deader than a doornail."

"Killed by the rival gang?"

"That idiot? Hell, no. He died in Jersey a couple of years ago. Massive coronary. Everyone saw it coming. Fat slob was big as a house. I swear he poured bacon grease over his morning cereal. Anyway, unintentional or not, Ben saved my life. You don't forget that. We occasionally traded information on stuff, worked together on a few things. Like I said, he's good people. He's no coward. He just goes by the book. If we can give him a little peace by blasting Haqqani, so much the better, the way I see it."

# CHAPTER TWENTY-SEVEN

Haqqani had just finished praying when he heard a knock at his door.

"Come in," he called.

The door opened and one of his men, an Afghan named Hamid, entered the room.

"It's as you suspected. They're coming for you."

Haqqani nodded serenely. "How soon?"

"An hour at the most. Probably much sooner than that," Hamid stated.

"How many are there?"

"At least half a dozen."

Haqqani nodded again.

"Thank you, my brother. Alert the others and let's prepare."

Hamid turned and left.

Within minutes Haqqani's lieutenant entered the room carrying a small submachine gun. Like Haqqani, he'd trimmed his beard close to the skin. He wore jeans, a short-sleeved casual shirt and tennis shoes. While there were many Muslims in the slums of Mumbai, Haqqani and his people were doing everything they could to not stand out.

During the past eighteen months, Haqqani had been moving people into position, allowing them to establish cover identities and lives in India. The last thing he wanted was to raise suspicions among Indian intelligence agents with a sudden influx of foreign Muslims. Most of his team hadn't met in person with one another since they'd come to the country, and they'd only occasionally communicated with one another during that time.

"I've been told," Haqqani said.

"What should we do?"

Haqqani shrugged. "We wait."


MASTERS KNEW HIRING mercenaries entailed risks. The ones who'd been kicked out of someone else's military were especially problematic. If they'd betrayed their own country, then they'd be only too happy to stick a knife in your back, too—if the check carried the right number of zeroes.

Masters realized that, of course, and tried to build safeguards into his plans.

This time, he'd recruited Mohammed Ayundev, a Chechen, for his team. Ayundev was up to his neck in the Chechen resistance and was well connected among Islamist groups. His main weakness was that he burned through money like flames through a bone-dry forest. He'd been kicked out of the Russian army for stealing AK-47s and selling them to the same people he was supposed to be fighting. It was a wonder his superior officer hadn't executed him on the spot.

The way Masters saw it, if anyone was going to feed information to Haqqani and his people, it would be Ayundev. He had the motives and the connections. Amazingly, though, the Chechen had proved surprisingly solid. Masters had put the man under near-constant surveillance within an hour of hiring him and had found no problems. He had put other members of the team under tight watch, too, though to a lesser extent than Ayundev.

As best Masters could tell, he had no moles in his organization.


TOM FERGUSON HAD NO CAPACITY for guilt, a characteristic that had served him well during his twenty-seven years.

He didn't mind doing the wet work for Masters. The gigs paid well. That they involved killing didn't bother him at all. Often the jobs led to some side work, too. In this case, the side work was betrayal.

It had been three days since Masters had hired him for the job and briefed him on the details. He'd sat on the information for a day or so, figuring that Masters was professional enough and paranoid enough that the Englishman would watch his people. As best as Ferguson could tell, Masters hadn't put him under much scrutiny, probably because the two had worked together enough times that Masters wasn't worried about where his allegiances lay.

Whatever, Ferguson had been only too happy to take the information from his briefing and sell it to Dadbhai Ayankar. He never knew what would ring the guy's chimes, but in this case, Ayankar had been particularly interested in Ferguson's information. He'd also paid him enough to alert him when the mission was under way.

Though he had no capacity for guilt, Ferguson occasionally felt regret. This was one of those times.

He wished he'd hit the Indian up for more money.

THE OLD TEXTILE PLANT stood silent. Steel bars or sheets of plywood covered the windows of the first floor. Sunlight and time had bleached the building's exterior from a deep brown to a dull tan. Smokestacks, the tips blackened with soot, jutted skyward.

Masters was seated in the back of a black Jeep Cherokee parked alongside an exterior fence that ringed the perimeter of the factory property. He stared at the dilapidated factory, sizing it up and ruminating over his plan one last time.

A vast ocean of pavement, cracked and faded, surrounded the place. There was no way to approach it at ground level, especially in daylight, without being seen by Haqqani's security team. That's why he'd opted for a more direct approach.

Sunlight glinted off metal from one hundred yards or so northeast, catching Masters's attention. He caught sight of a black car rolling across the parking lot toward them.

Masters shifted in his seat. It was probably Haqqani's security team wanting to ask some questions. Masters wouldn't stay long enough to provide answers.

"C'mon, lads," Masters said. "Let's go."

BY ANY TRADITIONAL MEASURE, Dadbhai Ayankar was an unlikely financier. A child of the slums, he'd spent his early years stealing food to survive, ending up in trouble with the police several times. He'd spent time in jail, where he learned to fight. It was there that another inmate had noticed his aptitude for numbers and had hooked him up with a local crime boss who had needed someone to track his illgotten proceeds.

Ayankar had taken to it immediately, realizing he enjoyed counting money better than getting tossed repeatedly into the cesspools that passed for jails in India, suffering beatings and other innumerable humiliations at the hands of inmates and guards. Like the inmate who'd first recruited him, those in the criminal syndicate noticed his facility with numbers immediately. They assigned him first with simple accounting tasks, but eventually gave him increasingly difficult financial work to accomplish. Finally, they taught him the black arts of money laundering, false corporations and offshore accounts.

After that, he realized that while he liked counting other peoples' money, he liked counting his own more. That was when he began skimming money off the top, eventually amassing a small fortune that he then grew into a large fortune by investing in stocks, properties and his personal passion, Bollywood movies. When his former employer discovered Ayankar's treachery, the old man had threatened to kill him. By that time, though, Ayankar had funneled millions of dollars into various Jihad groups. He considered their ideology complete bullshit. They had as much chance of establishing an Islamic caliphate as he did financing a Hollywood blockbuster. Still, he appreciated that their loyalty, driven by self-interest, made them willing to protect him from his spurned bosses.

The beauty, Ayankar knew, was that everyone underestimated him. In the circles in which he ran, they viewed him as nothing more than a money counter. While there was some truth to that, he had spent much of his youth on the streets and in prison, two places that hardened him. He never took his safety or his freedom for granted. Instead he protected his office and his home with a small army of mercenaries willing to take down anyone foolish enough to try to harm him.

YURI SOKOLOV COULDN'T wait to return to Moscow, take a hot shower and pick up his pay. The executive jet carrying him home had gone wheels up from Afghanistan forty-five minutes or so ago and was winging its way back to Russia. Leaning back in his seat, he stared out the window. They were cruising high enough that all he could see was the billowy white layer of clouds beneath the craft. A yawn rose up his throat and he clamped his hand over his mouth to stifle it. Noticing the sluggishness that had settled into his muscles, he shifted in his chair, hoping the movement might awaken him.

Glancing across the cabin, he noticed one of the scientists, the young woman, was also yawning.

She smiled at him. "It must be contagious," she said.

"Or perhaps it's the company," he said.

"No, no," she replied, flashing another smile. She turned her attention back to the book in her lap. Sokolov's gaze lingered on her for several seconds and he thought about the possibilities. He guessed she was twenty years younger. She looked slender and athletic, which was how he liked his women, even though he'd not exercised in more than a decade.

Another yawn. His eyelids felt heavier.

Turning his head to look at the young woman, he hoped to restart the conversation, perhaps with another joke. However, he saw that her eyes had closed and her head leaned forward. She hadn't bothered to remove her eyeglasses before falling asleep, which struck him as odd.

He turned his head and stared straight ahead. This time, the effort required to move his head seemed tremendous. His eyes stung and he struggled to keep the lids open.

Suddenly the plane jerked and the front of the cabin tilted forward sharply. What the hell? What was the pilot thinking? He wanted to have a look in the cockpit, make sure everything was okay. He considered grabbing the ends of the armrests and using them to push himself up, but his fingers didn't respond. His breathing became more shallow, his chest tighter. He struggled to keep his eyes open, a battle he ultimately lost. What the hell was happening? he wondered before losing consciousness.

*Moscow*

"WHEN DID IT GO DOWN?" Sasha Lebed asked.

"We lost contact less than an hour ago and got a ground confirmation five minutes ago," his intelligence chief, Lev Beria, told him. "I came here as soon as we confirmed the crash."

Lebed nodded. He was riding the elevator from his offices to his private garage. He wore black slacks and matching leather wingtip shoes and belt, a white cotton dress shirt and red necktie. Raising a forearm, he glanced at the gold

Rolex watch that encircled his wrist. He was late for an executive committee meeting, but they'd wait.

"What about the cargo?" he asked, referring to the Red Mercury. Lebed noticed that small beads of sweat had formed on Beria's upper lip and he avoided eye contact with Lebed.

"My sources tell me it's gone, too," the intelligence said. "You can probably expect the number of emergency response personnel to grow, though, if they get any hint of radioactive materials."

"Clearly."

"The attention won't help us at all, particularly if they realize the plane had been carrying radioactive materials."

"If the storage casing stayed intact, there'd be no reason for widespread leaks or contamination. In that case, no one would suspect a thing. If there are leaks, we need to contain it ourselves."

He turned to Beria and jabbed a finger into the smaller man's chest. "Your job is to get control of the crash site. We need to claim the wreckage as soon as possible."

Lebed saw Beria's cheeks flush red with anger, but he nodded in agreement. "Yes, sir."

"What do we know about the crash itself?"

Beria shook his head.

"Nothing much," he said. "Our maintenance teams checked the plane with a fine-tooth before it left Moscow. All the scheduled maintenance has been performed. It could be a while before we can nail down an actual cause of the crash."

"Haqqani did this," Lebed said, a trace of admiration in his voice. "That little fucker."

"Haqqani? Why?"

"He's covering his tracks," Lebed replied, shrugging. "He doesn't know about me. He doesn't know about the

Seven. He only knows Masters and the people who delivered the material to him."

"But why? If he succeeded in the attack, he'd claim responsibility."

"Maybe. But he doesn't want anyone to trip things up before he strikes. Alive, the people who sold him the materials are a liability. They might get arrested and talk about selling him the materials. Dead, they pose no threat. He only needed to buy himself a day or two. In his mind, he did that. He has a clear road to move forward with all this. It's not sophisticated by any stretch of the imagination. But it will be effective in the short run. Unfortunately it creates a problem for us, though."

"We need to cover our tracks."

"Exactly. Start making calls. What's wrong with you, anyway? You're sweating like a pig."

The other man wiped at his upper lip with his forefinger and opened his mouth, though no words came out. Fear flickered in his eyes as he seemed to grasp for an explanation.

The elevator slid to a stop. A bell pinged softly and the doors parted. Lebed's private garage was located in the tower's basement. Lebed whipped his head toward the garage and saw a figure dressed in jeans and a black turtleneck. A black knit watch cap was pulled down to just above the guy's eyebrows, and a kerchief obscured all of his face except for his eyes. The figure raised a gun and was drawing down on Lebed when the Russian reacted. His arm snaked out and he grabbed hold of the fabric of the sleeve of Beria's coat. With a hard yank, he brought the smaller man between himself and the shooter just as the gun, which was fitted with a sound suppressor, coughed out two rounds. Both slugs pounded into Beria's chest and his body jerked under the impact.

With his free hand, Lebed grabbed hold of another piece

of Beria's jacket and shoved him hard into the shooter. The move surprised the gunman, who tried to step aside. Beria's body crashed into the man, caused him to stumble and fall onto his back.

Lebed was already crossing the distance between himself and the assassin. He raised his foot and stomped down on the man's shooting hand, pinning the guy's wrist to the floor. The man let out a shriek of pain, and Lebed assumed he'd probably ground the man's wrist bones into dust.

Reaching beneath his jacket, Lebed drew the Stechkin pistol from its shoulder rigging. The gun roared once and a single round pounded into the man's shoulder, eliciting another scream from him. His fingers went limp and the gun fell from his grip. Taking his time, Lebed bent slightly at the waist, aimed the pistol at the man's heart and squeezed the trigger, unleashing another blast from the weapon. The man no longer posed a threat.

Zhukov, Lebed thought. That son of a bitch.

# CHAPTER TWENTY-EIGHT

*Mumbai, India*

The elevator carrying Bolan and Turrin opened into a wide-open expanse of office space. A single desk stood in the center of the room. To one side, two couches and several chairs were clustered together in a sitting area. Bolan rolled off the elevator first with Turrin a step behind him.

Both men swept their gazes over the place, sizing it up.

It hadn't been quite what Bolan had expected. Movie posters lined the walls, not only from films made in India, but also of several American films.

"Looks like our friend's a film buff," Turrin said.

Bolan nodded. The dossier supplied by Richards had included information that Ayankar had funded several films. Bolan guessed the attraction to films stemmed from a need for a money-laundering vehicle rather than some deep thirst for artistic expression.

He marched up to the desk. Resting his palms on the desktop, the soldier leaned over it and smiled at the woman seated there. The receptionist, a young woman, returned the smile.

"I want to see Dadbhai Ayankar," Bolan said.

"Do you have an appointment?" she asked in heavily accented English.

"No."

"You need to make an appointment."

"No, sweetie, I don't," Bolan said.

Her eyes narrowed. "Excuse me?"

"My name's Lou Antoniotti," Bolan said. He paused a couple of seconds, as though he expected the name to trigger instant recognition in the woman. "I said, Lou Antoniotti. I'm here from New York. To see your boss. And I will see him."

He paused and stared at the woman expectantly.

"Sorry, you still need—"

Bolan hit the desktop with the bottom edge of his fist. The woman jumped and her eyes widened.

"Pick up the damn phone and announce my arrival. It's a big deal. I'm a big deal."

The woman swallowed hard and reached for the telephone. Bolan guessed the woman was just trying to do her job, acting as Ayankar's gatekeeper. He didn't like to bully bystanders, though occasionally he found it necessary when he was using role camouflage as he was right now. Lou Antoniotti, a New York mobster, would have no problem leaning on her, and so neither could Bolan. He occasionally had to make those kinds of compromises in his War Everlasting.

The woman was still looking at him. Her manicured fingers had wrapped around the receiver, but she hadn't yet picked it up.

"The phone," Bolan said. "Now!"

She raised the receiver, brought it to her ear and pressed a button on the keypad.

"There's someone here to see you," she said. A pause. "No, sir, he doesn't have an appointment. Yes, I'm aware of how busy you are. I apologize, but he insists."

She paused again. "His name is—"

She looked up at Bolan.

"Lou Antoniotti," the soldier said again.

She repeated the name. "He says he is from New York. Yes, of course I can show him in."

Rising from her desk, the woman smoothed the front of

her skirt with her hands. She then gestured at the door behind her.

"Through here," she said. She walked up to the door and opened it.

"Mr. Antoniotti is here, sir," she said.

Ayankar was standing behind his desk, his arms crossed over his chest. Bolan noticed how coolly the guy appraised them and figured if he was going get any information, it wouldn't be easy.

Uncrossing his arms, Ayankar waved at several chairs ringing a small conference table.

"Sit," he said.

"We'll stand," Bolan replied.

Ayankar looked over Bolan's shoulder at the woman.

"That will be all," he said.

She nodded. "I'll make the call you requested."

"Fine, then take lunch."

"But, sir—"

"Priya, take lunch. And do it out of the office."

"Of course." The woman exited the room and closed the door.

Ayankar crossed his arms back over his chest. "I'm busy. If you could state your business and go on, I'd appreciate it."

"My business? My business is cleaning up your mess, Ayankar," Bolan said.

A smile played over the other man's lips. He uncrossed his arms and cocked his fists on his hips. "Really? Please tell me more."

Bolan marched up to the desk and walked around the edge of it, putting himself just a couple of feet from Ayankar.

"Tell you? Oh, I'll tell you, you douche bag." He raised his right hand and began poking the air between them with his index finger. "You don't know who I am, but I sure as fuck know who you are. You're a dead man walking, you little prick."

Whether conscious of it or not, Ayankar backed away from Bolan. The Indian's gaze stayed cool, though. The Executioner couldn't tell whether the guy was afraid or just wary of the aggressive man who'd just crossed his path. Bolan guessed that the years Ayankar served in prison had hardened him to idle bluster. The soldier figured he'd probably have to turn it up a notch or two before all was said and done.

"I still don't understand what you want."

"My people—"

"What people?" Ayankar asked.

Bolan ignored the question. "My people have an outfit that runs cigarettes throughout Asia. Two days ago, we lost a dozen trucks."

"Unfortunate," Ayankar said.

"Isn't it, though? It gets more unfortunate after that. Twenty-four hours after that, our local contacts find seven of the trucks outside Kabul. They were stripped of anything useful. All the cigarettes were gone. You starting to get the picture? Fucking gone. We lost a small fortune."

Ayankar heaved a sigh. "As I said, it's very unfortunate. But I don't see how this concerns me."

Bolan flashed the guy a wicked smile. "Hey, maybe you're right. Maybe this doesn't concern you. My mistake."

Bolan shot Turrin a glance. "Hey, looks like we made a mistake. Fuck it, let's quit badgering this poor bastard and go home."

Turrin grinned and shrugged slightly.

"You're the boss," Turrin said.

Bolan nodded. "I am the boss."

He stepped forward. His fist snaked out and he struck Ayankar with a jab to the mouth. The money guy stumbled back a couple of steps before he could get his footing. He raised his fists at Bolan and his eyes narrowed in anger. The punch had split his lip and a trickle of blood rolled down from the wound.

Bolan's hands dropped to his sides, his fists uncurling. He sneered at Ayankar. "You ready to listen to me now, you little shit? Or you want to keep playing games? Either way pays the same for me. And I'm going to have one hell of a good time breaking you."

Ayankar kept his fists up. "What do you want? I don't know anything about your trucks."

"That's bullshit on steroids," Bolan said. "But I don't care what you know about the trucks. I know you don't know about the trucks, idiot."

"What then?"

"Tell me what you know about Ahmed Haqqani."

A smile tugged at the corners of Ayankar's mouth. "You must be kidding."

"Do I look like it?"

Ayankar's smile widened. "You look like a man in over his head. Perhaps you and your friend should go home. This is—how do you Americans say it?—way above your pay grade."

Bolan's hands clenched back into fists. He stepped forward, buried his right fist into Ayankar's gut. The guy belched air from his lungs and folded at the waist, his hands coming up to protect his midsection.

"Hey!" Turrin said.

Bolan whipped his head in Turrin's direction. He saw his old friend pointing at a small video screen fixed on Ayankar's desktop. Displayed on the screen was the exterior office they'd passed through several minutes earlier. Only now a half dozen or so gunmen had stormed into the room outside Ayankar's office. A pair of them had positioned themselves on either side of the door, each holding one side of a small battering ram.

The Executioner reached under his jacket and drew his Beretta 93-R. Turrin produced a Glock 17. The pistol, chambered in 9 mm, carried nineteen rounds and had a muzzle velocity of more than 1,180 feet per second.

The battering ram thudded against the door, which shook under the impact.

A second strike caused the wood around the doorknob and locking mechanism to splinter. The door swung inward, hit the wall and bounced back.

One of Ayankar's men followed the door in, a pistol clutched in his hand.

Bolan raised his own weapon. From his peripheral vision he saw Turrin had already drawn a bead on the guy. The Glock cracked once and dispatched a 9 mm Parabellum round that drilled through the guy's temple, tunneled through his head and exploded from the other side in a spray of crimson and gore. Even as the guy's limp form folded to the floor, Bolan caught a second of Ayankar's hardmen coming through the door.

Unlike his colleague, though, this guy decided to come in shooting. A submachine gun cradled in his hands sputtered out three quick bursts. The bullets chewed into Ayankar's desk, splintered the heavy oak and pounded into leather-bound books lined up on a nearby bookshelf.

Bolan met the guy's attack with one of his own. He double-tapped the Beretta's trigger and it responded by coughing out twin bursts of death. Bullets stitched a line across the shooter's chest. The force punched him off his feet and knocked him on his ass. His body now operating on a death reflex, his finger tightened on the trigger and the SMG let loose with a more sustained burst of gunfire that angled upward, chewing into the ceiling.

Turrin fired off three more rounds through the doorway, driving back any more attackers before they could make it into Ayankar's office. Through the door, Bolan saw at least a couple of the shooters take cover behind a large couch.

Heading through the door in a crouch, Bolan hunted for more targets. One of the shooters popped up from behind the couch. The Uzi he held was chugging through the contents of its clip. Bolan threw himself to the ground. The murderous barrage sliced through the air just above him.

The Beretta moving in target acquisition, Bolan caught the shooter in his sights and fired. The rounds caught the guy in the shoulder, spinning him a quarter turn. Overloaded with adrenaline and the urge to survive, the guy ignored the wound and drew down on the Executioner. Before he could squeeze the trigger, though, Bolan fired off another volley from the Beretta, this time catching the guy in the bridge of his nose with the 9 mm rounds.

Gunfire crackled to Bolan's right, and he whipped his head toward the sound.

A squat man with the jowls of a bulldog crouched behind the receptionist's desk. His arm was stretched across the desktop, which he used to steady his aim. Bolan rolled along the floor, moving an instant before the guy squeezed off a couple of shots that drilled into the floor where the soldier had lain a moment earlier.

By the time he stopped moving, Bolan had drawn the Desert Eagle from inside his jacket. Raising the big-bore handgun, he fired two shots that caught Jowls in the center of his wide face, which disintegrated under the impact.

Bolan holstered the Beretta and rose in a crouch, still holding the Desert Eagle.

TURRIN FOLLOWED BOLAN as the big American left Ayankar's office.

He'd burned through the Glock's magazine while providing cover fire for the Executioner. He reloaded the pistol and allowed himself the indulgence of wishing he had brought the Benelli combat shotgun with him. Next time, he'd do just that. If there was a next time.

He dismissed the thought and kept moving.

The elevator doors opened and belched forth two more of Ayankar's shooters. As soon as they hit the room, they immediately separated. One of the guys was paunchy, with an upper lip shrouded by a thick black mustache. He swept the room's interior with the barrel of his pump shotgun. The second man, a big-headed shooter with the lanky form of a praying mantis, was running his eyes and the barrel of his submachine gun over his side of the room.

The Mantis was the first to spot Turrin, and he spun in that direction, the barrel of his weapon tracking in on the former deep-cover Fed.

Jagged muzzle-flashes lashed out from Turrin's pistol as he pumped out a pair of shots at the skinny guy. The bullets hammered into the gunner's ribs before bursting out the other side of his body. The guy's limbs went rubbery and he collapsed to the ground.

Turrin twisted at the waist toward the mustachioed thug.

The guy was already lining up the shotgun's barrel to squeeze off a shot at Turrin.

The little Fed acted first, firing the Glock and coring a single round through the guy's forehead. A death spasm caused the guy's finger to tighten on the trigger. The shotgun roared once and the blast ripped into the floor.

Turrin looked away from the dead guy. He glanced at Bolan and saw the soldier had just put down another of Ayankar's shooters. Then Turrin's mind jumped back to the man they'd originally come for, Ayankar.

When he reached the office, instinct told him to go through the door low, which he did. A shotgun roared and the blast tore a ragged half circle out of the door frame. Turrin heard the unmistakable metallic clack of someone working the slide on a pump-action shotgun.

He wheeled toward the noise in time to see Ayankar, who had walked around to the front of the desk. He was raising the shotgun, preparing to fire it again.

While not in Bolan's league, Turrin had survived more firefights than he cared to count and he had the combat reflexes to prove it.

He snap-aimed the Glock and fired it. One of the shots tore into Ayankar's hip.

The moneyman yelped in surprise and pain. The Mossberg discharged in his hand and a peal of thunder reverberated around the room. The shot had torn into the floor.

Turrin had the guy locked in the Glock's sights. "Drop it."

Ayankar, his teeth clenched, nodded and the gun fell from his hands.

Turrin noticed a bloodstain was spreading across the front of the guy's pants, from the site of the wound.

The bean counter grabbed the edge of the desk, using it to support himself. The Glock leveled ahead of him menacingly, Turrin moved in on the guy. With the toe of one of his black leather wingtips, he nudged the shotgun out of the other man's reach, bent and picked it up.

"On the floor," Turrin ordered.

The guy glared at Turrin, but, using the desk for support, lowered himself to the floor. A couple of times he squeezed his eyes shut and grunted. Turrin assumed the movement hurt like hell. Ayankar seated himself on the floor, but then lowered his torso to the ground and rolled onto his uninjured side.

Bolan rolled into Ayankar's office. He found Turrin standing over the injured man. Turrin apparently sensed someone approaching and his head whipped around. Relief was visible in his features when he saw Bolan.

The Executioner nodded at the little Fed, then brushed past him and stared down at Ayankar. The guy, his breathing coming in fast pulls, had pressed a palm over the wound. Blood seeped into view from between his fingers. Sweat was beading on his forehead. Reaching into his jacket, Bolan pulled out a folded handkerchief.

"I'm bleeding," Ayankar said through clenched teeth.

Bolan nodded.

Ayankar reached out a hand. "Give me your handkerchief. Now!"

"I'm curious," Bolan said, his voice wintry. "What's it worth to you not to bleed to death?"

"Maybe I won't. I don't have to. Give it to me!"

Smiling, Bolan shook his head slowly. "I wish it was that easy."

"What? Why?"

"I want to know something. You know it. I have something you want. See where all this is going?" Bolan asked.

"Bastard," the guy said.

"He's got you there," Turrin interjected.

Bolan threw Turrin a nod, then he dropped the handkerchief on the floor, a few inches in front of Ayankar's face. His hand lashing out, Ayankar gathered the cloth up and pressed it against his wound. The pressure against his injured leg elicited a gasp. It wasn't long before Bolan saw a crimson stain blossom on the cloth.

Bolan stepped back, crossed his arms over his chest and studied the man. Uncrossing his arms, he walked over to where he'd dropped his briefcase. He picked up the case, carried it over to Ayankar and set it on the floor next to the guy, but left it closed.

"Here's the thing," Bolan said finally. "That wound's bad, but not the worst I've seen. You get it cleaned up, maybe some stitches and antibiotics, staunch the bleeding, you'll be okay."

The soldier knelt next to his briefcase, spun it on the floor so the latches faced him and opened it. He rummaged around inside the case for a few seconds. As he found several first-aid items, he placed them on the floor between himself and the injured man.

Snapping on a pair of latex gloves, Bolan ordered Ayankar to move his hand from the wound. The guy complied, and the soldier pulled away the handkerchief, which was heavy with blood.

With the scissors, Bolan cut the fabric from around the wound, gently peeling it back from the bullet hole. He applied the compress over the wound and taped it down. Studying his handiwork, he nodded his silent approval. It was a quick job, but should do the trick, he thought.

Bolan packed the first-aid materials in the briefcase, which he closed and pushed away.

Rising to his feet, he peeled off the latex gloves and tossed them aside.

"Good news all around," the soldier said. "You'll have to have the bullet removed. But my friend here—" he jerked a nod at Turrin "—missed your femoral artery. Heard of that?"

Bolan didn't wait for a reply. "If the femoral artery gets torn, you're screwed. You can bleed to death in minutes. It's hard to rebound from that kind of injury."

The soldier shrugged as he dug into his right hip pants' pocket. "Where the hell did I put…? Yeah, anyway, if something happens to the femoral artery, you're fucked. Oh, wait, here it is."

He pulled his hand from his pocket, uncurled his fingers and showed Ayankar the switchblade he held. Pushing at a small stud on the hilt with his thumb, Bolan summoned the blade. He then closed his hands around the hilt, the blade jutting from his clenched hand.

"So, lucky break for you," Bolan said. "Crap like that happens all the time with bullets. You try to shoot someone in the gut, you hit them in the hip. You try to shoot them in the head, but you take off an ear. Shooting can be an inexact science, especially for him."

Bolan saw Turrin shoot him a scowl.

"Fortunately, with this blade, I can open up your femoral artery with one cut. Maybe slice open your jugular. Cause a big mess. But not much trouble. Pull up a couple of chairs, watch you bleed to death, if the mood strikes. Good times, right?"

Ayankar's eyes widened and he chewed at his lower lip. From Bolan's point of view, it looked like the sweating had intensified, accompanied by an occasional shudder.

Bolan peeled off his jacket and draped it over the guy, a move to keep him warm and stave off any shock.

"Don't pass out on me now," the soldier said in a grave-yard voice.

He knelt next to Ayankar and moved his face in close. Despite his injuries, Ayankar jerked back.

"The point is," Bolan said, "I want to know where Haqqani is. I asked you once. You played it tough and got carnage. Answer me this time and you live. Protect him and I'll cut you open and watch you bleed."

"There's an old textile plant…" Ayankar began.

# CHAPTER TWENTY-NINE

Bolan and Turrin returned to the penthouse. They changed their clothes, cleaned their weapons and packed more ammunition. The Executioner had stacked gun cases containing an M-16/M-203 combo and his H&K MP-5 on the granite counter, one on top of the other. Turrin lined up three speedloaders for his Colt .38 Detective Special on the counter. He slipped the pistol into a hip holster. The Glock rode in a shoulder rig.

"Nice job back there," Turrin said.

"What's that?" Bolan asked.

"Getting our friend to talk."

Bolan shrugged. "Comes with the territory."

"Of course, the crack about my shooting was way off."

"As is your shooting," Bolan said, grinning.

"I meant to shoot him in the hip."

"Sure you did."

"Seriously, a guy comes at you with a shotgun, you shoot him in the hip. Everyone knows that."

"Must have missed that lecture in basic training."

"Where do we go from here?"

"Hal called the CIA's liaison at the embassy," Bolan said. "She's lining up some wheels for us and promised she'd put a leash on the locals. Once the shooting starts, the last thing we need is to find ourselves up to our necks in cops."

"Agreed. Unless they're really hot lady cops."

The Executioner finished reassembling the Beretta 93-R.

Sliding it into the shoulder holster, he gathered up his gun-cleaning supplies and stored them in a plastic box.

"Do the locals know that friend Haqqani's skulking around Mumbai with nuclear explosives?"

"She might have left that out."

"Happens," Turrin stated.

"She told them we cornered a Hezbollah leader here," Bolan replied.

"He's not Hezbollah. He used to be with Lashkar-e-Taiba."

"My bad."

The little Fed smirked. "Well played."

Bolan shrugged as he slipped his cleaning kit in a canvas satchel. "India has a blood debt to settle with Lashkar-e-Taiba. The way I saw it, if we told them someone from LET—or any Kashmiri separatist—was on Indian soil, the arms-length treatment would be over."

"Understandably so," Turrin said.

"Yeah," Bolan replied, nodding. "They'd want to be kicking in doors with us. They'd want Haqqani for themselves. All of which I get, but none of which I can allow."

THE HELICOPTER SWOOPED down from the steel-gray skies, leveled off and skimmed a couple dozen feet above the factory rooftops of Mumbai.

Tom Ferguson checked the action on his Beretta 92-F, then slid the weapon into a thigh holster. He looked around the chopper's interior at the other grim-faced occupants.

One or two were completing last-minute preparations, taping down a loose item, checking the action on a weapon as Ferguson had himself done just moments earlier.

If the upcoming mission stirred any hint of fear in the men, Ferguson saw no sign of it in their faces or their movements. Whatever else could be said about the castoffs he'd surrounded himself with, they were professionals.

Ferguson shifted in his seat and devoted the next several seconds to listening to the whipping of the rotor blades.

Then the pilot's voice crackled in his headset. "We have a visual on the landing site," the pilot said. "Wheels down in less than two minutes."

HAQQANI STEPPED ONTO the rooftop. A hot wind blew hard across the elevated open space, tousling his hair. He pulled down the LAW rocket strapped across his back, telescoped it open and brought it to his shoulder. It took a couple of moments, but he lined up the chopper in his sights.

He wondered for a fleeting moment whether the pilot could see him standing there, weapon pointed at the craft, wondered if the pilot realized his death was at hand.

He could only hope.

Haqqani triggered the launcher, which spit out its payload. The rocket knifed through the air and burned a course toward the approaching helicopter. It punched through the aircraft's nose with a hard crack. Haqqani watched as the aircraft halted its advance, shuddered in midair before an explosion sounded from within the craft's metal confines.

The helicopter's Plexiglas panes burst out, accompanied by long tongues of flame. The rotors now dead, the craft plummeted to the ground, simultaneously spinning as it dropped. Even after the helicopter disappeared from sight, Haqqani heard it strike the ground, followed by another explosion that sent a column of smoke-tinged flame shooting skyward.

Haqqani allowed himself a smile.

"It's on," he muttered.

THE ABANDONED FACTORY looked every bit as decrepit as Bolan had expected, a sagging pile of rust, peeling paint and cracked brick walls. The rusting hulks of long-abandoned cars littered the grounds. It was the perfect place for vermin like Haqqani to hide himself, Bolan thought. He and Turrin stood outside the perimeter fence, looking in on the property.

"You think Ayankar called Haqqani to let him know we were coming?" Turrin asked.

Bolan lowered his binoculars and shook his head. "No. Even if he didn't bleed to death, he passed out. He'd lost a lot of blood."

"Maybe someone else dropped a dime on us."

"It's possible. You want to wait in the car? I've got this," Bolan stated.

"Funny guy."

"Just asking. I thought maybe retirement had left you a little too frail for this."

"It's semiretirement, Mr. Comedian."

"Sure."

Turrin glanced at his watch. "We should probably do this."

"Probably." Bolan looked at his old friend. The guy's gaze was pointed up, and he looked like he was scanning the top of the fence. Concertina wire ran along the edge of the fence and, in places, glinted in the sunlight.

"Are we going over this thing?" Turrin asked.

Bolan opened his mouth to answer. The sound of helicopter blades reached him and he checked his reply. Scanning the sky, he spotted a small black shape heading in the direction of the building. Raising the binoculars, he gave the approaching aircraft a closer look. The exterior was painted a dull black and, other than its tail numbers, had no other exterior markings that Bolan could discern.

When he heard the whooshing noise, he recognized it immediately as coming from a rocket launcher. Because that noise sounded much closer, he dropped the binoculars and stared up at the sky. He spotted the rocket burning its way toward the chopper, saw it strike the craft, the hulking machine transforming into a plummeting fireball that exploded moments later.

"Jesus," Turrin said.

"Come on," Bolan said.

He sprinted for the van that the local CIA station chief had loaned him. As in Karachi, the vehicle had been fitted with diplomatic plates, this time from Germany. While the station chief had promised to keep local police and intelligence agents at bay, Bolan had considered the diplomatic plates an additional safeguard against arrest were they to be stopped by the authorities for any reason. When a person was in a foreign country, it was never a good thing to be stopped with a vanload of automatic weapons.

Bolan climbed into the driver's seat and belted himself in. By the time Turrin had seated himself inside the van, the soldier was turning the key in the ignition. He put the vehicle in gear, twisted the wheel in the direction of the fence and gunned the engine.

The van's front end rammed into the gate, knocking it from its hinges, and roared into the parking lot.

"Subtle," Turrin said.

"Compared to crashing a helicopter, it's subtle," Bolan replied.

Before they could reach the building, the soldier saw half a dozen hardmen spill out of one of the side doors and down the concrete steps. Gunfire was spitting from the weapons of at least two of Haqqani's troops as they moved to defend their boss.

Bolan guessed the thugs only represented the first wave of gunners that Haqqani would send their way. Slamming his foot on the brake pedal, the Executioner jerked the wheel. Tires squealed against the pavement and the smell of burned rubber filtered into the vehicle while it ground through the hard turn. When the van came to a rest, the driver's side was facing the factory and Haqqani's small army of gunners.

Grabbing the M-16, Bolan poked the weapon's muzzle through the driver's window and squeezed off a couple of fast bursts. The shots flew wide of his adversaries, but close enough to drive them to ground.

In the meantime Turrin hefted the Benelli M-4 Super 90 shotgun that rested on the floor next to his seat. Opening his door, he jumped from the van and disappeared from view. Bolan fired off a couple of more quick bursts to buy his old friend some breathing room.

One of Haqqani's men got brave. He surged from cover and rushed at the van. While he moved, jagged tongues of flame lashed out from the barrel of his AK-47. A storm of 7.62 mm slugs pounded into the van's armored skin, generating sparks.

Bolan returned fire, maneuvering the M-16 in a tight sweep as it churned out a maelstrom of death. The 5.56 mm rounds drilled into the advancing hardman, tearing open his neck and torso. He withered under the sustained autofire, body crumpling to the ground.

The soldier spotted two more shooters popping up from behind an abandoned car, their weapons hurling leaden death. The Executioner triggered the M-203 grenade launcher, which drilled a high-explosive round at the gunmen. The bomb struck the ground a couple of yards from Bolan's adversaries, the explosion shredding the man closer to the blast, ripping flesh from his head and torso. The guy's body suddenly turned rubbery and he fell behind one of the derelict cars. The blast also caught the second man, though not as directly as the first. The skin on the man's arms and head had been peeled away by the explosion. He wheeled in Bolan's direction, his face a bloody mask.

By now the soldier had recharged the M-16 with a fresh clip. Aiming the weapon at the disfigured gunner, Bolan fired a fast burst from the assault rifle. The rounds pounded into the guy's chest and put him out of his agony.

The soldier peeled off his seat belt and he went EVA. Climbing past the console and over the passenger's seat, Bolan exited the vehicle and hit the pavement in a crouch.

He dropped behind the van's front tire as autofire continued to slap against the vehicle like hailstones. Bolan broke open the M-203, inserted a fragmentation round into the breech and snapped it closed. Popping up from behind the van, he balanced the assault rifle's barrel on the van's angled hood and tapped out another burst at a ragged line of shooters that was moving in his direction.

The bullets fell just short of his advancing adversaries and instead chewed into the asphalt in front of them. Two of the three held their ground and began unloading their AK assault rifles in Bolan's direction; the third man dropped back a couple of steps, but also triggered his weapon. The merciless onslaught of bullets pounded into Bolan's cover.

The Executioner's M-16 continued to belt out rounds and spit shell casings.

At the same time the bay doors on two more loading docks jerked into motion and began to rise. A half dozen men, their guns already blazing, marched from the building, ready to deal death on Bolan and Turrin.

TURRIN BROKE FROM COVER. The shotgun in his hands booming, he surged across the parking lot in the direction of the factory.

The rusting hulks of abandoned cars, tires missing, windows shattered, were arrayed on the grounds. The weeds that had broken through the asphalt stood up well past Turrin's knees, but they weren't concentrated enough to provide true concealment.

A storm of autofire blazed inches over Turrin's head as he ran across the open lot. When he reached a pile of cars, he dived behind it for protection. His back resting against one of the rusting wrecks, he took a moment to push fresh shells into the Mossberg. Grenade, he thought. Why didn't I bring a grenade? Or six?

He moved along the length of the car until he reached its front end. The hood was closed, but he hoped it still had an engine block under it to provide additional shielding against the hail of bullets hammering down on his position. The hard rain of bullets seemed to be striking the top of the vehicle instead of hitting closer to the front where he was crouched. Turrin took this to mean the shooters couldn't actually see him, which could mean they were laying down cover fire.

Still in a crouch, he poked his head around the vehicle's battered front end. He spotted a pair of Haqqani's shooters walking a few yards apart from each other, but closing in on his position. He put them at just a few yards away.

The man closer to Turrin caught sight of the American and swung his weapon in the intruder's direction. The little Fed's shotgun thundered out twin shots that caught the man in the gut, nearly cutting him in two and thrusting his broken body backward. Seeing his comrade go down, the second gunner whipped toward Turrin and squeezed off a burst from the AK-47.

Turrin jerked back behind the car a heartbeat before the bullets struck the spot where he'd just been. The near-constant blasts of close-range gunfire were robbing him of his hearing. Now that the shooter had an exact location on him, Turrin didn't want to risk a glance around the front bumper or over the hood of the car.

Then it dawned on him: going low was still a possibility.

The vehicle was propped up on stacks of concrete blocks, putting it well over a foot off the ground. Not enough space for a big guy like Mack Bolan, maybe. But for Turrin, it'd be enough. He crawled underneath the vehicle. Tufts of weeds and grass, along with the rough surface of the concrete, could be felt through the light fabric of his shirt.

Casting a look to his left, the Stony Man fighter could see the guy's feet as he moved closer. Raising the shotgun's forestock with his left hand, he drew down on the man's ankles and pulled the trigger. The shotgun roared. The blast disintegrated the fabric of the guy's pant legs and shredded the flesh of his ankles. His body crashed to the earth and he let loose with frenzied screams.

Turrin fired another shot from the Mossberg, this time catching the guy in the head and dispatching him to hell.

HAQQANI ALLOWED HIMSELF A moment to stand at the edge of the roof and stare down at the twisted mass of steel laying on the ground, engulfed in flames. He still had the rocket launcher balanced on his right shoulder and gripped it with his hand, steadying it. As an afterthought, he threw the launcher from the building and watched it plummet into the burning mass that had once been a helicopter. He thought of the men he'd just killed and indulged himself with a smile.

Turning on a heel, he headed back toward the stairwell. Obviously, with all the noise they had caused, he could expect the police to descend on the property at any time. He didn't want to be here when it happened, and he didn't want the Red Mercury here for them to find.

He wanted nothing more than to get away from the area so he could move forward with his plans to trigger the nuclear material.

Descending the steps, he found Mehta and two others from his crew standing on the landing, apparently waiting for him.

"We have a problem," Mehta said.

Haqqani scowled. "What now?"

"Someone just broke through the gate."

"Masters?" Haqqani queried.

"No, at least we don't think so."

"He could have planned a follow-up attack."

Mehta shrugged slightly. "Maybe. But it also could be the American, the one who killed Khan."

A cold chill ran down Haqqani's spine. Mehta already had told him about Khan's demise, describing in great detail the bloody swatch the American had cut across Dubai and Karachi. The kind of trouble Masters brought with him, Haqqani could handle. The man was a killer and a sneak. But the American was a one-man army. If he had come looking for Haqqani, it was possible the Americans knew of his attack plans. If they did, he might have to adapt on the run. Instead of traveling to Mumbai's financial district to detonate the Red Mercury, Haqqani may have to accelerate his plans and unleash the explosion here.

Pinning Mehta under his gaze, he nodded toward the front of the building.

"Lead a team outside," he said.

"The device?" Mehta asked.

"I'll deal with it. You just make sure they don't get inside the building."

Deep creases lined Mehta's forehead, and he stared at Haqqani with narrow eyes. Haqqani guessed that he wanted to question his decision, but he was a good soldier and knew to keep his mouth shut. Instead he turned and started down the stairs, followed by the other two Jihadists.

In a perfect situation, Haqqani would have taken time to pray, hoping that God would lead him down the right path. But he had no time for such a luxury. Instead he had to hope that he was interpreting God's desires correctly and move forward with them. If indeed it was the American, as Mehta had suggested, then Haqqani had to hope it was a good omen, that God had brought the infidel here to exactly the right time and exactly the right place to die. If Haqqani could kill an American agent while also striking a blow against India, so much the better. He would consider that a generous bonus.

Haqqani stopped by his quarters, where he found his AK-47 rifle cleaned and ready for battle. He slung the rifle across his back. Around his waist he wrapped a web belt that contained additional pouches of ammunition for the AK.

Exiting the room, he jogged through the corridors until he reached a large truck bay. The cavernous room stank of mold and diesel fumes. A large panel truck stood in the middle of the loading bay, radiator grille pointed toward the big doors. Two armed men were milling around the truck.

When Haqqani entered, both of the men turned toward him. One of them, a fellow Pakistani, was a hawk-faced man who had moved over to Haqqani's group from Lashkar-e-Taiba. The man had been a professional cricket player for several years before he became a militant. The other guard was an Afghan man, rail-thin and quick to anger.

Haqqani opened his mouth to speak, but was stifled by the crackling of gunfire outside the building. A second or two later his cell phone rang. He snatched it from his pocket and brought it to his ear.

"Yes?"

"We have at least two men attacking us," Mehta said.

"Two?" Haqqani replied. "Just two?"

Mehta hesitated. "That's all we've seen."

"Is it the Americans?"

"I don't know. Both are Caucasians, but that doesn't mean anything," Mehta stated.

"Of course."

"I don't recognize them, though."

"Deal with them," Haqqani ordered.

"Of course."

Haqqani slipped the phone back into his pants' pocket. He pinned both men under his gaze.

"We are under attack and the plans have changed. We need to do this right now."

Both men nodded.

"Good," Haqqani said. "If anyone comes in here, you kill them. Even if it's one of our brothers, you kill him. Understand?"

Without hesitation, both men nodded in silent agreement.

Stepping onto the truck's bumper, Haqqani climbed into the rear of the truck.

Inside the trailer was a wooden crate that stood at least up to his neck. Chains pulled over the top of the box and crossed in an $X$ shape were hooked to rings built into the floor of the trailer, holding the box in place. Haqqani unhooked the chains and let them fall to the floor. With that done, he picked up a screwdriver that lay next to the crate and began disassembling the box, a task he expected would take at least a few minutes.

Inside the box sat an improvised explosive device fueled by the Red Mercury. The device had been designed and built by a small crew of former Iraqi and Pakistani nuclear scientists and smuggled piece by piece into this country where it could be reassembled. It had cost an obscene amount of money, but his backers in Saudi Arabia had been only too happy to foot the bill. Of course, they'd also expected that he would give them the device so they could copy it. But he'd never quite been able to bring himself to do so.

While he worked, he considered what would happen in the wake of the blast. Today, he'd strike a blow against this godless country, help his homeland finally reclaim Kashmir once and for all. Once the Indians had a smoking, radioactive pit in the middle of their country, people burned and vaporized by the blast, the government would be paralyzed by fear, unable to act. The way he saw it, with part of one city destroyed, they'd never want to bring even more nuclear horror on their people. For that reason they'd never attack his homeland of Pakistan. Not only did they lack the courage to do it, but he also guessed the United States would step in and stop them from firing the first missile. Yes, the Indians would humiliate themselves by showing the world their cowardice. Haqqani only wished he'd be here to see it happen.

He pulled out the last screw securing the top of the crate and began to lift the lid, the anticipation almost unbearable. It took several more minutes before he'd peeled away the sides of the wooden crate to reveal the improvised device that would trigger the Red Mercury.

The apparatus didn't look like much, a steel cylinder that had the circumference roughly of a car tire. Metal tubes jutted from the top and sides of the cylinder and stretched into a steel box topped by a control panel outfitted with gauges and brightly colored buttons, including a numeric keypad.

Walking to the control panel, he began to punch in the arming code.

THE VEHICLE THAT HAD been following Masters suddenly broke off the chase. Rubber squealing against the pavement, the vehicle whipped into a sharp turn and darted back toward the factory.

What the hell? Masters wondered. Apparently, Haqqani had summoned his people back for some reason. Why else would the guy break off the chase?

By now, Masters's drive had put two blocks between them and the factory. Twisting in his seat, the Englishman could peer out the rear window and see the factory poking its head above several other buildings. He also could see the helicopter bearing in on the factory, growing larger by the second.

"Stop the fucking car," he said.

The driver obeyed, slamming on the brakes and guiding the car up to the nearest curb.

"Maybe they got called back because of the helicopter," Masters said to no one in particular.

"Too little too late," the driver said. "By the time they get there, the team'll have swept the place out. It'll be a damn bloodbath."

Masters nodded, but said nothing. A tickle of excitement sparked in his stomach, though. Within moments the chopper would land and the men would disembark. The whole bloody thing would be over. He only regretted that he couldn't be there to watch it up close. By this time tomorrow, the Russian would even have slipped a few extra dollars into Masters's account.

Yeah, all was right with the bloody world. At least for the moment.

Masters guessed the whole thing would be brutal. The mercenaries would have a fight on their hands. From what he understood, Haqqani's men weren't pushovers. They'd spent years training in small camps and running insurgent operations against the Indians. They knew how to throw a punch, he guessed. At the end of the day, though, his hand-picked group would burn them down with deadly efficiency, butchering everything in sight.

At first, what he saw made no sense. A dark object, white smoke trailing it, suddenly angled up from the rooftop. It slammed into the helicopter's nose. Fire erupted at the point of impact, accompanied by a thunderclap. The flames continued to boil and swell as they swept through the craft's interior. The craft shuddered and plummeted from view.

"Shit," Masters muttered.

The driver, who was twisted around, his arm draped over the back of his seat, opened his mouth to speak.

Masters held up a hand. "Go back there."

BOLAN DARTED LEFT. HIS M-16 stuttered out short bursts of death at the half dozen gunners who were rushing his way. The bullets were hastily aimed and flew wide of their intended targets, though the onslaught of lead caused the oncoming gunners to hesitate instead of drawing a bead on the big American.

At least one of them broke ranks and sought cover. The soldier fired off an HE round from the M-203 that sailed into a knot of men. The ensuing blast ripped through flesh and tore limbs from bodies.

Three down.

At least two of the remaining hardmen decided to apply some overwhelming force of their own to Bolan, unloading weapons at him from different angles. The Executioner sprinted behind a steel trash bin. He rode out the initial wave of gunfire and used the time to load another HE round into the launcher. With the weapon recharged, he whipped around the side of the bin. A man dressed in jeans and a polo shirt was moving toward his position, an Uzi held in one hand and a small, dark object that Bolan pegged as a grenade in the other. The soldier squeezed off a searing burst from the M-16 that chewed into the man's chest and stomach, jerking him in place as though he'd been seized by an electrical charge. Another of Haqqani's thugs darted into view, seemingly from out of nowhere. The M-16 once again uttered its death call, the bullets stitching an angled line across the guy's midsection.

The M-16 cycled dry and Bolan pulled back behind cover so he could reload. A deadly rain of gunfire began to fall as the remaining shooters continued to assail him with sustained bursts from their assault rifles.

Pulling himself to his feet, the soldier moved in a crouch to the other side of the trash bin and away from where the thugs were concentrating their fire. Gliding along the side of the big steel box, he reached the edge of it and peered around the side. From his vantage point, he could see one of the shooters standing behind an old wrecked car.

The soldier let loose with another burst from the M-16. The onslaught of bullets hammered into the guy's skull and neck, knocking him to the ground. Two more men broke from cover, their weapons grinding out punishing barrages of gunfire at Bolan. The Executioner mowed them both down with sustained autofire from the M-16.

The thunderclap from a shotgun cracked behind Bolan and caused his heart to skip a beat. He whipped around, his eyes sweeping for a threat. A few yards away he spotted a man lying facedown. The man was missing part of his midsection, as though a shark had taken a big bite out of his body. Blood was quickly pooling on the ground around the guy. Farther back yet, the soldier saw Turrin standing there, a curl of smoke rising from the barrel of the shotgun.

"No need to thank me," Turrin said.

"Thanks," Bolan replied, "for the heart attack."

# CHAPTER THIRTY

The van roared across the grounds. Bolan, who had reloaded his M-16, nudged Turrin with an elbow and nodded at the approaching vehicle.

"Not friends," he said.

"Good guess," Turrin replied.

Bolan wheeled around toward the factory and sprinted forward, Turrin falling in a couple of paces behind him.

"Not going to see who it is?" Turrin asked.

Bolan shook his head. "I want Haqqani. He's got the nukes."

When they reached the sprawling building, Bolan eased open an exterior door and slipped inside. Turrin stayed a couple of steps behind, occasionally casting glances over his shoulder to make sure no one followed them inside.

The plant's interior was dimly lit. Most of the windows had been boarded up. Sunlight poked in through holes in the walls or through windows where the boards had been pried away. Every third ceiling light shone down. From farther ahead, Bolan could hear a steady mechanical whirring that he guessed belonged to one or more generators.

The M-16 snug against his shoulder, the soldier headed through a maze of rooms, then down a long corridor. He knew he was heading in the general direction of the loading bays.

From somewhere deeper in the building, he heard talking. He shot a glance at Turrin, who nodded. The two men crept down the corridor until they reached the room from which the sound had emanated.

Bolan glanced around the door frame and saw a man he recognized from photographs as Haqqani, flanked by two other men, each armed with an AK-47. One of the shooters broke away from the other men, walked to a loading-bay door and jabbed a button affixed to the wall. The door jerked into motion, and daylight immediately flooded in from underneath the door as it opened.

Bolan turned toward Turrin again, flashed the guy some hand gestures to indicate that he planned to go through the door first. The little Fed nodded and took a step forward so he could provide cover to his partner as he went through the door.

The Executioner surged into the room.

The man who'd just opened the garage door turned around in time to catch a round in the bridge of his nose from Bolan's M-16. The weapon's sharp crack prompted Haqqani to spin toward the Executioner. At the same time, the other guard reacted more quickly. He wheeled toward the intruders, his AK-47 flaming to life and loosing a line of 7.62 mm rounds.

MASTERS CLIMBED FROM the rear of the SUV, an FNC assault rifle in both hands. His breath came in loud, rapid pulls caused not by exertion but rage.

He didn't mind losing the team, though he hoped like hell Lebed didn't try to force him to pay for the helicopter. The mood he was in, that might just cause him to put a bullet through the Russian's forehead, something Masters had considered on more than one occasion.

What really burned his ass, he knew, was being beaten. Not this way and especially not by some American cowboy who parachuted out of nowhere to make his life miserable. Even worse was having some backwater terrorist like Haqqani get the best of him.

So, yeah, he was going to burn both these bastards down, take the Red Mercury and get it the hell out of India. Maybe he'd sell it to the Iranians or the Saudis, take the money to Thailand or the Dominican Republic, someplace where he could live the high life until things cooled down and he could go back to doing what he did best.

But first things first, he told himself.

As he neared a steel trash container, he saw a pair of feet jutting from behind it, heard the low moaning of a man in pain. Moving around the big steel box, Masters found a man lying on his back on the ground, blood-soaked hands clamped over his belly as he apparently tried to hold his shredded entrails inside his body.

Masters stood over the guy. As he ran his gaze from the top of the guy's sweat-soaked head to his booted feet, Master's let the FNC move in concert with his eyes, as though he were deciding just where to plant a bullet.

The man returned Masters's stare.

In the guy's eyes, Masters saw the stark terror of a man on his way out of this life, poised at the edge of hell, ready to take a final plunge. All he needed was one final nudge.

Masters knelt next to the guy. "How we doing, lad?"

The guy's lips moved, but the only sound that escaped was a sickening croak. The creases on Masters's forehead deepened as he studied the man for a few moments before recognition came.

"You're Mehta, aren't you?" Masters asked. "Look at you. Gut ripped open, lying here on your back like a damn turtle on its back. Can't say I'm surprised. That treacherous bastard Haqqani probably did this himself, didn't he? You want to deal with someone with a little more honor, you deal with the Brits. Hell, I'm as trusty as the day is long. At your fucking service."

Masters leaned in a little closer,

"See, the whole martyr thing loses its appeal when it takes time to die, right? I can fix that, though. Help me out and I can get you help in two shakes." Masters nodded at his driver, who was standing by watching the whole exchange. "My friend here is a medic. He can patch you up, toss you into my car and get you some help. You want that?"

The man nodded once, clenched his teeth and drew a sharp intake of air. Masters assumed it was the pain of moving when your guts were hanging out, though he'd never had the pleasure himself.

He gestured at the factory with the FNC's barrel. "Haqqani. Is he inside?"

"Yes," Mehta replied, his voice faint.

"Is he alone?"

Mehta shook his head once and winced in pain.

"Fine," Masters said. "There's a good lad."

The former SAS officer returned to standing. He looked down at Mehta, who stared back at him.

Mehta mouthed the word *help.*

"Sure," Masters said.

The FNC chugged out a short burst. Bullets ripped through the man's gut and severed his spinal cord. Shell casings rained down from the assault rifle, tinkling and bouncing as they hit the asphalt.

"There's your help," Masters said. He stared at his handiwork for a couple of fleeting seconds.

"Nice," he said. "Very nice."

THE REMAINING GUARD squeezed off a fast burst from his weapon. Because of haste or stress, the bullets missed Bolan and chewed into the concrete-block walls. The soldier triggered his own weapon and the burst hammered into the guard's torso, striking the man's hip and stitching a line to his shoulder.

Bolan surged to the truck. Looking in the rear of the vehicle, he saw Haqqani standing next to an odd-looking machine. The Pakistani whirled in Bolan's direction, raising his hand. The soldier fired his M-16, the sustained burst chewing into the man's center mass, the force of the bullets jerking him in place for a stretched second before he collapsed. His fingers opened and a small silver box fell from his grip.

The Executioner climbed into the rear of the vehicle, picked up the box and examined it. He guessed it was a detonator, though he couldn't be sure.

He keyed his throat mike.

"Striker to base," he said.

"Go, Striker," Barbara Price replied over their satellite connection.

"We have the device."

"Is it armed?"

Bolan studied the control panel, but saw no signs that it included a timer.

"Looks like it was detonator-operated."

"Clear. Who has the detonator?" Price asked.

"That'd be me."

Bolan heard the relief in Price's voice. "Good," she said. "We're sending in the decommissioning team."

"Right."

"Good work, Striker."

TURRIN INITIALLY WANTED to follow Bolan into the back of the truck to provide some backup for his old friend. He squelched the impulse, remembering that they'd seen someone else approaching the factory. Enough time had passed that the new arrival either could be in the building or about to enter. Either way, Turrin had worked with Bolan long enough to know that the guy would want him to make sure their six wasn't exposed instead of pulling a mother hen routine.

With the Mossberg up at his shoulder, the little Fed moved toward the door, his eyes searching for any sign of someone closing in on them. A shadow on the wall. A shoe sole scraping on the floor. Whatever. He neither heard nor saw anything.

The stocky little Fed went through the door in a crouch, the Mossberg leading the way. From inside the hallway he spotted two men walking several paces apart. The smaller man, the one holding the FNC, Turrin made immediately as Masters. Turrin didn't recognize the other man, a lanky guy with spiky black hair. The guy was holding a pistol, and he brought his shooting hand up quickly. Turrin squeezed the combat shotgun's trigger twice. Two crimson wounds burst open on the guy's midsection, the force from the twin blasts shoving him back. His pistol cracked as his finger squeezed the trigger one last time in a death reflex.

Masters reacted quickly. Flames lashed out from the FNC's barrel. The maelstrom of bullets was intense enough to force Turrin to dart through a nearby doorway.

The former SAS commando unloaded his assault rifle into the wall. Bullets ripped through the plasterboard, kicking up geysers of white dust. A sudden pause in the shooting told Turrin that Master's rifle had run dry. He'd either need to reload it or switch weapons.

If he got the chance. The stocky little Fed raised the shotgun and fired shot after shot into the tattered wall, which disintegrated under the onslaught. When the gun clicked dry, Turrin let it fall loose on its strap and drew his Colt Detective, thumbing back the hammer.

He stepped into the corridor, the Colt held in front of him in both hands. He swept the weapon's barrel over his surroundings. White dust, wood splinters and pieces of plasterboard littered the floor. Motes of dust danced in shafts of light filtering into the hallway from a skylight and a couple of windows.

Something hard hit him in the back of his skull. A white light exploded behind his eyes and he staggered forward, his legs suddenly weak. He sank to his knees. The Colt had dropped from his hands and had skidded along the floor several feet. He could see it, but never reach it.

A shadow came around from behind, and suddenly he found Masters in front of him. The former paratrooper looked down at Turrin and shook his head with pity. He snapped a new clip into the rifle and smiled down at his prey.

"I'd like to say you were a worthy adversary," he said. "At least then you could die feeling better about yourself."

Masters chambered a round in the FNC. Before he could point it at Turrin, the stocky little Fed, his body fueled by adrenaline, surged up from the ground. He lunged forward and wrapped his arms around Masters's knees, using his weight to knock the guy to the ground.

Masters swung the barrel of his rifle at Turrin, who batted it aside. At the same time, he yanked a knife from his belt, drove it into Masters's throat and twisted it. The assault rifle fell to the floor. Blood pumped from the wound, pooling on the floor. Masters struggled. His arms flailed as he tried to strike Turrin a couple of times in the head and face. The Stony Man warrior batted aside the blows and eventually the Briton's body went still. His sightless eyes stared at the ceiling.

Turrin felt a presence behind him. Turning his head, he saw Bolan standing there.

"I think he may be dead," the little Fed said.

# CHAPTER THIRTY-ONE

Konstantin Zhukov read the email once. Unable to believe his eyes, he read it again. During the second read, his heart began to race and the inside of his mouth went dry. This was bad, he told himself. The assassin he'd hired to kill Lebed had failed. His tongue suddenly felt too large and seemed stuck to the roof of his mouth.

Chances were good that Lebed already knew who'd sent the killer. Not that there was a shortage of people who wanted the bastard dead. Most just weren't willing to take the risk. Zhukov figured Lebed would want retribution and he'd likely not wait to get it, especially with so many things falling apart.

Zhukov paced his office while his mind raced through his options. Should he call Lebed, feign surprise when he heard of the attack? Zhukov rejected the idea outright. Lebed was many things, but not a fool. He'd see through such a thin ruse easily.

He could make another try at Lebed. What was the expression? The best defense is a good offense. If that was true, he'd best start combing around for someone else to take the guy out. He still had friends at the Kremlin, too. They might be able to stop this through some back-channel negotiations or by neutralizing Lebed outright. Zhukov preferred to know Lebed was dead and rotting in a landfill somewhere. Failing that, though, he could live with an uneasy peace between them, as long as Lebed was willing to do the same.

It was an unlikely outcome. He had to acknowledge that from the outset. Lebed had long ago abandoned any pretense of pragmatism or civility, choosing instead to indulge in his bloodlust. But it might at least buy him some time. All things considered, a little time was a good thing. If nothing else, it gave him the chance to come up with a better contingency plan.

Walking to his desk, he jabbed the intercom button on his phone with a finger.

"Yes, sir?" his secretary asked.

"Send Illya in here," he said.

"Of course."

In less than five minutes a young man in a tailored gray suit entered the room. Illya Kosygin, Zhukov's security chief, was a tall man with thinning blond hair, pale skin and unforgiving blue eyes.

"Sir?" Kosygin asked.

"I have a problem," Zhukov said.

He told the younger man about the attempt on Lebed's life and his worries that Lebed might accuse him of ordering the hit.

"Did you order the hit?"

The question surprised Zhukov.

"No," he lied. "And even if I did, why would it matter?"

Kosygin shrugged. "It doesn't."

"Then why ask?" Zhukov queried.

"I overstepped my bounds. My apologies."

"Focus, damn it!"

Kosygin shifted in his chair. "What do you need me to do?"

"You still have contacts at the Kremlin?" Zhukov asked.

"Of course."

"Good. So do I. I will need you to begin making calls. I want them to know I had nothing to do with this. Understand?"

"Certainly," Kosygin replied.

"And I want them to tell that to Lebed. I know how he operates. He's probably angry and will try something. I don't want a war with him." He paused after he heard those words come out of his mouth, realizing how they sounded. "What I mean is, it doesn't do either of us any good to fight each other. It's a distraction from what we're trying to accomplish here."

"I understand. I do have one other question, if I may?"

Zhukov nodded.

"Head or heart?"

A cold chill raced down his spine. "What?"

Kosygin reached beneath his jacket and withdrew a PSM pistol. The small gun, chambered in 5.45 mm ammunition, was fitted with a sound suppressor. He aimed it at Zhukov.

"Head or heart? Mr. Lebed wanted me to ask."

A scream welled up inside Zhukov. Before it could burst free, though, the PSM coughed. A single bullet crashed into the old man's forehead, killing him.

*Stony Man Farm, Virginia*

AARON KURTZMAN, HIS FACE bathed in the glow from his computer monitor, read the news alert flashing on his screen and let out a low whistle.

Turning his head, he saw Price and Brognola across the room, discussing a small pile of intelligence reports.

"Hey," he called.

The two looked up from their work and he beckoned them with his finger. By the time they reached him, Kurtzman's eyes were already glued to the monitor again.

"What is it?" Brognola asked.

"This," Kurtzman said. He tapped the screen with his index finger. "It just came across the wires, or whatever the hell they call it in the internet age."

Brognola and Price leaned forward and read over Kurtzman's shoulder. While they did, he skimmed the article again.

Russian Tycoon Found Murdered
MOSCOW—Russian millionaire Konstantin Zhukov, who helped build much of the country's telecommunications infrastructure after the fall of the Soviet Union, was found murdered in his office.
Zhukov was 67.
He died from a single gunshot to the head, said a Moscow police official who requested anonymity because he was not authorized to discuss the case.
Zhukov, a former Communist Party leader turned businessman, spent decades in the Soviet defense sector before the Soviet government collapsed. He went on to make a fortune installing fiber-optic cables and cellular phone towers throughout the country. A staunch nationalist, Zhukov maintained close ties with the Russian government in the post-Soviet era.
Two years ago, he was quietly expelled from the United States after authorities there leveled spying charges against him.

Brognola nodded once when he finished reading the story. "Okay," he said as he pulled himself away from the screen. "So what?"

"The 'so what' is this guy has long-time ties to Sasha Lebed," Kurtzman said.

"Business dealings?"

"Yeah, business dealings. But both these guys did a ton of advocacy work in Russia. Zhukov used his own country's military as well as those in other countries to channel contracts to Lebed. According to the reports I'm seeing here, they both also encouraged Russia to take a much harder stance against the States. Capitalism was good to them, but they still missed the old days of the Soviet Union, at least as far as the power it enjoyed. They wanted to take our country down a peg or five."

"What do you make of this?" Brognola asked.

"Here's the thing," Kurtzman said. He maneuvered the computer's mouse around, opened up a program window that contained a flow chart with photos of four men and one woman.

"These five people have major holdings in some of Russia's biggest industries—defense, manufacturing, media, transportation," Kurtzman said. "You name it, they own it or at least have a piece of it. They also have a lot of shared business interests, investing in each other's companies, forming joint ventures, the works. The enterprises look legitimate, at least on the face of it."

"But?" Price asked.

"Well, all these executives have hard-line nationalist views, some might say fanatical beliefs," Kurtzman said. "They've written newspaper and journal articles for years, demanding that Russia start kicking us in the groin. When the U.S.S.R. collapsed and we stepped in to help secure their nuclear stockpiles, these clowns threw a fit. Publicly, they criticized the efforts. Privately, they lobbied the government to back out of them. There's been speculation that over the years they've used their money and influence to acquire those materials themselves rather than letting the U.S. anywhere near them."

Brognola turned his gaze to Price. "What do you make of this?" he asked.

"If you mean the murder, it's possible that it's part of an internal squabble. With the pressure on, they could be having some friction with each other."

"How probable is it, though?" Brognola asked.

She shrugged. "Depends on how much pressure they're

under. With Striker on their trail, my guess is the pressure's pretty damn heavy."

Brognola nodded. "Well, let's see what we can do to make things a little worse for everyone involved."

BROGNOLA WENT TO THE office he used when at the Farm. Without thinking, straightened his tie and rolled down his sleeves, buttoned them at the cuffs. He needed to call the President of the United States. Dropping into the seat, he reached for the secure line that went directly to the White House.

An aide answered on the first ring. Brognola gave the guy the right code word. The aide thanked him and within two minutes the Man was on the line.

"Hal?"

"Sorry to disturb you, sir."

"Always happy to hear from you. But, if you're calling, it's probably bad news."

"I want to do something, sir. I need you to sign off on it. Unofficially, of course."

"I give you complete autonomy, Hal, just like my predecessors. You know that."

"And I appreciate that, sir. It makes our job here a lot easier. But this is one of those things where it could cause you a headache. Nothing huge, but it will piss off some folks in Moscow."

"I'm no stranger to headaches. What did you have in mind?"

Brognola told the Man his idea.

"That *will* piss some people off." He sounded more amused than concerned.

"I know, sir. Unfortunately we've asked the Russians to provide as much information as possible. It's my professional opinion they've fallen far short of that. Some very dangerous people armed with dangerous weapons are running loose because of it."

"Do it, Hal," the President said. "I'll take the heat for it. You want a written order or is verbal okay?"

"Verbal's fine," Brognola said. "I doubt I'll get hauled before Congress for this."

*London, England*

TAMARA GILLEN HAD JUST stepped from the shower begun drying off when her phone rang. Of course the phone rings now, she thought. She wrapped the towel around her rib cage so it fell to the tops of her thighs. Stepping from the steamy bathroom, she felt a blast of cool air as she walked into her hotel suite. She padded across the thick carpet to the bed, where her phone lay. A look at the screen told her the caller had the number blocked. She answered anyway.

"Hey," a voice said.

"Jack? Is that you?" Unbidden, a smile formed on her lips and she brushed a few strands of hair from her face.

"How's London?" Grimaldi asked.

"Fine, I guess. Haven't seen much of it. Your friends whisked me out of the airport, drove me to the hotel and locked me in my room, which is very nice, by the way. Unless there's a fire, I have a feeling I'm stuck in here until morning."

"So, you have some time on your hands?"

"I was taking a shower."

"Shower? Like naked?" Grimaldi asked.

"Nothing gets past you."

"Hey, I need a favor. And not the naked kind."

"A favor? I did you a favor when I left Dubai," Gillen told him.

"Okay, then, I need another favor," he said.

She heaved a deep sigh, but mostly for effect. She was too intrigued not to let him make his request.

"I have a story for you to write," the Stony Man pilot stated.

She scowled. What kind of propaganda was he going to ask her to spout?

"I don't take dictation," she said. "I write real stories based on real facts." Heat was radiating from her cheeks and without realizing it, she had put her free hand on her hip.

"What if I told you it was all true?"

"I'd say let me dry my hair. Then tell me more."

So he did.

*Stony Man Farm, Virginia*

AARON KURTZMAN WAS TAKING a bite from his turkey sandwich and scrolling through the internet when he first saw the headline: Dead Tycoon Had Ties to Crime, Russian Government.

He read the first few paragraphs and grinned.

Exclusive
By Tamara Gillen
Staff Writer
MOSCOW—A Russian tycoon shot to death in his office here had been under investigation for selling sensitive components used in nuclear weapons, officials said.

Konstantin Zhukov, 67, who died today from a single gunshot wound to the head, was former Russian defense official and continued to maintain close ties to the Kremlin, according to U.S. officials. It is believed those ties to the Russian government put him in close proximity to technology used to make nuclear weapons, said the official, who spoke on condition of anonymity. It was unclear whether Zhukov had access to nuclear fuels, a key component used in making nukes.

An official with the Russian embassy in London called the allegations "an outrageous attack on a patriot," but declined further comment.

Zhukov was part of a group of wealthy ultranationalists who advocated publicly and privately that the Kremlin take a more adversarial approach to what they viewed as the expansion of American power.

"Wow," Kurtzman muttered, "some heads are exploding in Moscow right now."

BROGNOLA RETURNED TO his Farm office, a cup of coffee in one hand, a folder filled with reports in the other.

Setting the coffee on an end table, he sat on a couch and rubbed his eyes, which felt grainy and swollen from lack of sleep. Balling his hands into fists, he pressed the exposed parts of his palms into his eyes to relieve the strain. How many days had it been since he'd been home? Two? Three? He'd lost track. Fortunately his wife, Helen, was out of town this week, visiting friends in Massachusetts, salving a little of the guilt he felt over being away from home for several days in a row. At least this way, he knew she wasn't alone, worried about his health and safety.

The secure line from the White House trilled. Brognola pulled his hands from his eyes and scowled. The Man didn't *always* call with bad news, just usually.

Grabbing his coffee, he rose from the couch and walked to the secure phone. Picking up the receiver, he brought it to his ear and spoke.

"Mr. President."

"Hello, Hal. You sitting down?"

"Yes," Brognola lied.

"I got a call from the Kremlin. Who called probably isn't

important, but the person had interesting things to say. As you can imagine, the Kremlin isn't happy with the article."

"I'm sorry to hear that, sir."

"I'm sure you're very broken up. The point is, this Kremlin official, who's very high up, assured me that whoever leaked that information had it all wrong."

"Really?" Brognola replied, his disbelief audible.

"They swear the Russian government broke off ties with Zhukov, Lebed and their associates years ago."

"I stand corrected."

"And, of course to show us how mistaken we are, they offered to provide us with a packet of information about Mr. Lebed and the others," the President said.

"Generous."

"This person assured me the packet will include information on Mr. Lebed's current whereabouts. According to their information, he has been summoning the others in his circle to an estate he owns in Costa Rica."

"It's always good to get away," Brognola said.

"Like either of us would know."

Brognola let loose with his first laugh in what felt like forever. "Isn't that the truth?"

"I'd suggest you take a vacation, but why waste my breath? Watch your email. You'll have the whole packet in a few minutes."

"Thank you, sir."

"And, Hal?" the Man said.

"Yes, sir?"

"I want them gone. Every last one of them."

"I think we can accommodate you there."

# CHAPTER THIRTY-TWO

*Mumbai, India*

Bolan navigated the car through the small executive airport on the outskirts of Mumbai. Turrin, who was riding in the passenger's seat, had just finished a phone call with Barbara Price at Stony Man Farm and was slipping his phone into his jacket.

"Barb says she has some information for us," Turrin said. "She's sending us some of it in an e-mail, and she's going to give us a video briefing in about an hour."

Bolan nodded. He cut the wheel to the left and turned into the parking lot in front of a small hangar. He saw Grimaldi standing outside, leaning against the building, smoking a cigarette. Bolan parked the rental car and he and Turrin disembarked from the vehicle.

"Hey, Sarge," Grimaldi said. "I'd offer to take your bags, but I know you don't travel light."

He nodded at Turrin. "I see you brought a carry-on, though."

"Oh, sure," Turrin said, "go with the little-man jokes right out of the gate, you skinny bastard."

"Just plucking the low-hanging fruit, my friend." He came off the wall and punched Turrin in the arm. "How you been?"

While the two men continued to banter, Bolan popped open the trunk and began unpacking the weapons cases and carrying them to the Gulfstream jet. Grimaldi and Turrin offered to help, but Bolan waved them off. Though physically tired, he wanted to keep his body moving and he didn't feel like talking.

He was glad to have taken out Khan, Masters and Haqqani. But, as important as those strikes had been, he now had to deal with the man driving all the carnage over the last few days, Sasha Lebed. The soldier never considered killing someone a pleasure. But if he got the chance to kill Lebed, the soldier wouldn't think twice about it, either. It was time to end this thing, one way or the other.

He sensed Grimaldi a second or two before the guy brushed by him. The pilot slapped him on the shoulder as he passed.

"Look alive, ladies," Grimaldi said. "Next stop Costa Rica."

SEATED IN THE CABIN OF the C-37A, Bolan drank some coffee and listened to the twin Rolls-Royce turbofan engines whine as the plane powered up. He guessed Grimaldi and the copilot, a blacksuit named Tom Staples, who occasionally assisted on long flights, were running the craft through its last-minute checks before taking to the sky.

Bolan and Turrin had each been given laptops hooked into the plane's secure communication system. On Bolan's laptop, a black program window fixed in the center of the screen suddenly winked to life, filled with Price's face. Web cameras fitted on the machine beamed the two warriors' images back to Stony Man Farm.

She flashed Bolan a smile, exposing perfect white teeth.

"Striker," she said, "it's good to see you. And you, Leo."

Turrin made a gun with his hand, thumb cocked back like a pistol's hammer. When the thumb dropped, he winked and made a clicking noise with his tongue. "Right back at ya, Barb," he said.

"Smooth as glass, Leo," Price said. "Anyway, we have

some information for you. And, really, Aaron should be the one sharing it, since he and Jack did the most to uncover it."

"But you're better to look at," Turrin said.

"Can you do something about him, Striker?" Price asked.

Bolan shook his head. "Other than shoot him, no. A lack of sleep is only making his deviant nature worse. And I'd hate to waste the bullet."

"Wonderful," Price said. She scowled, but Bolan saw the amusement dance in her eyes, and he heard it in her voice.

"Well, let's get this briefing behind us so you two can grab a few hours' sleep," she said. "According to the Russians—yes, I said the Russians—your friend Lebed has a lot more going on than just running a defense contracting company and smuggling weapons on the side. While his allegiance to the former Soviet Union is debatable, his belief that the United States shouldn't be the sole superpower is not. And he has surrounded himself with several like-minded people in high places in Russia, all of them willing to put their time and money into doing what they can to knock us off balance."

"How did the Mumbai mission further those goals?" Bolan asked.

"Your guess is as good as mine, but the working theory is that he wanted to create a sense of insecurity and instability in Asia."

"So his security company could fill the void," Bolan suggested.

"Right," Price said. "According to what we're piecing together, he planned to step in and upset Haqqani's plans with his crew of killers. But it went much deeper than that, at least according to what the Russians are telling us. Apparently he thought the threat of a nuclear explosion in Asia would weaken America's position there."

Bolan turned his head slightly to the left in a questioning gesture. "Not sure I follow," he said.

"The theory right now is that he could do this in a couple of ways. One, he would make the U.S. look ineffectual and weak by having the Russians step in to save the day. The cover story was going to be that the weapon traveled through Afghanistan and Pakistan on its way to India."

"Forcing people to ask why the U.S. didn't know about it," Bolan said.

"Exactly," Price said. "But it gets worse."

"Of course it does," Bolan said with a rueful grin.

"They were going to pin the weapon transfer on us," Price said. "We've been thinking they killed Lang because he figured out too much about the whole operation. That was partially right, though they added a sick twist to it. They planned to blame Lang and a handful of alleged 'rogue' CIA officers with providing the weapons. The other officers were working deep-cover assignments overseas, a couple of them were highly decorated."

"We know this how?" Bolan asked.

"An analyst at Langley got busted several hours ago for stealing the names of overseas operatives. Long story short, he was dipping his wick where he shouldn't have been and got blackmailed for it. He gave the security people who busted him the name of the blackmailer. It was a woman with fairly extensive ties to Lebed."

"So they'd kill the undercover guys and pin the transfer on them. And with the accused dead, it'd be hard for the U.S. to refute the allegations."

"Making us as popular as the plague," Price said.

"So Lang basically died for nothing," Bolan stated.

"Don't they always?" Price replied. "As if all that's not bad enough, we're worried what the guy may have told them while he was being interrogated. His last hours on Earth sound pretty hellish."

Bolan nodded. "I'll make sure Lebed and his people get no use out of it."

The soldier realized Turrin had been uncharacteristically quiet during the briefing. He cast a glance at the man and saw his head lolled to one side, his breathing heavy.

"Well, look at that," Bolan said. "A little ride and he's out like a light."

"They're so cute at that age," Price said.

# CHAPTER THIRTY-THREE

*Costa Rica*

Sasha Lebed stood in his walled courtyard, an ice-cold gin and tonic in his grip, and pondered his next move.

He guessed that the American, Matt Cooper, was coming for him. The man had proved too tenacious to do otherwise. And Cooper had to know his location. Masters probably had betrayed him. Or maybe Khan. But someone along the way had to have told him what they knew, blurted out some piece of valuable information to buy themselves a few precious seconds of life. In his experience, it was a rare man willing to take a secret to his grave if he could trade it for money, sex or another breath. The few who did keep their mouths shut usually did so because they died suddenly and alone.

He sipped the drink and enjoyed the tang of the lime, the feeling of a cool drink trailing down his parched throat. Dressed in lightweight brown slacks, a sky-blue polo shirt and a pair of moccasins, he looked like any other tourist in Costa Rica. The twin micro-Uzis he carried, holstered in a cross-draw position on either hip, however, dispelled any notion that he was in the country to take in the sights or shoot photos of monkeys and waterfalls.

He had always carried a sidearm, of course. But with Matt Cooper breathing down his neck, he felt no need to skimp on firepower. He hadn't lived as long as he had, in the world he inhabited, by being passive or unprepared.

The thumping of helicopter blades reached his ears. He

turned and looked toward the noise, but was unable to see the approaching craft because of the tall trees surrounding his sprawling home. Winding his way between the arrayed patio furniture and past the Olympic-size swimming pool, he made a beeline for the helipad, the rumble of the helicopter growing in volume as he did. Stepping out from the tree line and into the sunlight, he saw a large chopper lowering to the helipad, the down draft from the chopper's rotors flattening vegetation and causing tree leaves to shake. The noise also drowned out the cacophony of bird calls and other wildlife noises that usually provided an aural backdrop for the estate.

Bending, he set the empty glass on the edge of his flagstone patio. Returning to his full height, he marched for the helipad. By the time he reached it, the pilot had cut the engine and the spinning rotor blades had begun to slow.

The helicopter's side door slid open. Two of Lebed's gunners, each armed with an AK-47, climbed from the craft. One of the men extended a hand back inside the helicopter and a second later, a tall, slender woman came into view. The blonde held the man's hand as he helped her from the craft.

In her mid-40s, the woman, Nikkita Altinov, looked many years younger. She wore a skirt that rose a few inches above her knees, highlighting well-shaped calves and thighs. Her skin was tanned a golden brown. Altinov had been a high-ranking official in Russia's information ministry, but more recently had focused her energies on running the media holdings her family had built once the Soviet Union had fallen. Her father, a founding member of the Seven, had died two years ago from a massive coronary, leaving her to take his place.

Two men, both in their sixties, disembarked from the helicopter. Both were former intelligence officers, first from the KGB and later from the GRU. An elderly man with stooped shoulders shuffled into view, his movements supported with a wooden cane. One of the guards helped the old man down. He immediately slapped away the guard's hand the moment his feet touched the earth. Vladimir Penkovsky glared at Lebed, who shrugged.

Altinov broke away from the men and quickly advanced on Lebed. She hugged him and pressed a lingering kiss on his lips. She stepped back, opening a few inches between them, her hands holding on to his biceps. She gave him a wide smile, exposing perfect white teeth. Dazzling though her smile was, it didn't reach her eyes. That came as no surprise to Lebed, who knew that, while not all women used their beauty and charms as a tool, Altinov did. No, more like a truncheon to get men to do her will. It was a behavior so deeply ingrained in her, he doubted she even was aware of it. But it had made her extremely valuable to Lebed when he had needed someone to manipulate and bend tycoons and world leaders to the will of the Seven.

"So good to see you, Sasha," she said.

"And you, Nikki. I trust your flight went well?"

She gave him a throaty laugh and a smile. "My fellow travelers behaved themselves, if that's what you mean." She leaned in close and in a whisper said, "Look at them. I don't think they have any choice to behave. Not like you."

The banter continued for another minute, light and easy. Though Lebed played along, he also was watching the old man begin to fidget impatiently, his irritation obvious as he glared at Lebed.

Finally, Penkovsky stamped the tip of his cane against the earth.

"You'd better have a damn good reason for dragging us out here, my friend," he said. "You just about have exhausted my goodwill and my patience."

Lebed looked away from Altinov's face and cocked an eyebrow at the old man. He smiled, but his left hand, which was jammed in his pants' pocket, balled into a fist. "Thanks for the warning, Vladimir. I'll try to remember it."

As expected, that wasn't enough. The old man lifted his cane and, wobbling on unsteady legs, jabbed it at Lebed.

"Try to remember it? Try? Fuck you, punk! Who do you think you are? We have worked for years on this organization, building up our wealth, power and influence." He stopped speaking and pressed the cane back to the earth for support. He took a couple of gulps of air before he continued. "Now you, through this insane plan of yours, have unleashed hell on us. We're being hunted like animals. Some of the most powerful people on Earth and we're being hunted. Do you get that?"

Lebed held up a hand to silence the old man, who did stop to again catch his breath.

"Of course, Vladimir. You raise valid points. Please, come inside, get comfortable, and I will be happy to listen to your complaints. We can work this out."

The old man opened his mouth to speak, but stopped as though the conciliatory words had just sunk in. His rheumy blue eyes bore into Lebed's face, searching for some sign of deception or derision from the Russian.

Lebed nodded in the direction of the house. "Please, my friend."

The old man nodded and stepped forward.

The big Russian gave the old man a smile. "There you go. We can work this out."

Lebed turned toward the house.

In the next instant his left hand whipped across his chest. Fingers encircled the butt of one of the micro-Uzis, and he yanked it from the holster. Whirling, he centered the Uzi on the old man's torso. Flames stabbed out from the barrel, and 9 mm Parabellum rounds drilled into the old man's body, shredding flesh before they burst from man's frail back in a spray of blood and bone fragments.

The bullet-riddled body collapsed to the ground. Lebed swept the barrel over the other men.

"Anyone else have anything they'd like to share?"

The men looked stunned, their eyes bulging in fear. They all assured him they had nothing to say.

He smiled. "How nice. The perhaps we can adjourn inside for a drink? Put this unpleasantness behind us."

Lebed turned back toward the house and squelched a desire to laugh.

# CHAPTER THIRTY-FOUR

Bolan moved through the jungle undergrowth, not quite silent, but nearly so. He was again dressed in the blacksuit, combat rigging layered over top of that. The Beretta 93-R and the Desert Eagle were holstered in their familiar spots, shoulder and hip, respectively. The warrior also carried an MP-5 submachine gun.

His job was to plow his way into Lebed's compound so the others could follow him inside. While Turrin and Grimaldi had experience under fire and plenty of guts, jungles were Bolan's specialty. He wanted to move quickly and his fellow warriors might slow him under the circumstances. He had heard helicopters thunder overhead, but had only glimpsed them briefly because of the canopy of leaves above him.

Still moving, he keyed the throat mike. "Striker to base."

"Go, Striker." It was Barbara Price.

"I'm within a quarter mile of the target. What's new?"

"You heard the choppers?"

"I did."

"One of them just landed on the premises. Satellite readings indicated seven people disembarking from the craft. The second copter hasn't landed yet. It just keeps circling the estate. NSA is picking up some communications between the ground and the chopper. It's feeding us live audio, but—"

"But it's all in Russian."

"Exactly. Their linguists are trying to provide a real-time

translation, but it's slower than we'd like. As best we can tell, it's jammed with security people and maybe an assistant or two. But the people on the ground won't give them permission to land."

"Any video or images of the people from the first chopper?"

"Nothing worth talking about. Whether by design or not, I have no way of knowing, but Lebed has a lot of mature trees with big tops and several wide canopies lined up one after the other. It makes it hard to get decent photos of his friends."

"My guess is it's by design," Bolan said. "I don't think Lebed does anything by accident."

"Any theories?"

"If I had to guess," Bolan said, "it's probably his fellow travelers from the Seven. Someone called a meeting, and someone is going to get roasted alive for the disaster in India."

"Lebed?"

"Probably not. They're a smart group of people. If they wanted to kill him, they probably wouldn't come to his house or do it in person. They'd have hired it out."

"Wouldn't he do the same?"

"Maybe," Bolan said. "Probably not, though. Lebed's an arrogant son of a bitch. He could have hired it all out, sure. But he would probably rather be there when it happens. He thinks he's better than the rest of these guys. What better way to prove it, in his eyes anyway, than by bringing them to his place and killing them?"

"Pretty sick."

"You think?" Bolan said.

"Sorry," Price replied, a smile in her voice. "I have a poor track record when it comes to reading men."

"But you're an ace when it comes to picking them," the soldier said. Bolan had shared a bed with the beautiful and intelligent mission controller on more than one occasion. And, while they had no commitment to each other, they did have a mutual respect and affection.

"We've got three on the screen, just ahead," Price said, a no-nonsense tone back in her voice.

"Thanks," Bolan said. "I'll work on getting a visual. Striker out."

Bolan continued toward the estate. Finding Lebed's hideaway had been surprisingly easy. Once confronted by the U.S. about the Seven's actions, the Russian government had been only too happy to give up whatever intelligence they had on Lebed, including some of his off-the-books land holdings, aircraft registered to his various shell corporations and his list of overseas accounts. Kurtzman and the Farm's cyberteam had worked miracles taking the information, along with intelligence from various U.S. agencies, to figure out that Lebed had chosen this as his hideout. As far as Bolan was concerned, the fact that Lebed had chosen Costa Rica, a country so close to the United States, as a place to hide, spoke volumes about the man's arrogance and disdain for those tracking him.

Getting to the coastal island had posed no challenge. Bolan and the others had used a raft to access the beach in the predawn hours. While Bolan was supposed to perform a frontal assault on the estate, Grimaldi and Turrin were looping around to approach it from a different direction. This allowed Bolan to travel light, which he preferred, and also positioned the others to hit the facility from another direction, if possible. Bolan wondered how the others were faring.

"This camouflage itches," Turrin said. Hooking his finger into the collar, he pulled the fabric away from the skin of his neck.

"Forgot about your delicate skin," Grimaldi muttered.

"I'm just saying."

"All right. You said it."

Both wore jungle camouflage and combat boots. Turrin had loaded up with the Glock 17 again, along with his Colt Detective. Grimaldi had opted for the M-16/M-203 combo. His 9 mm SIG-Sauer was holstered on his thigh. Both had streaked their hands and faces with green, tan and black camouflage paint.

"I usually wear a nicer class of clothing," Turrin said. "That's all I'm saying."

"Would you feel better if I told you the camouflage cost two grand and Gucci made the boots?"

"Funny."

"I'm just saying," Grimaldi replied, grinning at his old friend. "Look at me, I haven't had a cigarette in a couple of hours. It's killing me."

Turrin and Grimaldi were approaching the estate from the northeast, which would take them to the rear of the facility. They'd been walking through the jungles for more than an hour by that point. Grimaldi estimated that the estate lay about a tenth of a mile ahead. He was about to confirm this with his GPS unit when a buzzing noise, faint and mechanical, caught his ears.

He shot a questioning glance at Turrin, who confirmed with a nod that he had heard the noise, too. Grimaldi strained his ears, but the noise emanated from too far away for him to pinpoint the source. Since it seemed to be gaining in volume, though, he guessed it was coming from one or more approaching vehicles. The birds populating the branches overhead continued to make noise, and he heard the occasional crash of a monkey or another large animal moving among the branches.

Grimaldi keyed the throat mike.

"Eagle to Striker."

"Go," the familiar voice said.

"I hear something. Sounds like a vehicle coming our way."

"Any visuals?"

"Negative. I can hear them, but I can't see them."

"Roger that. I took out a couple of their guys over here. Possible that they're searching for them."

"Or looking for the guy who took out their buddies."

"Or that," Bolan agreed. "Try to get as close as possible to the estate before you do anything. But if you need to engage, do it."

"Roger."

By now the pair had reached a clearing. They stopped at the edge and waited. After a couple of minutes the noise had gained enough volume that Grimaldi could begin to dissect it. A high-pitched whine that sounded like it came from one or more motorbikes. The lower-pitched growl was probably being generated by a truck, he thought. A trail lay about twenty yards to their right. The pilot assumed the riders would use trails instead of trying to navigate the dense growth covering the jungle's heavily rutted floor.

"Motorcycles," he said to Turrin.

"Yeah."

"If they stay on the trail, we should be able to avoid them."

"Probably will," Turrin agreed. "No way for a motorcycle to get through this terrain."

"The big thing—whatever the hell it is—worries me more."

"Right."

After a couple of minutes the whine from the motorcycle engines had intensified to a point where Grimaldi guessed they were only a short distance away. Both men crouched into the thick vegetation and scanned their surroundings for some sign of the threat.

Moments later they heard the low growl of a much larger

engine, accompanied by the sound of snapping branches. As the sound intensified, Grimaldi realized there was more than one large vehicle coming their way.

He shot his partner a look. "This sounds bad."

Turrin nodded.

Grimaldi cracked open the M-203 grenade launcher and switched out the smoke round it contained for a high-explosive one. Seconds later the pilot saw one of the trucks crest a small hill that lay just ahead. It was a pickup with massive tires built for off-road riding. The driver gunned the engine and the vehicle raced down the hill toward them. It mowed down small trees and shuddered and rocked from side to side as it rolled over the uneven ground before it shot into the clearing. Two men stood in the bed of the truck, each gripping an FNC assault rifle in one hand and the roll bar painted in the greens, browns and blacks of camouflage in the other.

A second truck raced into view. Plumes of black smoke boiling up from behind the vehicle, it hurtled into the clearing before it ground to a halt.

Grimaldi dropped to his belly and crawled along the jungle floor. Turrin had moved in the opposite direction and had already disappeared.

"You there, Leo?"

"Yeah. I figured we could hit them from separate directions."

Grimaldi stopped crawling, stretched out on his belly and aimed the M-16 at the nearer truck, which stood a dozen or so yards away. The vehicle idled, the heat rising from its hood causing the air to shimmer. The gunners in the back of the truck climbed down from its bed, their eyes sweeping their surroundings. A couple of seconds later two more gun-wielding thugs, presumably from the other truck, stepped into view. Grimaldi watched as the four men shouted at one another, gesturing occasionally at the surrounding vegetation. He couldn't hear what was said over the rumble of the idling truck engines.

Grimaldi tightened his hold on the M-16. He guessed the men were looking for Bolan, or more generally whoever had killed the guards at the estate. At the end of the day, though, Grimaldi knew it didn't matter who these heavies were looking for. If they found him and Turrin, they'd just as quickly put a bullet in them.

Well, he figured, at least they all were on equal terms. Grimaldi tightened his hold on the M-16 and began to slowly pivot the assault rifle's barrel toward one of the hardmen who'd broken away from his crew and was moving toward him.

As the Stony Man pilot lined up the shot, the passenger's door of the truck swung open and another man, a burly Caucasian with his curly black hair cut short, exited the cab. Once his feet were on the ground, he turned and reached back inside the jacked-up vehicle, the bottom of which stood just below the guy's chest. He withdrew something from inside the truck's cab. When Grimaldi saw it, a cold chill of fear raced down his spine and he felt the inside of his mouth go dry.

The apparatus the guy brought out consisted of a pair of tanks hooked together and fixed to a metal frame. A hose ran from the tanks into a long tube with a pistol grip jutting out from the bottom. The guy began shrugging on the flame-thrower's harness.

The pilot activated his com link.

"You seeing this, Leo?" he asked.

"Yeah."

"You want this one?"

"No, thanks. I like watching you work."

"You're a freaking gem. If I end up extra crispy, it's your fault. Stay down. I'm about to light these bastards."

Lebed's shooter was closing in. Grimaldi squeezed the

M-16 and the weapon loosed a punishing burst of autofire, stitching a short line across the gunner's chest. The guy's eyes widened in shock, and his body wavered for a heartbeat before collapsing in on itself.

Even before the corpse the crumpled to the ground, Grimaldi was swinging the M-16 toward the guy with the flamethrower. The guy was twisting a knob on the side of the tank to open up the flow of gas. The pilot triggered the M-203 grenade launcher and an HE round sizzled from the weapon's muzzle. It knifed through the air just past the walking torch and slammed into the truck behind him. The round exploded with a roar, and flames ripped through the truck's interior. The fire lashed out from the vehicle and heated the fuel tanks on the firebug's back. Grimaldi let the M-16 fall from his grip, buried his face in the ground and covered his ears with his palms. Thunder pealed again through the jungle as the fuel tanks ignited, engulfing the firebug in flames. As the explosion died down, Grimaldi pulled his hands from his ears and grabbed the M-16. Another of the shooters, his body engulfed in black-tinged yellow flames sprinted toward Grimaldi. The man screamed and slapped at his burning flesh.

The pilot fired a mercy burst into the guy's torso to end his suffering. The man fell to the ground in a boneless heap, the flesh of his flame-ravaged remains puckering and turning black. Grimaldi averted his gaze and rose to his feet. By now fire had consumed the truck's interior, the flames choking the sky with a thick column of black smoke.

On the move again, the pilot was trying to put some distance between himself and the burning truck. The flames, he guessed, would reach the pickup's fuel tank any second and cause a secondary blast.

A voice buzzed in his earpiece. "You okay?" Turrin asked.

"Yeah."

"Good. The rest of these guys are pissed off."

Grimaldi got proof of that a moment later when one of the shooters emerged from the haze. When the hardman saw Grimaldi, the guy whipped the FNC's barrel toward the pilot. The assault rifle chattered as it cut loose with a deadly volley of bullets.

Before Grimaldi could react, another gun report sounded, drowning out the crackling of the various fires burning around him. Lebed's shooter suddenly stiffened, a bullet exiting his chest, and pitched forward.

Turrin emerged from the smoke, the Uzi clutched in his right hand. When he saw Grimaldi, he shot the guy a wink.

"I think they know we're here," he said.

They continued their march toward the estate. A minute or so later another explosion ripped through the jungle. Grimaldi flinched, but kept moving. He noticed Turrin didn't miss a beat, either. He guessed the flames of the burning pickup had finally reached its fuel tank and caused it to explode.

Considering all they had yet to do, he guessed the mayhem was just starting.

BOLAN HAD BARELY COVERED another thirty yards before he heard someone cough. Pressing on for another several yards, he caught a traces of fresh cigarette smoke wafting through the jungle, though he couldn't see it.

He crouched and scanned his surroundings. Several yards away, he spotted a man standing with his back toward Bolan. The guy was shifting his weight from foot to foot nervously, the move causing his upper body to weave rhythmically, like wheat stalks blowing in a light breeze.

Still in a crouch, MP-5 leading the way, Bolan crept up on the guy. He split his attention between his target and his surroundings, wondering where the hell the other two figures had disappeared to.

The sentry pulled the campaign hat from his head and wiped the sweat from his gleaming, bare scalp with a white handkerchief. He wore brown khaki shorts and a white T-shirt with the Paradigm Systems logo emblazoned across the back.

Slipping the hat back on his head, he wadded up the handkerchief and jammed it back into his pocket. Suddenly he hissed something under his breath. Bolan recognized a couple of the words as Russian, but couldn't hear the whole muttered phrase. The irritation in his voice was obvious, though. Seconds later a second man emerged from some nearby bushes, zipping his fly, apparently having just relieved himself.

Unlike the first gunner, the second guy was facing Bolan's direction and spotted him instantly. Shouting in Russian, the man pointed at him with one hand and began grabbing for a pistol holstered on his hip at the same time.

Bolan tapped the MP-5's trigger and it coughed out a fast burst that ripped apart the man's torso. The other gunner spun in the soldier's direction, clawing at his hip holster. Bolan leaned on the trigger. The subgun chugged out a murderous burst of 9 mm slugs that chewed a diagonal line from the man's right hip to his left shoulder, shredding flesh and causing geysers of blood to erupt from beneath his skin. The guy crumpled to the ground in a dead heap.

Something sizzled through the air just in front of Bolan's face. The Executioner dropped into a crouch, his eyes searching for his assailant. A withering burst of autofire sliced through the air just in front of the soldier as the other gunner apparently got a better line on him.

The Executioner whipped the MP-5 in the direction of the hardman and, firing the weapon with one hand, laid down a barrage of autofire that shredded the third shooter's torso.

Though he couldn't see it through all the dense vegetation, Bolan guessed the estate lay another one hundred yards or so ahead. Under normal circumstances, he could cover the distance in no time. But the numbers were working against him at this point. He'd just taken out some of Lebed's forces, and the rest of the security force would have heard gunfire.

In other words, it was time to step things up.

# CHAPTER THIRTY-FIVE

Bolan reached the estate, but stayed hidden in a line of trees while he sized up his target.

From his position he could see one story of a three-story building, its red-tiled roof poking above a stone wall that surrounded the property. Three guards, all of them armed with what Bolan guessed were FNC assault rifles, stood outside a guard shack. A window air conditioner jutted from the side of the guard shack, humming and dripping condensation on the concrete pad on which the small building stood. A green SUV with tinted windows was idling. From his position, Bolan couldn't tell whether a driver was seated inside the vehicle or whether he was among those milling around outside the gates.

The soldier emerged from the trees and sprinted across the lawn. The first guard to spot the big American spun in his direction. The guy shouted a warning to his comrades and raised his FNC assault rifle. Wielding the MP-5 with one hand, Bolan cut loose with a storm of slugs that caught his opponent in the right hip and chopped a diagonal line up to his left shoulder. With his free hand, the Executioner palmed an M-67 fragmentation grenade, pulled the pin with his teeth and hurled the bomb. It hit the ground just a couple of feet from the guards and bounced a couple of times. In the same moment, whoever was behind the wheel of the SUV gunned the vehicle's engine and it lurched forward.

The grenade blast unleashed a maelstrom of razor-sharp shrapnel that shredded the guards.

In the meantime the vehicle's engine roared as the SUV bore down on the Executioner. He loosed a sustained burst at the oncoming vehicle as he launched into a sprint. The 9 mm slugs drilled through the SUV's steel skin or occasionally glanced off its hide and spun away.

The SUV whipped past Bolan and he leaned on the trigger again. This time the relentless volley of slugs lanced through the side windows, causing a dozen spiderwebs to suddenly appear.

Bolan glimpsed the driver, his head and body rent by the hail of bullets, collapse onto the steering wheel. The vehicle suddenly angled away from the soldier, and it careened into a circular wall of red bricks that surrounded one of several fountains that dotted the landscape. The SUV shuddered to a violent halt.

The soldier moved up to the vehicle. He opened the passenger's door and looked inside. The driver hung forward, suspended in place by his safety harness, his body ravaged by gunfire. Leaning his upper body into the truck, Bolan reached across the seat and snatched a key card that was pinned to the man's left breast pocket.

When he exited the vehicle, he turned and saw Grimaldi and Turrin emerging from the tree line and heading toward him. The three men moved along the exterior wall until they reached the gate. Bolan swiped the card through the reader, and the gate parted at the middle and began to fan outward. He and the other two men slipped through the entrance, guns held at the ready.

LEBED STOOD, HIS ARMS crossed over his chest, and stared at the people arrayed around his study.

The youngest of the men, Olav Andropov, sat in a leather recliner. His legs were crossed, right ankle on top of the left knee, his forearms positioned on the armrests. A pistol of some kind hung in a shoulder holster. A slight smile curved his lips and he looked almost bored, as though he were there as a dispassionate observer.

Lebed knew nothing could be further from the truth.

The other two men had seated themselves on opposite ends of a couch, one had fear in his eyes, the other murder. One shifted nervously in his seat while the other stared down into a tumbler of Scotch whisky that Lebed had poured for him.

The latter two, frankly, disgusted Lebed. Both had millions of dollars and dozens of guns for hire at his disposal. But they both looked deflated and defeated. Andropov, on the other hand, looked amused and maybe a bit curious about the turn of events.

Lebed guessed that was a good thing. Judging by their facial expressions and their body language, anger and fear had consumed the other two men. High emotion made men dangerous, cost them their judgment and warped their motivations.

But Andropov seemed to be keeping his cool and Lebed guessed he would stand beside anyone willing to shell out the right amount of money. No loyalty borne of emotion. No patriotism. No desire for revenge. Just a willingness to look out for Number One and to adapt to the changing circumstances set out in front of him. From Lebed's way of thinking, that made him a valuable ally—as long as the checks kept coming.

From the corner of his eye he noticed Altinov staring at him. He turned and shot her a wink before returning to his drink. She'd been sitting at the bar, nursing a rum and cola. A large mirror ran along the wall behind the bar and she stared into it, studying her reflection, occasionally brushing a curl of hair from her eyes or pulling at the hem of her skirt, smoothing it.

She had known ahead of time that Lebed had planned to wax the old man. If seeing the old man's body chewed by bullets bothered her, she'd showed no outward signs and she'd remained silent ever since they'd come inside.

Andropov spoke again. "Look, I have no trouble with you plugging the old man. Really, I don't. But why? Was it just because he was a shrill little man? Or is there something else at work here?"

"You ask a lot of questions."

"Indulge me," Andropov said, shrugging.

Lebed heaved a sigh. "I'd rather thought it obvious, but apparently you need it laid out for you." He shot a look at Andropov to see if the dig had angered the man, but his expression remained inscrutable.

"His day has come and gone," Lebed stated.

"Obviously."

"I mean, his kind has had its day. His generation lost the cold war and left the Americans standing as the world's sole superpower."

Andropov grinned and gestured at their lavish surroundings. "It hasn't been all bad," he said. "This beats living with ten relatives in a crowded Moscow apartment, right?"

"Granted. But defeat is defeat. Loss is loss. If you accept it, you just get more of it."

"We lost in Mumbai."

"Just a setback, I assure you. This isn't a strategic defeat by any means. Penkovsky couldn't see that. He panicked, hell, had a tantrum. That kind of cowardice repulses me. I won't tolerate it, not when we have so much work to do here."

One of the men on the couch spoke up. "Where's our staff, our security teams? They were right behind us."

Lebed shrugged. "They're dead."

The man stiffened and his eyes widened. "What? Dead?"

The other Russian, the one who'd been fidgeting, stopped moving and stared at Lebed. "Why did you do that? You have no right. We're all equal partners in this. We're supposed to be working together."

"I'm tired of working together," Lebed said. "You act like a couple of old women, shivering and sweating at the sight of your own shadows. Look at Nikki, at Andropov. They're not panicking. Those are the sort of people I need in my operation."

"You had Zhukov killed, too, didn't you?"

"Yes, I did. It was a rather nice piece of work."

"You're insane."

Lebed smiled. "Hardly. I'm just adapting to changing circumstances. Zhukov tried to have me killed and failed. I returned the favor. I won't work with people I can't trust, and I won't passively accept someone trying to kill me. I have come too far to be stopped by anyone."

"What about the American?"

Lebed's smile faded and his eyes narrowed. "I'm not worried about him."

The door opened and one of his guards rushed into the room. The man's cheeks were flushed scarlet and he was breathing heavily.

"Sir! We have a problem."

"What do you mean?"

"We've lost contact with perimeter security."

"Which team?" Lebed pressed.

"All of them."

Lebed swore under his breath. "Cooper," he said. "It has to be him."

One of the men seated on the couch opened his mouth to speak. Lebed whipped around the Uzi, squeezed off a sustained burst and hosed down both men with a screaming storm of lead.

Turning away from the two dead men, Lebed pinned his guard under his gaze.

"Mobilize everyone who can carry a gun. Now!"

BOLAN SURGED ACROSS THE lawn. Grimaldi kept up with the
big American, while Turrin lagged a couple of steps behind.
The front door of the house whipped open and gunfire immediately erupted from inside the sprawling mansion. Bullets tore into the ground several yards ahead of the Stony
Man warriors, kicking up small explosions of dirt as they
chewed into the ground.

The gunfire stopped just long enough for one of Lebed's
shooters to race out the door. A submachine gun held in
close to the guy's body spit fire and death. From the corner of his eye, Bolan saw Turrin drop to one knee, bring his
M-16 to his shoulder and cut loose with a barrage of autofire. The bullets from Grimaldi's weapon riddled the running man's torso and brought his sprint to a shuddering halt.

By now, more gunfire was lancing out of the windows
at the Stony Man warriors. With Grimaldi and Turrin laying down cover fire, Bolan ran in a zigzag pattern toward
the house. Ripping an M-67 grenade from his web gear, he
pulled the pin, tossed the bomb through the doorway and
dived to the ground. Thunder crashed inside the house as
the grenade unleashed its deadly payload. Bolan surged up
the short flight of stairs leading to the porch that ran the
length of the front of the house.

A man, his shirt shredded, his face and arms flayed by
the razor wire from the grenade, stumbled through the door.
Bolan squeezed off a quick burst into the guy's center mass,
putting him out of his misery. The soldier found a second
man lying on the ground, his body convulsing from his
wounds. Likewise, the soldier delivered a fast flurry of bullets into the man's torso, killing him.

A volley of bullets screamed past the soldier's ear, orig-
inating from his right. He spun in time to catch another
member of Lebed's security team firing from a corridor to
his right. The soldier swept his MP-5 in a tight horizontal
swath, scything the man down.

Turrin and Grimaldi had followed the soldier inside the mansion. The little Fed had moved to Bolan's nine-o'clock position and was searching for targets with his shotgun. Grimaldi was sprinting up the stairwell, the M-16 leading the way.

Moving into a large room, the walls lined with bookshelves, Bolan swept his eyes and the MP-5's barrel in unison over its interior. Sudden motion flashed to his right. He whirled and caught one of Lebed's hardmen popping up from behind a couch, his Steyr chugging out a volley of slugs that were cutting a horizontal line toward the Executioner's midsection.

The burst flew wide, and Bolan's MP-5 chugged out a blistering reply to the assault. The maelstrom of slugs chewed into his opponent, taking the man down.

A twin thunderclap erupted behind Bolan and he felt his heart stop for an instant. He wheeled around in time to see a man armed with a Steyr, the flesh of his midsection torn open, teeter in the doorway. When he collapsed, Turrin, his shotgun barrel still smoking, came into view. Bolan nodded a silent thanks at his old friend before kicking back into motion.

Two more shooters surged into the library, their weapons grinding out deadly volleys of autofire. The bullets flew wide of Bolan and ripped into the shelves, shredding the books into confetti. The soldier hosed them down with a sustained burst from the Heckler & Koch subgun.

A quick search of the lower level revealed no other targets. Bolan climbed slowly up the stairs, where a cacophony of gunfire was already ripping through the air. When he reached the upper level, he found Grimaldi taking down two gunners with a concentrated burst from his M-16. The soldier spotted a figure across the room and recognized him as Lebed. The soldier started after the Russian, who immediately disappeared through a doorway.

Without warning, something hard hit Bolan in the midsection and knocked him to the ground. The MP-5 slipped from his hands. Bolan's fist lashed out and he struck his opponent in the mouth, bloodying the man's lips.

The guy went with the hit, falling off Bolan and rolling a couple of yards away before coming up from the ground, a knife clutched in his hand. Bolan recognized him from the background briefing as Olav Andropov. The Russian kicked Bolan's MP-5 away and coiled his body to strike.

# CHAPTER THIRTY-SIX

Lebed knew he had to move.

The Russian surged through a door and down a set of stairs. The sounds of chaos—gunshots, screams and alarms—rang in his ears. His mind raced as he rolled through his options. He could stand and fight, maybe put the Americans in a situation where he could take them down one by one.

Or he could run.

Fuck it, he'd run.

He reached the bottom of the stairs and sprinted across the huge living room. Shell casings crunched under his feet. Flames chewed through the curtains that hung from the windows, filling the room with a noxious black smoke.

Three of his gunners lay in various spots around the room, each dead in a pool of his own blood. Lebed barely noticed them. He wanted only to get to the front door and out of the house. It wasn't cowardice that drove him for the exit, he assured himself. It was a strategic retreat. Live to fight another day and all that.

Along the way he stopped at the bar and grabbed a bottle of vodka by the neck and whipped it hard against the burning drapes. The glass exploded and blue-yellow flames blossomed up from the splattered alcohol. He liked the effect enough that he threw a bottle of Scotch whiskey into the fire, intensifying the flames even more. It likely wouldn't stop Matt Cooper and his associates. But if the fire spread fast enough it could at least slow them by forcing them to look for another exit. By then, he'd be gone.

Lebed headed for the door, reloading the Uzi on the run.

THE YOUNG RUSSIAN SLASHED at Bolan with the combat knife. The blade's tip sliced through the air, inches from his face, forcing him to step back. The soldier balled his hands into fists, raised just below chin level. As they circled each other, Bolan sized up Andropov. He knew his opponent was younger than him, a few inches shorter, a few pounds lighter. If it were a bench-pressing contest, the soldier probably could make the guy look like the proverbial ninety-eight-pound weakling.

But it was combat, and sheer strength alone didn't win fights.

The Russian moved in fast, taking a jab at Bolan's face. Knuckles connected with the soldier's chin, and he rolled with the punch. His opponent struck again, this time with his knife hand snaking out, the blade carving a path toward Bolan's heart. Figuring the shot to the jaw was a distraction, Bolan had expected the follow-up attack. He caught the thrust with his forearm. At the same time his fist rocketed out and he pounded Andropov's mouth, splitting the man's lips and drawing blood.

Andropov fell back another step, dragged his forearm across his busted lip and glanced at the blood smeared there. He looked up at Bolan, raised the knife over his head and surged forward again. As he rushed forward, he slashed downward, the gleaming knife angled toward his adversary's heart.

The soldier pivoted from his attacker's path and drove a fist into the guy's ribs as he passed. Andropov belched a lungful of air and the force of the blow caused him to stagger.

In the same instant Bolan grabbed a combat knife from his web gear, stepped forward and drove the blade at an upward angle under Andropov's ribs, the tip piercing his heart. The Executioner twisted the blade.

The Russian's eyes bulged in shock, a gasp escaped his lips and his body went slack. His fingers opened and his knife fell from his hand. As Bolan yanked the blade from his opponent's body, the other man crumpled to the ground, dead.

Returning the knife to its holder, Bolan drew the Desert Eagle and thumbed back the hammer. He swept his gaze over the mayhem that surrounded him. Grimaldi, his M-16 held at hip level, was hosing down two other shooters with an onslaught of autofire. Bolan didn't see Lebed anywhere.

The Executioner stalked forward, searching for targets with the Desert Eagle. He saw a pair of Lebed's thugs churning out punishing hails of autofire at an overturned table and a couch. The twin fusillades splintered the table-top and sliced through the back of the couch like a buzz saw. From Bolan's vantage point, he could see Turrin huddled behind the pile of furniture.

The soldier drew a bead on the nearer of the two shooters and double tapped the Desert Eagle's trigger. The weapon roared and the slugs ripped through the man's spine, violently shoving him forward in a pile of broken flesh and bones.

Whether prompted by the thunderous Desert Eagle or by the sight of his comrade falling to the ground, the second shooter whirled. Even as he swung the assault rifle in Bolan's direction, the guy squeezed the trigger on the weapon and unleashed a burst of fire that was cutting its way toward his adversary.

Too little too late.

Bolan already had lined up his shot on the other guy. The hand cannon roared once, the shot catching the guy in the mouth and coring through the back of his skull.

Turrin poked his head around from behind the table's

chewed-up remains and gave Bolan a thumbs-up. The soldier saw the relieved expression on his friend's face suddenly melt away. Something sizzled through the air at eye level, just inches from him.

Bolan pivoted and saw a woman, a nickel-plated handgun clutched in her hands. Her blond hair was disheveled, and splatters of blood and smudges of dirt covered her clothes. She was readjusting her aim, lining up a better shot on the soldier.

The Executioner set aside chivalry and shot her once in the chest with the Desert Eagle. Climbing to his feet, he began to look for Lebed.

LEBED SPRINTED FOR THE helicopter. His heart slammed in his chest and his throat felt parched. Cooper was cutting down his men—an army of trained warriors—like a scythe through wheat. The Russian had worked with some of the world's best mercenaries and he'd never seen fighting chops like those displayed by Cooper.

When he got to within a couple dozen yards of the helipad, he spotted three of his soldiers hoofing it toward the lift-off site. One of the mercenaries glanced over his shoulder and spotted Lebed. He stopped in his tracks and shouted for the other two to do the same.

Lebed rolled up on the gunmen, a pair of Russian Spetsnaz soldiers and a former Georgian army captain. A group of unnatural allies to be sure, but money made for strange bedfellows.

The Russian who'd first spotted Lebed had turned to face the man. The merc carried an AK-74 in both hands, the barrel pointed at the ground at a forty-five-degree angle. He was less than six feet tall, slender, like someone who ran a lot. His blond hair was cut into a flat-top and his face had been burned red from the Costa Rican sun. A beer belly ringed the other Russian's midsection, but his arms, shoulders and chest were thick with muscle. His black hair was pulled back into a ponytail that hung down between his shoulder blades. His eyebrows were thick and unruly and his forehead and chin jutted unnaturally far, giving his face the shape of a crescent moon. He sucked in deep pulls of air, apparently winded by the short sprint from the house to the helipad.

Similarly, the Georgian was stout, the fabric of his polo shirt straining at the seams by his wide midsection. Rivulets of sweat streamed down the man's forehead and his cheeks and forehead were flushed scarlet from the heat. The ripped fabric of his shirt exposed a nasty gash where a bullet had grazed his rib cage.

Lebed trapped the men under his gaze. "Where the hell were you going?"

The young, fit Russian looked in the direction of the house and spoke. "We lost communication with you," he said. "You were nowhere to be found. We—" he nodded at the other two men "—wanted to see if you'd made it to the chopper."

Lebed's eyes narrowed at the man. "You're a lying dog," he snapped. "Get your asses back to the house and fight. What else am I paying you to do? More important, if something happens to me, who the hell's going to pay you? Go!"

The man hesitated for a couple of beats, apparently considering his options. Finally he nodded in agreement.

"Yes, sir," he said.

He looked at the other two and nodded at the house. "Let's go."

The three men started for the house, the injured Georgian bringing up the rear, one hand clamped over the open wound on his side. Lebed stared after them for a couple of seconds and a smile ghosted his lips.

Idiots, he thought. Were the situation reversed, he would have put a bullet in his boss's head, stolen the guy's wallet and headed out in the chopper. Live to fight another day. He expected—no, demanded—that kind of loyalty from his people. But he certainly didn't consider it a particularly admirable or practical trait, only a weakness in others that he could exploit.

Pivoting toward the helipad, he took off in a dead run.

A glance over his shoulder assured him that the Americans weren't on his trail. If they did make it from the house, which he doubted, they would still have to tear their way through another wave of gunmen. By then, Lebed would be on his chopper and safely airborne. It would be easy to disappear for days, weeks, even months or, if necessary, years. Over the decades, he'd created a worldwide network of safehouses, bank accounts and weapons caches that he could hide indefinitely. All he needed was enough time to regroup, to rebuild the organization. This time it would have a much more personal purpose, though. No longer would he waste money or endanger himself in pursuit of some lofty geopolitical goals, games of treachery and deceit that, like the heads of a hydra, just continued to multiply.

No, this time, he'd keep it simple. He'd dedicate every dime he had, every bullet, every ounce of blood that coursed through his veins, to destroying Matt Cooper and the country that had dispatched him.

He'd unleash waves of horror on America, selling biological weapons and suitcase nukes to the antigovernment crazies or the Jihadists with their visions of an Islamic caliphate. Such useful idiots always would be willing to provide cannon fodder for a man like him, one with the brains, money and resources to make things happen. He'd be only too happy to push them into the meat grinder if it meant taking down Cooper.

The whine of the chopper's engine intensified and drew his attention back to the present. A figure stepped into view in the helicopter's side door. At first, Lebed assumed the man was there to help him climb inside the aircraft. Lebed tried to remember whether the man was a pilot or another gunner.

He poured on the speed, closing the gap between himself and the aircraft.

The man's eyes locked with Lebed's just for an instant before the man disappeared from view. Though he couldn't hear it over the sound of the engines, Lebed saw the side door slide forward and slam shut.

What the hell?

The ear-splitting whine hit a higher pitch and the rotor blades had gained speed.

The helicopter lifted off from the ground.

Fuck!

Enraged, Lebed triggered one of his Uzis and flames leaped from the SMG's barrel. Slugs pounded into the bottom of the helicopter, ripping open a line of small black holes in its skin. The Uzi's magazine cycled dry. The Russian ejected it and slammed another into the weapon's grip. In the meantime, the aircraft had leveled off and shot forward. Lebed watched as the machine disappeared over the treetops.

"That has to hurt," a voice said from behind.

Lebed whirled, the Uzi leading the way. He saw Cooper standing there.

BOLAN HAD THE DESERT Eagle trained on Lebed, his body tense as he waited for the other man to react. Lebed jerked up his Uzi, the weapon spitting fire and lead from it. A horizontal line of a tracking fire cut a swath toward Bolan.

Given less than a second, Lebed would correct his aim and cut Bolan down with a withering fusillade.

Given a second.

Bolan tapped the Desert Eagle's trigger. Thunder pealed from the pistol and a long tongue of flame lashed from the muzzle. A single .44 Magnum round pounded into Lebed's face just to the right of the bridge of his nose, coring through his skull before exploding out the back of his head.

The corpse teetered for a moment before falling to the ground. Bolan holstered the Desert Eagle, turned and marched back to find Grimaldi and Turrin.

* * * * *

# The Executioner®
## Don Pendleton's
### FATAL COMBAT

After a number of civilians throughout Detroit turn up dead from knife wounds, a red flag is raised in Washington. Concerned the city has become a testing ground for low-budget, low-tech domestic terrorism, the President wants those responsible brought down. And there is only one man who can get under the radar to do it—Mack Bolan.

*Available November wherever books are sold.*

## Don Pendleton
# TERMINAL GUIDANCE

### A fresh wave of terror is unleashed across the Middle East...

U.S. intelligence agencies are picking up chatter about something big coming their way. When a series of calculated executions of undercover intelligence personnel occur in key cities, the Oval Office is convinced this is the attack the world has feared. The Stony Man teams deploy to the hot spots, seeking to smash a deadly alliance of terror....

# STONY MAN®

*Available December wherever books are sold.*

# JAMES AXLER

# DEATH LANDS®

## Lost Gates

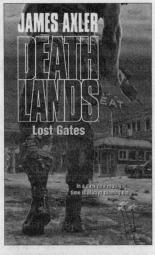

**A deadly cult goes on a killing spree in Detroit...**

Baron Crabbe is dangerously high on legends of the Trader and rumors of a secret cache. His ace in the hole is Ryan Cawdor and his band — his prisoners. Ryan knows the truth, and it won't help Crabbe, but the only option is to play along with the crazed baron's scheme. Staying alive is all about buying time — waiting for their one chance to chill their captors.

*Available November 2011 wherever books are sold.*

# TAKE 'EM FREE

## 2 action-packed novels plus a mystery bonus

## NO RISK
### NO OBLIGATION TO BUY

## AleX Archer
## CRADLE OF SOLITUDE

**A treasure of the revolution...or of ruin?**

It was dumb luck, really, that archaeologist Annja Creed happened to be in Paris when the skeletal remains of a confederate soldier were discovered. But this was no ordinary soldier. Now Annja is unraveling a 150-year-old mystery and a trail of clues to the treasure...but she's not the only one looking....

*Available November wherever books are sold.*

**www.readgoldeagle.blogspot.com**

GRA33

# James Axler
# Outlanders®

## INFESTATION CUBED

**Earth's saviors are on the run as
more nightmares descend upon Earth…**

Ullikummis, the would-be cruel master of Earth, has captured
Brigid Baptiste, luring Kane and Grant on a dangerous pursuit. All
while pan-terrestrial scientists conduct a horrifying experiment
in parasitic mind control. But true evil has yet to reveal itself, as
the alliance scrambles to regroup—before humankind loses its
last and only hope.

*Available November wherever books are sold.*

Or order your copy now by sending your name, address, zip or postal code, along with a check or
money order (please do not send cash) for $6.99 for each book ordered ($7.99 in Canada), plus
75¢ postage and handling ($1.00 in Canada), payable to Gold Eagle Books, to: